Books by Norman Kalloch:

A Long Way to Walk
45th Parallel
Life in the Backwoods
Stranded
Last Hike

WASHED OUT

Norman R. Kalloch, Jr.

Washed Out
Copyright © 2025 Norman R. Kalloch, Jr.

ISBN: 978-1-63381-456-1

All rights reserved. No part of this book may be reproduced in any form or by any electronic or mechanical means, including information storage and retrieval systems, without permission in writing from the author, except by a reviewer, who may quote brief passages in review.

This is a work of fiction. Names, characters, places, and incidents either are the product of the author's imagination or are used fictitiously, and any resemblance to actual persons, living or dead, is coincidental.

Cover drawn by Wesley V. Kalloch
A special thanks to Jonathan Miller for reviewing the manuscript

Designed and produced by:
Maine Authors Publishing
12 High Street, Thomaston, Maine
www.maineauthorspublishing.com

Printed in the United States of America

This book is dedicated to the two hundred residents of Bigelow, Dead River, and Flagstaff who sacrificed their heritage for the greater good of the people of Maine.

To the Editor,

Your recent article on the benefits to be received from building the dam on the Dead River makes me shake a wrathy fist at you people who are so in need of more hydropower that we must sacrifice our homes and lands to it. To us who have put all our love, labor, and earnings into the lands that have been in our families for years there can be no compensation for their loss.

It seems a sad and selfish thing when the need of urban dwellers becomes more demanding as, cause to be obliterated two communities where inhabitants live in greater happiness, satisfaction, and far more tranquil peace of mind than you harried city folks can imagine.

Another shake of my fist at the companies involved in the proposed project for keeping us "on the fence." Since twenty years ago when first mention was made of the dam, we have been given no assurance that its construction was or was not a sure thing. Our region in a sense, has been devastated. Farms that the company bought then were abandoned and left to grow up to bushes and scrub. The buildings ransacked and looted, finally fall in, to become eyesores to us all. Homeowners hesitant to repair, paint, or plan for far reaching enterprises. We hardier souls built new homes and set our roots deep are still "on the fence."

Why not print an article in your paper presenting our side of the situation? Or print this letter so the people can read the dam will not be a wonderful thing for all concerned.

Mrs. Frances S. Taylor
Dead River, Maine
June 29, 1948

Letter to the Editor (unedited), *Lewiston Daily Sun*, July 1, 1948. Frances Taylor's response to the paper's editorial extolling the benefits of building Long Falls Dam. However, the paper failed to acknowledge the upheaval the dam would cause residents of the Dead River Valley. Frances Taylor was born in Flagstaff, Maine, in 1916 and died in Skowhegan, Maine, in 2013 at 97.

TABLE OF CONTENTS

Introduction 1
Prologue 5

Part One: Washed Out

Chapter 1 17
Chapter 2 25
Chapter 3 31
Chapter 4 69
Chapter 5 81
Chapter 6 95
Chapter 7 113
Chapter 8 119
Chapter 9 127
Chapter 10 139
Chapter 11 157
Chapter 12 187
Chapter 13 197
Chapter 14 205
Chapter 15 211
Epilogue 219
Afterword 221

Part Two: An Abbreviated History of Politics and Water Power in the 1920s as It Relates to the Construction of the Long Falls Dam

Acknowledgments 247
Glossary 249
Bibliography 251

Maps

West Side of the Dead River Valley Pre-1950 22
East Side of the Dead River Valley Pre-1950 23
Grand Falls and the Dead River Region 36
Dead River Valley Post Long Falls Dam 218

INTRODUCTION

World War II had ended, and people felt good about themselves and their country. The U.S. had defeated two evil empires. Other than the attack on Pearl Harbor, the homeland came through four years of war relatively unscathed. Patriotism was everywhere. Factories shifted from manufacturing materials to support the war effort to turning out consumer goods, and people were buying them, and most ran on electricity. Washing machines, hair dryers, and mixers needed a reliable, cheap energy source. And hydroelectric power could do the job. Large areas of rural Maine in the 1940s still had not been electrified. To meet the demand, the state was scoured for potential dam sites that would hold turbines to produce the millions of kilowatts needed to energize the state's expanding electrical grid.

Walter S. Wyman was the man to make it happen. Wyman and his business partner, Harvey Eaton, bought dozens of small independent power companies. In 1910, the Central Maine Power Company was formed. Gobbling up small hydro and steam generator plants was only the beginning for the two businessmen. In 1928, Wyman announced that the company would construct a 72-megawatt hydroelectric dam on the upper reaches of the Kennebec River. The dam was completed in 1930 and was named for Wyman.

A storage reservoir needed to be built to ensure the turbines ran at maximum capacity in low flow. The Dead River Valley was the ideal site for such a reservoir.

The construction of the Dead River Reservoir, today's Flagstaff Lake, would prove to be no easy task for Wyman. Central Maine Power Company needed approval to dam the Dead River at Long Falls. To complicate matters, the site of the proposed dam was owned by the State of Maine. Gaining support for the project became a tug-of-war between Wyman, the State Legislature, and Governor Percival P. Baxter. And caught in the middle were the nearly two hundred people who lived in the villages of Flagstaff, Dead River, and Bigelow.

In a sense, the 170 residents in the Dead River Valley became pawns in the feud being played out in Augusta. Not only did the families in the three communities wrestle with the possible loss of their ancestral homes, but they also needed to cope with the anxiety that rose and fell with each political move and countermove by Wyman and Baxter. Part 2 of *Washed Out* traces the argument over water rights among the Central Maine Power Company, the legislature, and Governor Baxter.

Percival Baxter was not against hydropower. Nor was he particularly concerned about the dozens of families displaced in the Dead River Valley if the dam at Long Falls should be built. However, he held the steadfast belief that Maine citizens owned the state's natural resources and were entitled to compensation if a private company wanted to monopolize them for financial gain.

Baxter was also adamant that electricity produced in Maine should stay in Maine to benefit Maine people. For each end run Wyman made to get around Baxter's demands, Percival was there to head him off.

Flooding the Dead River Valley to create a 20,000-acre reservoir had been discussed for a quarter of a century, so much so that some of the valley's residents felt it would never be built. However, in the minds of most residents, there was always a degree of uncertainty, wondering if one day they would have no choice but to sell their houses to Central Maine Power Company and find a new place to call home.

Washed Out is a tale of mystery, but it is also a fictionalized account of the uncertain times for the people of the Dead River Valley as they tried to live their lives while in the shadow of a company's determination to flood their land. For nearly twenty-five years, the residents of Flagstaff, Dead River, and Bigelow wondered if someday there would come the dreaded knock on the door, and a Central Maine Power Company appraiser would hand them a take-it-or-leave-it offer for their property.

PROLOGUE

I loved my hometown. I suppose many people feel the same about where they grew up. However, my life in the Dead River Valley was exceptional. Although I admit that living there for the first seventeen years of my life didn't seem that memorable. It just felt normal. Growing up, my brothers and sisters and I often heard our parents tell us that some people don't appreciate what they have until it's gone. Now that I'm some distance beyond age sixty, I understand what they meant. Life was good growing up in the Dead River Valley, and at the time, we didn't appreciate what we had.

I lived in Dead River Plantation. Our farm was at the base of Mount Bigelow and about 600 feet back from the Dead River. The river divided Dead River from the village of Flagstaff. It sounds somewhat confusing, living in a town with the same name as a river, doesn't it? I was born at home in 1932 and lived in the same house until my family was forced to leave in 1949 when the Central Maine Power Company built Long Falls Dam. I have many wonderful memories of growing up in the Valley.

We never had much money, even though my father worked six days a week on the farm or in the woods. Things changed after World War II, with more goods to buy and more money to make. Even then, if we did have a little extra, being thrifty was so embedded in my parents' psyches that they rarely spent it—and never on themselves. Most families in the Valley were careful with their money. Thriftiness was ingrained in children as a way of life by parents of past generations. During the war, the slogan was "Use it up, wear it out, make it do, or go without." Valley families had followed that code for three generations. People made do with what they had. No one used the term *frugal*; instead, they called it cutting the coat to fit the cloth. You make do with what you have. My grandmother, who lived with us, took frugality to the extreme, at least as far as her cooking went. She made the most delicious apple pies. She refused to make another until the last piece was eaten. No reason to waste sugar, she would say. My sister and I would lift the crust to check for green mold before we took the last piece.

In Dead River, most houses were scattered along State Route 144, the only tarred road in the Valley. There was no downtown to speak of. Flagstaff village had a main street with a general store and a post office tucked in the corner. Flagstaff even had a pool hall. Although I was never allowed to go inside, I did peek in the windows a few times. It all looked pretty harmless to me. People mostly farmed, some worked in the woods, and all were fiercely independent of Augusta and Washington.

Like most small towns in Maine at the time, everyone looked out for each other, and usually folks got along. I'm not saying life was perfect. The Valley had its share of gossip. My father told us more than once that a rumor started at the general store would be known by everyone in the Valley by nightfall. Small-town petty jealousies and even a dust-up of sorts happened on occasion. But overall, it truly was life in the slow lane.

As much as family, friends, and community influenced our young lives, our environment also impacted our upbringing.

When I was a teenager, my aunt Ethel gave me a book about famous alpine climbers. I don't remember much about the book, but I've always remembered one sentence: "A mountain has no need for people, but people do need mountains." I believe in that quote with all my heart. Mount Bigelow dominated the landscape, both physically and emotionally. The 14-mile Bigelow Range was an eye-catcher every day of the year.

It might be a farmer haying on a hot July day, stopping for a drink of water and gazing at Bigelow's summit locked in a summer haze. Perhaps someone's mother at the clothesline dropping clothespins into a bag, thinking how nice it would be sitting on its summit taking in the 360-degree view, or perhaps a child, dreaming about someday being a fire warden, watching for forest fires from the tower on West Peak. Everyone had their thoughts about Bigelow; some shared, and others held them tight to the hearts. The mountain was the common denominator among the 200 souls that lived in the Valley.

Mount Bigelow was our 4,000-foot-tall meteorologist. If the upper slopes glistened with an early-morning frost, it was time to cover the tomato plants at night. A dusting of snow on its rocky summit in late October meant the Valley would receive its first snowfall two weeks later. When the ridgeline disappeared into the clouds on a scorching summer day, it was almost guaranteed that a thunderstorm would soon burst over the summit and drench our parched fields with much-needed rain.

Mount Bigelow had a long reach. Each October, our father would take us partridge hunting, often miles away from the Dead River Valley. Through nearly every notch in the mountains, we could see Bigelow. Father would always tell us, "There's home. I can see your mother feeding the chickens in the yard."

On special occasions, we would borrow the neighbor's car and ride to Farmington to visit my mother's side of the family. I was always anxious to see my cousins, but something never seemed quite right. Instead of seeing "my" mountain, I saw rolling hills dotted with fields and white farm buildings. Nice, but far less inspiring than the towering twin peaks of Bigelow.

Bigelow was everyone's playground. Adventures to the top exploring caves and crevices for mountain lions and she-bears, though we never found either one. Summer hikes to the top for family picnics and snowshoe expeditions in the winter, although our legs gave out before we ever reached the top. Once, as teenagers, we slept out at the Horns while taking turns keeping watch for porcupines so they wouldn't get into the food we had hung in a bag from a tree. The next day, we hiked all the way to Stratton and called home, hoping someone would drive over and pick us up.

Bigelow was more than entertainment. Its maple and beech warmed dozens of Valley homes during the seemingly endless winters. It also provided jobs cutting spruce logs and hard- and softwood pulpwood. In the winter, my father and many other farmers would leave the care of the farms to their wives and older children while they worked six days a week in a logging camp somewhere high up on Bigelow and other mountains far away from home. Teams of horses hauled the four-foot pulpwood on scoots to the river's edge, where other men muscled the wood onto long, high rows parallel to the river. In the spring, as soon as the river was free of ice, the pulpwood was pushed into the river for the long ride down the Dead and then the Kennebec to the mills in Madison and Waterville to be made into paper. The white birch went to Harry Bryant's sawmill at the outlet of Flagstaff Pond, where it was made into dowels and squares and sent by truck to Bryant Pond, Maine, to be milled into wooden toys and novelties.

November was a time to fill the family's larder with venison. My father taught my brothers and me how to hunt deer and the best areas on Bigelow to find them. As my father grew old, he left hunting for the boys, saying that trudging up and down the steep slopes was for younger legs.

Mount Bigelow was my inspiration. Many mornings, I would lie in bed looking out the window, waiting for the first rays of a new day to touch Avery Peak. At first, a small wedge of sunlight hit the highest points on the mountain. Then, in an instant, the entire mountain would burst into daylight. The scene was one I never tired of seeing. On starry nights, Biglow's silhouette seemed to fill the southern sky. During a full moon, it was haunting to see the moonlight reflect off the mountain's barren top.

The Dead River was an essential part of our lives as well. The river lived up to its name most of the time, slowly meandering west to east through the Valley before swinging north toward Long Falls. Some of the river's twists and turns were so sharp it appeared that it had turned back on itself and then, seemingly having a change of mind, abruptly swung back to the east. I remember one canoe trip in high school. A group of us decided to make a quick, easy trip on the Dead. We started behind the Dead River School and planned to paddle as far as the Fud Taylor Farm, two miles in a straight line. We made it, but it took most of the day. There was a sandbar at every turn, perfect for another swim. Maybe that had something to do with us not getting to Uncle Fud's until suppertime.

At times, the Dead was anything but. The March 1936 flood was the worst. All the intervals flooded, and many of the homes in Dead River had water on the first floor. Our house was the exception. I remember coming down the stairs and seeing water between the cracks of the pine-board floor. A flooded cellar, but our home remained dry. The high water destroyed the only bridge that connected Dead River to Flagstaff, the so-called Big Bridge. The only way across was by boat. The entire village of Flagstaff was under water. People canoed down Main Street for three days after the rain ended. Across the street from the flooded general store, a canoe came through the front door of Hazen Ames's Pool Hall. I have a picture showing two men with their paddles raised. Finally, the water retreated into its channel, and people returned to the day-to-day business of living.

The spring pulp drive was one of the most fascinating events I ever saw while living in the Valley. Thousands of cords of pulpwood plugged the Dead River, held in place by a boom chain connected to opposite banks. When conditions were right, men would open the boom, and the mass of four-foot wood would begin to move. Word that the drive was underway spread like wildfire. Hearing the news, our teacher would call off school and take us down to the river to watch. As ten-year-olds, we were fascinated by the sight of thousands of pieces of wood as far as you could see, slowly parade past us. Only the dull thud of sticks of pulpwood bumping into one another broke the eerie silence.

Seventy-five people lived in Dead River, not enough population to support a store. When our post office closed, most families drove to Flagstaff to get their mail. A tiny area was partitioned inside Leavitt's Store, and Mr. and Mrs. Leavitt served as postmaster. The store carried some groceries. It was where we bought the basics like bread and butter. We never had a car, so we couldn't drive to Madison or Kingfield to shop. Instead, we purchased our apples, meats, and eggs from the peddlers who drove up from New Portland and Farmington, selling their goods door to door.

Dead River did not have a high school. Students wanting to go beyond the eighth grade went to school in Flagstaff. I often heard other parents say they hoped their Johnny or Jane could transition from eighth grade to high school and not get in with the wrong crowd. That was never an issue in the Dead River Valley. Our graduating class in Dead River had a total of eight students. The entire student body at Flagstaff High was nineteen. Everyone knew each other. Some of us from eighth grade had even played on the high school's basketball teams, so there would be enough people on the roster to play a game. Occasionally, an older student might pick on a freshman, but Mr. Taylor, the principal, would quickly straighten things out.

Winter was a time for basketball. Boys and girls played in the high school gym, which was the school's basement. Stratton was our biggest rival. Many friends lived in Stratton, but they were enemy number one when it was time to play them.

It seemed like the entire population of Dead River, Flagstaff, and Bigelow Township attended the games. Going to see a basketball game beat sitting home reading a book by the light of a kerosene lamp, my mother told me. My parents would ride to every home game with friends to watch me play, even if it was five below zero or a near blizzard. To light up the gymnasium, power to the homes in the town had to be cut. Once the game was over, the lights in town would snap back on. I should mention that DC electricity was generated by waterpower from a waterwheel at Bryant's Mill. In Dead River, where our family lived, no one had electricity—or indoor plumbing, for that matter.

When the basketball season ended, Saturday night dances filled the winter void. They were sometimes held in the hall above the general store but most often in the high school gym. Young and old would be on the floor dancing to piano music played by one or two local women. Later on, the high school bought a record player. We thought dancing to modern music rather than just "Lady of the Lake" and "Boston Fancy" was much more fun.

Mud season was the Valley's fifth season, wedged between winter and spring. It generally lasted three weeks or more. Cars and trucks constantly became stuck in the springtime ooze. Nearly every road in the Valley was dirt, and when the frost left the ground, they turned to soup.

One night in early April, my sister and I begged Father to take us to a movie in Stratton. He did not want to drive fifteen miles after dark and risk becoming mired. Finally, he relented and borrowed Uncle Ned's DeSoto to take us to the six o'clock show.

After the movie, we started home. There must have been six cars returning to Dead River or Flagstaff. The problem began when the lead vehicle slipped into a rut and became stuck. With no room to go around him, we could only sit in the dark and wait for him to find a farmer to pull him out with his tractor. An hour later, the car was dragged onto firmer footing, and the procession resumed the trip home. The farmer waited until all six vehicles cleared the mud hole in case someone else needed a tow.

People were more trusting than they are now. It was a different time. No one locked the door when going downriver for the day to shop or when they turned out the lights at night. There was no reason to. Leaving doors unlocked assured visitors they were always welcome.

Mother never worried about us playing outside, even when we were small. If we turned up missing, she'd call the neighbors to ask if they had seen us. Invariably, someone would report we had just walked by or they had seen us playing with the neighbor's children in the field across the road. We were constantly being watched even though we never knew it.

Central Maine Power bought up properties as they came onto the market long before the dam was a sure thing. Some residents were glad to have had the opportunity to sell, move out of the area, and start a new life. Some felt pride in sacrificing their way of life so others in the state could have electricity. I was not one of them. I saw all the CMP people running around the Valley as an invading army trying to destroy our land and us. When the time came to leave our homes for the last time, even the dam supporters had second thoughts, wondering if they had made the right decision.

The scariest days of my life happened in the summer and fall of 1949 when hundreds of men were cutting all the trees below what would be the waterline of the lake to be created by the dam at Long Falls. Once the trees were removed, the slash needed to be burned. The fires would get out of control almost daily and burn everything in sight as they roared through the Valley. I can still see the billows of black smoke and the orange glow of the fires as they came closer and closer to people's homes. My mother was constantly going outside to check what direction the fires were headed, ready to grab us kids and escape if needed. Many people did just that, not daring to take a chance of becoming trapped by the inferno. Once the threat passed, they returned home. My father said it was as if the Valley had been cursed, between the fires and the impending flood. The summer of 1949 was stressful for my parents, between the fires, moving to our new home in North Anson, and all the time knowing our lives were forever changed because of that dam.

PROLOGUE

About a year after the dam's gates had closed, I visited the Valley for a final time. I wished I hadn't. It was June 1950, and what was now known as Flagstaff Lake was half full. My father, one of my brothers, and I took a small boat powered by an outboard motor to where we had once lived. My mother refused to go with us. She wanted to remember life as it was before the dam. Father launched the small boat near where the Ledge House once stood. We dodged floating lumber from shattered buildings and trees that escaped the fires. Everything looked so different. Most buildings were gone, either burned, demolished, or hauled off on flatbeds to a nearby town.

Ten minutes later, Father shut off the engine. I asked why he had stopped.

"This is the homestead. We're sitting on top of where the house stood. The barn sat about fifty feet behind us."

I was horrified. Everything was gone. "Are you sure this is our place?" I asked.

Before my father could answer, I saw proof that this was once our home. There was one building on the property that the wrecking crews had left. It was the chicken coop. It sat on a knoll behind where the barn had stood. I knew it was ours. I could see the faded blue paint on the door. I had painted that door when I was eleven. Now, the flood water had risen halfway to the top. Soon, it would lift from its rock foundation and drift away, eventually breaking apart into boards and timbers. Seeing that last tangible remnant of my life in Dead River being slowly consumed by the rising water was like the final curtain dropping at the end of a three-act play. So sad.

Dead River, Flagstaff, and Bigelow disappeared three months later. One hundred years of Valley history is now under thirty feet of water. My hometown may be gone, but I will always have the memories, and they are all happy ones.

—Anonymous

PART ONE

Washed Out

1.

The story of flooding the Dead River Valley starts with the construction of Wyman Dam on the Kennebec River. Without Wyman, the dam at Long Falls likely would not have been built, and the nearly 200 residents of the Valley would not have lost their homes.

Kennebec River, one mile above Bingham
June 1908

A lone fisherman paddled his canvas-covered canoe along the east shore of the Kennebec River, pausing occasionally to cast a dry fly behind a sunken tree or into the tailwater of one of the boulders that dotted the river. The mayfly hatch that had begun an hour earlier made him optimistic. At any moment, a trophy-sized native brook trout could rise to the fly, and the fight would start to determine the victor. His casts were long and precise, the imitation Mayfly striking its intended target every time. However, despite his impressive fly-casting technique, his mind and heart wandered elsewhere. The trip to the Bingham area meant more to Jim Kelleher than merely catching fish. It provided a break before heading to the Dan Robinson farm in Pleasant Ridge to visit a woman he had met at dinner at his sister's house in Waterville a week before. He'd quickly become captivated by her beauty and charm. Kelleher checked his pocket watch. He needed to be at Angie's parents' home at six p.m., which gave him enough time to paddle to the base of the rapids and make a few more casts before heading back to his car.

Kelleher worked as an accountant for the Maine Central Railroad, headquartered in Waterville, Maine. He was ambitious and good at his job. When not working for the railroad, he maintained two apartment buildings in the neighboring town of Winslow.

He found the electrification of Maine fascinating. Until recently, electricity had been generated only for towns fortunate enough to have a nearby stream that could be dammed, allowing water to be diverted through a turbine. The primitive distribution system of poles and wires was limited to neighboring homes. The use of electricity had surged dramatically in recent years, resulting in the need for greater capacity to meet demand. Large dams and complex distribution lines became necessary to power lighting and new electrical appliances that were becoming commonplace in every home throughout the state.

As Kelleher neared the head of the rapids, he observed how the river narrowed, forming a natural bottleneck of soil and rock. The steep banks on either side made it an ideal site for a dam. The more he studied the landscape, the more he was convinced that a hydroelectric dam blocking the Kennebec River at this point would produce a tremendous amount of electricity, enough for dozens of towns and cities. Kelleher needed to tell someone about his discovery...

The first person he thought of was his brother-in-law, George Hegarty. George worked for Walter Wyman, an entrepreneur in small-scale hydro projects in the Waterville area. George convinced Kelleher to talk to his boss about his idea and offered to set up a meeting between Kelleher and Wyman.

On a hot July afternoon, the two men met in Bingham. Kelleher drove Wyman first to Pleasant Ridge to look at the dam site from the west and then to Moscow to get a perspective from the east side. Kelleher said little, wanting Wyman to decide if the site had as much potential as he believed.

After a few moments, Kelleher could no longer contain himself. "I was thinking a dam twenty-five to fifty feet high could easily fit between the two mountains."

"Kelleher, you don't think big enough. A dam a hundred to a hundred and fifty feet high is what I would build. The more water you store, the more electricity it can generate, which means more customers."

Wyman unrolled a 1905 topographic map and traced a contour line up the valley and down the other side. "Based on a hundred-and-fifty-foot-high dam, I'd estimate that the reservoir would reach Caratunk and be ninety feet deep at the dam. A reservoir of that size, Mr. Kelleher, would generate a significant amount of electricity."

Wyman and his business partners, Harvey Eaton and George Hegarty, established the Robinson Land Company and appointed Kelleher president. The newly formed company began acquiring land and water rights. Central Maine Power Company was established two years later, and the Robinson Land Company was subsequently purchased. Over the next eighteen years, CMP continued to acquire properties that would eventually be flooded once Wyman Dam was constructed. The first property sold to the Robinson Land Company was the Dan Robinson Farm. Although Angie Robinson and Jim Kelleher's romance didn't last, it was the catalyst for building Maine's largest hydroelectric dam.

Central Maine Power Company Headquarters
313 Water Street, Augusta, Maine
May 3, 1923

"Mr. Wyman. Mr. Buckingham and Mr. Mason are here to see you," Walter Wyman's secretary announced over the intercom.

"Good morning," Wyman greeted the two men as they walked into the private office of the president of Central Maine Power Company. Wyman sensed they had something to show him and gestured toward the large oak conference table.

Mason, Central Maine Power's Chief Engineer, removed the cap from a tall brown tube and shook it, coaxing out a large, tightly rolled drawing. He unrolled the easel-sized paper and taped it to the desk.

"Frank has been thinking of ways to optimize the turbine output in the new hydro dam we'll build in Moscow. I think you'll find his plan quite intriguing," said Everett Buckingham, the new vice president of the power company.

The two men stood on either side of Mason, their hands braced against the table's top, staring at the map.

"As we know, for maximum productivity, the turbines at the Moscow Dam must operate at full horsepower as continuously as possible. This is feasible when there is enough water behind the dam. However, during the summer months, when runoff is at its lowest, and during prolonged droughts, low-flow augmentation is necessary to keep the turbines running at full power. The only way to achieve this is by creating an upstream reservoir, either on the upper Kennebec or the Dead River, and releasing the water as needed," Mason said.

"We know that," Wyman said, thinking Mason was plowing old ground. "Last month, you said we could construct a dam at The Forks to harness the flow from the Kennebec and the Dead Rivers. So why aren't we doing it?"

"I did say that, but that was before I calculated the costs. The Valley is too wide. Building a dam would be incredibly expensive, at least fifty million dollars. Even if it were feasible to construct, rerouting the highway around the impoundment would cost millions. The Forks site offers more costs than benefits."

"So where does that leave us?" Wyman asked.

"There are two alternatives. One is on the Moose River, and the other is on the Dead River. We need both reservoirs. However, the better site of the two is on the Dead," Mason said, pointing to Long Falls. "It's about thirty miles above The Forks site. Long Falls is a natural choke point," Mason continued, still pointing at the spot on the map. "A structure could be built here for a fraction of the cost compared to building at The Forks. A thirty-foot-high dam would store 275,000 acre-feet[1] of water, enough to run the new Moscow dam's turbines at no less than ninety percent capacity during periods of low runoff."

"How large will the impoundment be?" Wyman asked. His analytical mind operated on facts; the more information he received, the faster he could determine CMP's course of action.

"The dam would create a lake twenty miles long and up to six miles wide, or 20,000 surface acres when at capacity. It will be the fourth largest lake in Maine."

Wyman studied the map. "It looks to me several towns would be flooded out."

"Yes. Flagstaff, Dead River, and Bigelow Township. Let me clarify that: Flagstaff is the only true town, or I should say, village. The other two, Dead River and Bigelow, are sparsely populated, mainly along the road to Stratton."

"How many people live in the three towns?"

"About two hundred."

"How many more megawatts would the new dam produce with the extra water?" Wyman asked.

Mason flipped through his notes. "About an eighteen percent increase…another eight megawatts. And that doesn't account for the increased production at the other downstream facilities that would also utilize the water."

Wyman looked at Buckingham. "The more water we can put through those turbines, the more power we have to expand our service area."

Everett Buckingham smiled and nodded. "And the happier our shareholders will be, as well."

"Good work, Frank. Do what you need to do in the field to gather the information required to develop the preliminary figures for the dam at Long Falls. Be discreet about it. I don't want the

---

1. One acre-foot: the volume of water covering one acre one foot deep (43,560 cubic feet).

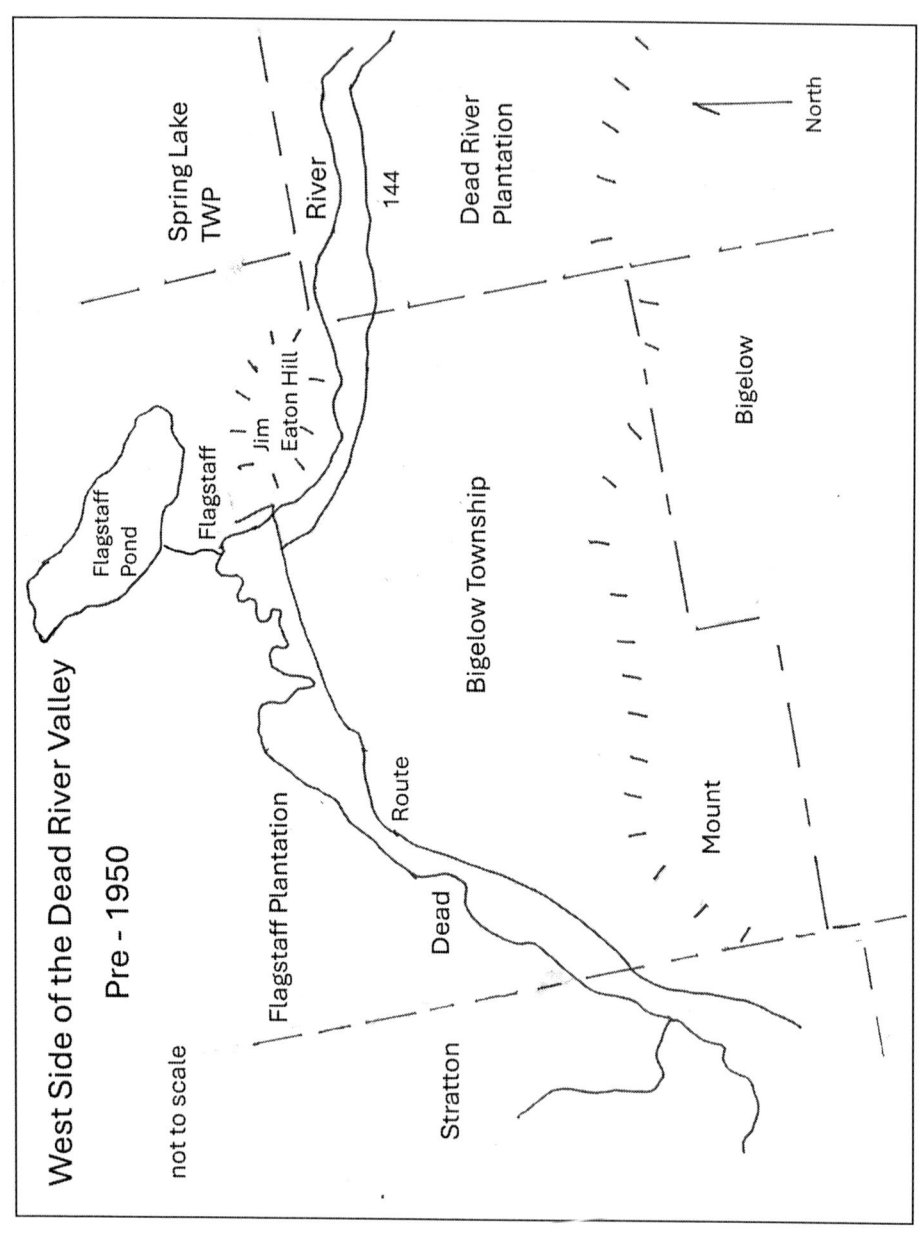

PART ONE: Washed Out   23

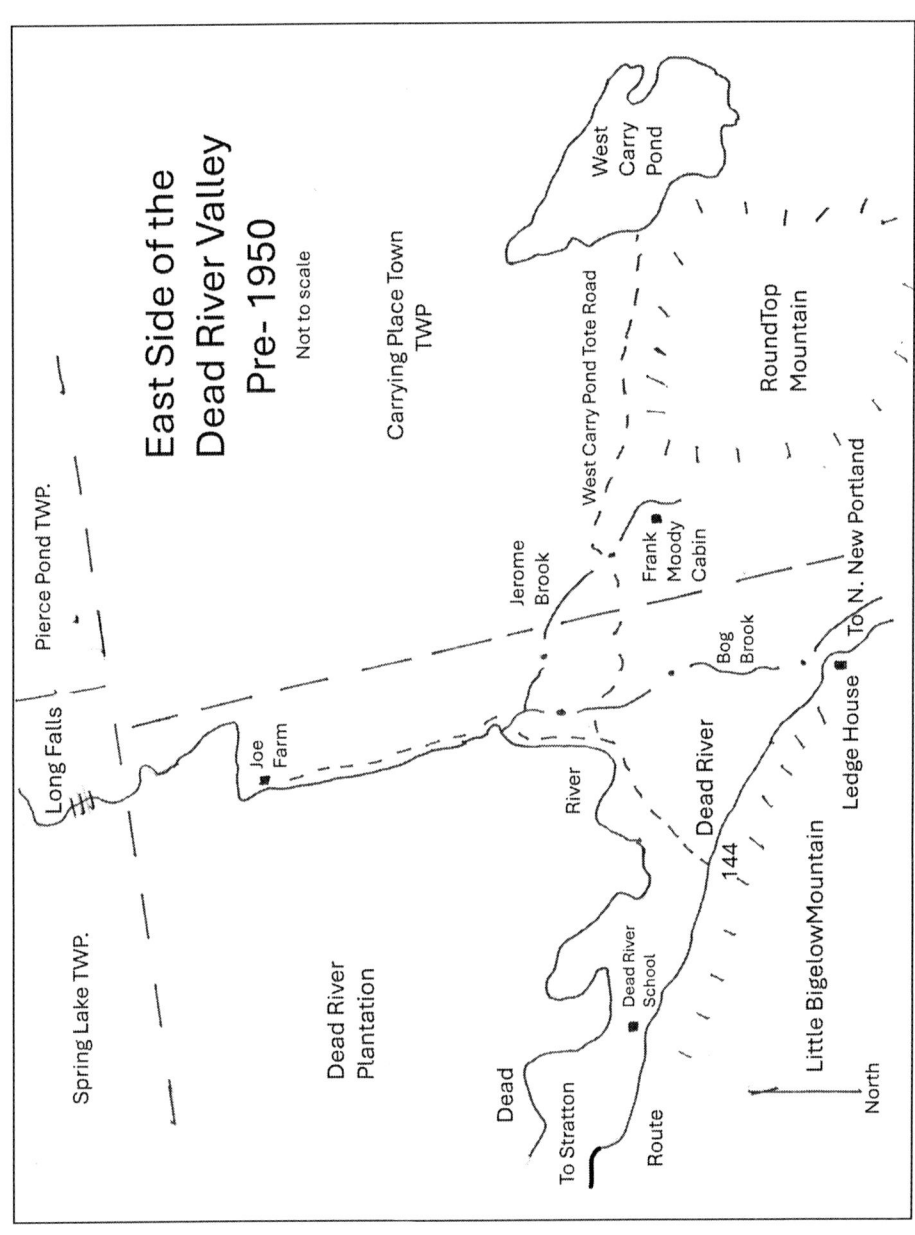

locals to get anxious seeing a group of surveyors moving around their land. Also, have your engineering department work with accounting. I need the estimated costs to buy out the residents of the three towns. Can you provide that for me in three months? We'll need the documentation to present to the legislature to obtain a charter from the state for the project."

Mason said he could, rolled up his map, and left the office. Buckingham waited for the door to shut before speaking. "What Mason said makes sense. However, I have one question: What if those people won't sell? Or worse yet, they petition the State to stop the project?"

"They'll sell."

"Why so sure? Getting ten people to agree on anything is almost impossible, let alone two hundred. It will never happen that they all agree to give up their farms to a power company."

"Everett, didn't you take a basic sociology course in college? Studies show that people in small towns are very patriotic. And the further those towns are in the willy-whacks, the more patriotic they tend to be. And, there are very few towns deeper in the woods of western Maine than those in the Dead River Valley."

"I still don't get it."

"I'm saying that we will appeal to their patriotic spirit when the time comes. We'll tell them it's for the good of the state and the country. They'll be helping their fellow citizens to get out of the dark ages and put the working man on a path to prosperity never seen before. I guarantee they'll be ready to give up their land for a cause that benefits the country, the state, and themselves. And if not everyone is willing to wave the flag, then I know just the ticket that will get them on board."

2.

Ed Morrison's hayfield
Flagstaff, Maine
July 7, 1923

"What the...? Who are those two fellers standing at the edge of the woods?" Ed Morrison asked his hired hand.

"Don't know, Ed. Never seen them before," said Bill.

Ed watched one of the men pointing into the distance, first one way and then another, while the second man studied something laid out on the hood of their truck.

"Looks to me that the one standing next to the truck is looking at a map of some kind. Seeing they're on my land, I think we ought to see what those two birds are up to."

Ed and Bill dropped their scythes and worked their way across the field, careful to sidestep the windrows of freshly cut timothy.

Seeing the two farmers walking toward them, the strangers hurriedly rolled up their map and started toward the doors of the black Ford panel truck.

"Whoa, there! Just a minute, boys. Don't be in such a hurry to leave," Ed called, running as fast as his fifty-year-old legs would carry him.

Trapped, the two men closed the truck doors and waited.

"What are you two characters doing? Did you get permission from the landowner before you trespassed?" Ed asked, gasping for air.

The men knew enough not to try to bluff their way out of the situation and admitted they didn't know who owned the land.

"I own it from where we're standing to the Dead River, including that patch of woods you were eyeing. And I don't want you two on it. Anyway, what kind of map is that?"

"It shows elevations," the man holding the map tube replied.

"Elevations of what?" Ed asked.

"If you want more information, call our office in Augusta." The man passed the long tube to his partner, tore a page from his survey notebook, scribbled something on the paper, and passed it to Ed. "Call this number and ask Mr. Simmons, if you want to know more."

"Really? Well, I don't have a phone."

"Then I'd suggest finding someone who does," the man snorted as he settled into the driver's seat. As the vehicle pulled away, the neatly painted words on the driver's door caught Ed's attention: *Kennebec River Reservoir Company*. Ed and Bill watched the truck bounce across the rough field and disappear in a cloud of dust down the gravel road.

"Now, there goes one perfect gentleman," Ed said.

"A perfect something, all right, but it ain't a gentleman," Bill responded, spitting his chew onto the cut grass.

"Come on, Bill. Let's go down to the store and see if Jim knows anything about those two birds. By the looks of that thunderhead, we're about done haying for the day."

The sign above the entrance to Leavitt's Store said it all: THE BEST DAMN STORE IN TOWN. And since it was the *only* store in town, that slogan held true. Jim Leavitt had taken over the store after his father died while assisting a neighbor shingle a barn roof. No one survives a thirty-foot fall onto a stored two-bottom plow and lives to tell about it. After his father's death, Jim felt compelled to leave his job at the Farmer's Union in Farmington and return home to care for his mother while continuing the family business. As the only storekeeper in town, he knew everyone in the Valley and all the latest gossip.

Jim took pride in knowing the names of all the families, from the widowed grandmother living alone in a sprawling farmhouse by the Dead River to the twelve kids of the Olsen family, who lived at the end of Parsons Road on the far edge of town. Jim and his wife, June, served as the postmaster and postmistress of the cubbyhole-sized post office tucked away in the back of the store. All mail sent and received from Flagstaff, Dead River, and Bigelow Township passed through the eight-by-eight-foot cubicle.

The sleigh bell hanging over the door jingled as Ed and Bill entered the store.

"Hello, Ed. What brings you two into town? I thought you'd be making hay on a nice drying day like this," Jim remarked.

"We were until we got rudely interrupted."

"Ask him, Ed," Bill prodded.

"Ask me what?"

"About an hour ago, Bill and me caught two characters on my land. I'd never seen either of them before. When I asked what they thought they were doing, they clammed up. Never did give me a straight answer. All they said was they were looking at elevations, whatever that means. One of them was a real wise guy. I thought you might know something about it, seeing you talk to about everybody in the Valley at one time or another."

"Was 'Kennebec River Reservoir Company' spelled out on the truck door?" Jim asked.

"I knew you would know what they were up to! Yes. That's exactly what it said."

'I don't know for sure, but I have suspicions. Anyway, Bert Morris came in yesterday telling me the same story. He said he saw them in one of his pastures, and when he approached them, they drove off."

"So, what do you think is going on?"

"I think they're surveying for when they build a dam at Long Falls and flood us all out."

Leavitt had just finished ringing up a customer when Asa Ferrin rushed into the store all excited.

"Guess who had a run-in with two surveyors today?"

"Who?" Leavitt asked.

"Arapaho Nell. According to Larry Connor, who heard it from the Sheriff's deputy, she caught the same two surveyors Ed saw a couple of weeks back walking across one of her fields. Only she didn't ask questions. Nell grabbed her rifle and marched across the field to cut them off. She took that German shepherd of hers along with her for safety. I don't know which one of the two is the crazier, her or the dog. That canine had just as soon bite you as to look at you. I'd shoot the mangy son of a bitch if it were mine."

"Asa, stick to the story. What happened?"

"The deputy told Larry that she got about fifty feet from the two, raised her gun, and ordered them to turn around and go back to their truck, or she'd plant a .22 long between their ears. They tried to reason with her, but she wouldn't have any of it. Old Nell ordered them to shut up and move out. As the two walked past her toward the pickup, the taller one made a wisecrack that set Nell off. Nell told the Sheriff that Pretty Boy pulled the leash from her hand and that she never meant for the dog to bite one of them on the calf. Well, I don't condone siccing a dog on anyone. However, maybe it sent a message to those two birds that you don't go traipsing across someone's land without first asking," Asa said.

While Asa told Leavitt about the incident between Nell and the land surveyors, a passerby stopped at the general store to buy coffee for the drive to Stratton.

"That Nell seems like quite a character," the stranger remarked, listening to the conversation as he waited at the counter to pay for his drink.

"A complete fruitcake would be more descriptive," Asa said.

"How so?" the man asked, taking a swig from his coffee. "I've always been intrigued by human nature. She reminds me a lot of a couple of characters in my town. Although the two I'm thinking of wouldn't threaten anyone with a rifle. Sic a dog on someone, maybe."

"Well, to start with, nobody knows what ever happened to her husband. Bill went into the service right after high school. After being discharged, he returned home with Nellie, his new bride. No one knew where she hailed from. We all figured it was Louisiana or Alabama by her accent. Anyway, things seemed to be fine for a time. They lived with Bills parents until they passed away. Then the farm belonged to Bill. That property has some of the best-drained intervale land in the Valley. Every farmer in the area would have given their eye teeth to own that land. About two years after Bill and Nell took over the place, Bill disappeared. Not a soul knew it until the town meeting in March. Bill always went to the annual meeting. Always had something to say, too. Real civic-minded, Bill was. Anyway, after the meeting, the first selectman paid a call to the farm to see if Bill was okay. Nell met him at the door. She said Bill had gone to Farmington for some tractor parts. Well, Clyde Donahue, the selectman, knew that wasn't true, but he played along. He told Nell that Bill had forgotten to pay last year's poll tax and to ask him to stop by the selectmen's office when he returned. Of course, he never showed up at the town office or anywhere else in the Valley, for that matter. It was as if a spaceship came down and took him."

"Did anyone call the police?" the passerby asked.

"There's no police in the Valley. No need. If someone does something wrong, a couple of us give them a good talking-to, and everything gets straightened out…one way or another. We did call the County Sheriff in Skowhegan, though. He never drove up to check things out. As far as he was concerned, Bill could have left on his own free will. There was nothing he could do until there was evidence of a crime. One of Bill's neighbors even went to the Registry of Deeds in Skowhegan to see whose name the farm was in. Nellie owns it fair and square. Her name is on the deed. Bill deeded it over to her about two months after he inherited it from his folks."

"Any idea what happened to him?"

"Everyone has their own idea. Most think Nellie killed him for his money and buried him somewhere on the property. But who knows? Maybe he did leave willingly to get away from the old bat."

"How does she act when people see her in town?"

"No one's seen Nellie in three years. At least until the incident I told you about. She holes up at the farm. When she needs things from the store, she pays one of the neighbor's kids to get them for her."

Leavitt interrupted the two. "Asa, weren't you supposed to pick something up for your wife?" He thought Asa had already shared more than enough about the townspeople's business with the stranger.

"Holy old Mackinaw, that's right! Ellen is going to kill me when I get home. I've got to get going. I'm gonna grab a can of brown bread to go with the homemade beans she's having for tonight's supper. I'll be back tomorrow to pay you, Jim."

"I've got to go along as well. I'm supposed to be in Stratton in an hour. Good luck with Nell," the man said with a smile, and disappeared out the door.

3.

"The last of the Hayden Logs on the Dead River was rolled in Friday the 16th—two and a quarter million. It was a dangerous place to work, and men were glad when they saw the last of it. It has been the scene of a series of accidents. Some 22 years ago, Hayden was killed there; afterward, Hunnewell was drowned there; a little more than a week ago, O'Donnell was caught by the rolling logs and killed, and a few days after that, Frank Davis of Solon, head man on the landing had his leg broken."

—*Lewiston Evening Journal*
May 27, 1873

Logging is hazardous. A crushed foot by an obstinate horse, a deep gash from an errant swing of the ax, and bloody wounds from a two-man crosscut saw were some of the risks of working in the woods. Each logging operation occasionally experienced a fatality due to a tree falling in the wrong direction or a team of horses sluiced while descending an icy road, with the driver crushed by the overturned load. An even greater risk was after the wood was delivered to the landing, where it sat in massive piles until the river was free of ice. Rolling logs into the river and the drive itself were where most fatalities happened. Dead River and Flagstaff men were just as vulnerable to fatal accidents as anyone else who cut wood for a living.

Most people living in the Dead River Valley made a living by farming, working in the woods, or supporting the two industries. Bryant's sawmill at the outlet of Flagstaff Pond bought and cut white birch. The blacksmith shop in the center of the village kept tools and equipment repaired, and Leavitt's Store sold the saws and axes for the woodsmen to use in the backwoods operations. The same was true of farming. Nearly everything the farmer needed, from fertilizer to baling twine, was funneled through Leavitt's Store, and without local labor, farms couldn't prosper.

After high school, many young men in Flagstaff, Dead River, and Bigelow, at least those who didn't go into the military, went into the woods. Those who quit school made the transition to logging quicker.

Isaac Blanchard graduated from Flagstaff High School in 1940. The day after graduation, he began working at Joe Farm as an assistant herdsman, caring for the fourteen teams of horses that the logging companies kept there for the summer. At the same time, he waited, hoping to be hired by one of the jobbers who had a winter contract to cut spruce in Pierce Pond Township. Isaac's father and grandfather earned their living by cutting wood, making it seem only natural for Isaac to carry on the family tradition. Only now, most of the large trees nearby had been cut, forcing the logging operations into more remote areas.

In October, Isaac finally received the letter he had been waiting for. He was to report for work at the Stony Brook Camp on the Dead River on November 2, where he would work as a chopper and perform other duties as assigned. He would be working for the Moxie Gore Logging Company based in Bingham, one of the largest logging contractors in Somerset County. Isaac couldn't wait to return home and tell his parents the good news.

His parents and grandfather were having supper when Isaac burst through the door and immediately told them about his first real job. His father, Harry, listened but didn't share his son's excitement, and his grandfather also appeared less than enthusiastic about the announcement.

"Do you know the area they'll be cutting?" Harry asked.

"The letter said the north side of Hurricane Mountain."

Isaac's father fell silent momentarily, casting his father a brief, serious glance.

"That means they'll haul the wood to Hayden Landing."

"I guess."

"Son, Hayden Landing is cursed. Bad things happen there. It's not a safe place to be."

"Come on, Father. What do you mean, cursed?"

"Your father's right, Isaac," Harry's father said. "There have been way too many accidents there to be a coincidence."

"Like what?"

"To start with, it's how Hayden Landing came by its name. Back in 1853, a young man about your age, Oswald Hayden, drowned after slipping off a log he was standing on trying to push the logs away from shore with a pike-pole[2] far enough so the river current would grab them and send them on their way down the rapids. He wasn't fifty feet from shore when he surfaced. He didn't see that raft of logs pushed by the current headed right at him. The men standing on shore saw what was going to happen. All they could do was watch as the entire mass of tangled logs drifted right over him, pinning him beneath the water. There was no way out. Eventually, the men separated the mess enough to pull Hayden's body out of the water. So, in memory of the boy, they named the log landing Hayden Landing. A name that has stuck for over ninety years."[3]

"That was a terrible thing to have happened. But I don't see what a curse had to do with it."

"Hayden's accident was the first of many at the landing. Two years after Hayden was killed, a spruce log fell from a scoot being

---

2. See Glossary for definitions of logging terms used in Chapter 3.
3. Hayden Landing remains a feature on present-day USGS Topographic maps.

unloaded when the binder chain snapped. The man never knew what hit him," Harry said.

"And ten years ago, an Irishman named O'Donnell was daydreaming and didn't hear the foreman yell to stand clear just before the crew knocked out the key log, causing the stack of logs to roll into the river. The men who dug him out of the pile said every bone in his body was broken. Two weeks after O'Donnell died, the scaler broke his leg when a log rolled just as he was stepping over it. And just last spring, a French logger from Quebec was working in a bateau trying to break a jam when his pick pole got stuck between two logs. As he struggled to free it, a raft of logs struck the bateau, causing the Frenchman to lose his balance and fall overboard. Before the men in the boat could rescue him, he slipped beneath the knotted pile of logs. The searchers discovered his body a week later in a pile of debris entangled around Elephant Rock, four miles downstream. I know for a fact that those accidents happened, son. I've heard of others over the years being maimed or killed at Hayden Landing as well. So that's why I say the place is cursed."

Isaac's mother, Sarah, gazed at her plate, listening to her husband recount the accidents. When he finished, she set down her fork. Still staring at the table, Sarah spoke for the first time since Isaac had come home.

"Isaac, I don't claim to understand everything that goes on when cutting wood. And I certainly don't know anything about any curse. I do know logging is dangerous work, and men can get hurt or killed on the job. Curse or not, I need you to promise your father and me that you *won't* work anywhere near that log landing. Do you promise?"

Isaac looked at his grandfather, hoping he would tell his parents they were overreacting. However, his grandfather did not come to Isaac's defense. Instead, he glanced at his daughter-in-law and said, "You need to answer your mother, Isaac."

"Okay," Isaac conceded. "I promise I'll say no if asked to help start the drive. But I don't like it. I'm seventeen and should be able to do anything I want, including launching the logs at Hayden

PART ONE: *Washed Out*   35

Landing. Now, I'm going up to bed. I need to be back at the Joe Farm tomorrow at six to tend to the horses." Then he flew up the stairs to his bedroom, slamming the door behind him.

"Does the boy remind you of anyone you know?" Isaac's grandfather asked, looking at his son.

"Maybe," Harry said. "Is there any pie left, Sarah?"

At last, November arrived, and Isaac set off for his new job in the woods. Stony Brook Camp was twenty-five miles downriver from his parents' home in Dead River. The all-day trek followed an old tote road past Joe Farm, Long Falls, and Grand Falls. The sun had dropped below the tree line when Isaac stepped from the uninterrupted forest into an open area about four miles downriver of Grand Falls.

Hayden Landing, he supposed, seeing several well-used haul roads converging on the break in the forest canopy. Isaac studied the area, thinking it didn't look hazardous. He watched the water rush past the landing, tumbling over boulders, speeding toward The Forks, where the Dead joined the Kennebec River. As Isaac stood looking out over the opening, he noticed what seemed to be a wire running parallel to the river, silhouetted against the darkening sky and then vanishing into the shadowy forest. Isaac couldn't waste precious daylight investigating the purpose of the aerial wire; he merely found it strange to see it in such a remote area. He quickened his pace, unaware of how much farther he had to go to reach Stony Brook Camp. One thing he was sure of was that his parents had greatly overestimated the danger of Hayden Landing.

Later, Isaac learned that the single strand of wire stretched twelve miles between Stony Brook Camp and the Dead River Dam above Grand Falls. Once the spring drive started, the camp boss would hook up his phone and call the dam workers to tell them to open the gates and for how long. The head of water would flush the logs down the Dead River. Once that wood was washed out, the process was repeated.

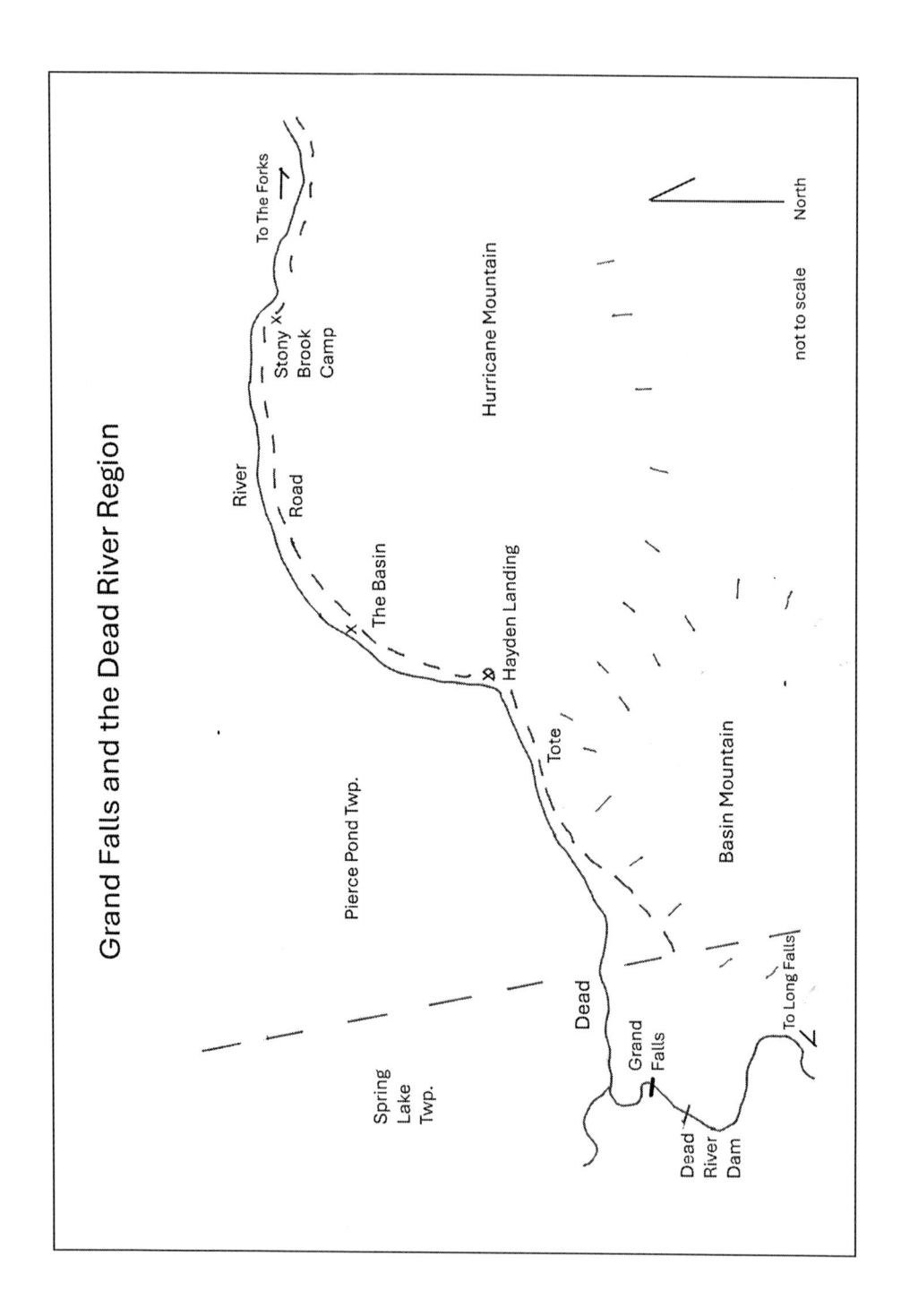

Grand Falls and the Dead River Region

To The Forks

Stony X
Brook
Camp

River

Road

Hurricane Mountain

The Basin
X

Hayden Landing

Tote

Pierce Pond Twp.

Basin Mountain

Spring
Lake
Twp.

Dead

Grand
Falls

To Long Falls

Dead
River
Dam

North

not to scale

The sun had set by the time Isaac arrived at what would be his home in the woods for the next four months. Curls of wood smoke spiraled upward from the stovepipes of two of the largest log buildings. Isaac presumed that one log structure was the bunkhouse, and the other was the company dining room.

Isaac had wanted to work in the woods for as long as he could remember, and now that day had finally arrived. The work would be hard, and the days would be long, but the pay was decent, even though he wouldn't see his money until the operation shut down in the spring. Isaac could hardly wait to head into the woods to begin cutting the giant spruce, promising himself to become the best man with an ax who ever worked for the Moxie Gore Logging Company.

In the distance, he could hear the unmuffled bark of the diesel generator powering the dining room lights. Men walked past the windows carrying plates of food. It struck him as odd not to hear voices penetrating the log wall. The only sounds he heard were silverware scraping against metal plates and the occasional clatter of tin coffee cups hitting the table.

Suddenly, Isaac lost confidence in becoming the best woodsman to swing an axe. He was about to enter a room full of men he didn't know—strangers of all shapes and sizes who were well-seasoned in the logging trade. Experts at swinging a double-bitted ax and drawing a two-man crosscut saw, each strong as an ox. Isaac was worried that he might not fit in. Maybe he wouldn't be able to pull his own weight. Perhaps they wouldn't take kindly to a scrawny, inexperienced kid from Dead River slowing down the woods operation. He stood at the dining room door, gathering the courage to enter. At last, he lifted the latch, crossed the threshold, and hoped for the best.

Isaac didn't need to worry. No one paid any attention to him. They were all too busy devouring their meal. Isaac would soon learn that talking was not allowed while eating. The camp cook expected the crew to go to the dining room at the sound of the bell, fill their plates, eat, and then leave. Anyone who didn't follow these rules would hear directly from the cook and might even get a rap on the head with a frying pan—the camp cook's word was law.

"Hey, you. Over here," came a commanding voice behind Isaac.

Isaac turned to see a short man, the owner of the booming voice, dressed in a large white baker's cap and apron.

"You late! You come to eat when the cookee rings the bell at five-thirty. Breakfast is five—same thing. You hear bell, you come in and sit. No talk, eat," the French camp cook said. "What's your name?"

"Isaac Blanchard. I'm from Dead River Plantation."

"Did I ask where you live? I don't think so," the cook said, running his finger down a list of names on a piece of paper nailed to the cabin wall.

"Okay. The cookee will fix a plate for you. Just remember what I told you. Next time you late, you don't eat. Remember, you live in woods, not Dead River Plantation, wherever that is."

Isaac took his plate and sat at a table near the back of the dining room, looking around as he ate. There were four sturdy tables, each about twenty-two feet long, flanked by two equally long plank benches. To the side of the tables were two woodstoves, one for heat and the other with an oven for cooking. A shelf ran between them with firewood stored underneath. The rest of the dining room was dedicated to the kitchen, except for a small walled-off area that served as the cook and cookee's bedroom.

The door swung open just as Isaac finished his second slice of pie, and another latecomer stepped into the dining room. He received the same reprimand from the cook that Isaac had gotten twenty minutes earlier. The cook checked the list to verify he worked for Moxie Gore Logging Company and then piled his plate with food. The man made his way toward the tables to sit. Isaac recognized the newcomer.

"Jimmy! Jimmy Parsons! Over here," Isaac called out.

Jimmy smiled and hurried to Isaac's table and sat across from him.

"Boy, am I glad to see you!" Isaac said. "I was afraid I wouldn't know anyone here."

"You and me both," Jimmy replied.

"I thought that after graduation, you said you were going to Skowhegan to work at the shoe shop."

"I did."

"So, what happened?"

"What happened was that I hated it. All I did all day was hand-stitch work boots. The pay was decent, but the job drove me crazy. And when I wasn't working, there was nothing to do. I went to the movies a few times, but there are only so many Hopalong Cassidy films a guy can stand. So, I quit and moved back home. At least in Dead River, I could go fishing and shoot partridge.

"My mother was constantly on my back about getting a job. I knew Moxie Gore was hiring, so I came here for the winter. Next spring, after the fish stop biting, I'm going to join the navy and see the world. The way I figure it, they will flood the Valley sooner or later, so why stick around?"

"Maybe it won't happen," Isaac said. "My father says if people stand together and fight it, they might stop the dam from being built. He says people are too quick to say okay to something that's being crammed down their throats."

The conversation abruptly ended when the dining room door opened. A tall, lean man with a gray beard and mustache entered, glanced at Isaac and Jimmy, and then walked over to the list of names pinned to the wall. He exchanged a few words with the cook, who pointed out Isaac and Jimmy as they were about to leave the dining room. The man intercepted them just as they approached the door. "Which one of you is Isaac Blanchard?"

"I am."

"Then you're Jimmy Parsons," the man said, looking at Jimmy. "I'm Virgil Trundy, foreman of this operation. So, you boys want to cut wood for the Moxie Gore Logging Company for the winter." Without waiting for them to answer, Trundy looked at Isaac and asked, "Have you cut wood before?"

"I cut and split firewood for my family. Ten cords a year," Isaac said.

"I mean *big* wood, like seventy-foot-tall spruce and pine, three foot on the stump. How about you, Parsons? Do you have any experience working in the woods?"

"No, sir."

"Pretty much as I expected. You two will help swamp roads. Be at the horse hovel in the morning and every morning at six. David Daigle will show you where you'll work."

"But I thought I'd be cutting wood," Isaac said.

"I've got twenty experienced choppers. There's no openings for a novice."

"But I signed up to cut wood," Isaac protested.

"Read the letter the company sent you. It says, 'and all other jobs assigned.' And this is your assignment. Now follow me, and I'll show you where you'll bunk."

Trundy used his flashlight to lead Isaac and Jimmy to the bunkhouse behind the dining room. Groups of men stood along the path, quietly talking while they enjoyed their last smoke before going to bed. Some conversed in French, while others spoke in English. This would be the last evening of idle conversation. For the next four months, six days a week, most of the men would head for their bunks soon after eating, too tired for small talk.

Isaac and Jimmy followed Trundy into the ram pasture—so-called by the loggers. The three walked between the two rows of bunks to the far end of the building, where Trundy lit a kerosene lamp. He lifted the lamp high so the boys could see where they would sleep. It wasn't by accident that Isaac and Jimmy had been given the bunk furthest from the bunkhouse door. Beds closer to the door were reserved for veteran woodsmen to give them a head start to the backhouse if the urge hit them during the night.

"That's your bed. You'll be sharing the double bunk. There's a blanket for each of you in the trunk. The outhouse is around the back, and the wash basin is at the other end of the room, next to the door. Any questions? Good. Make sure you turn off the lamp when you're in bed. We don't want the bunkhouse to burn down, if it tips over."

The straw boss opened the bunkhouse door at four the next morning and started hollering at the sleeping men. Six mornings a week, it was the same wake-up call, a ritual that gave him great pleasure.

"Everybody up! Look lively now. It's going to be a fine day to bring daylight to the swamp. Up! Up! Up!"

The generator roared to life as the obnoxious straw boss called reveille, illuminating the dining room and the foreman's office. It turned into a frantic rush to the outhouse to claim one of the eight holes. Inside the bunkhouse the men lined up at one of the two sinks, which could accommodate five men at a time. On the woodstove, two kettles of hot water, with two barrels of cold water beside the sink ready to wash and rinse away the grime from the previous day. Not every man made time to wash, though many wished they had, especially as winter dragged on. At five o'clock, the pace quickened at the sound of the cookee ringing the bell, signaling the men to head to the dining room for breakfast. At breakfast for the first time, Isaac realized how many woodsmen worked at Stony Brook Camp. The four tables were packed with men who, for the next four months, would cut the standing spruce and transport it to the river to be stacked in mammoth log piles that would be toppled into the river once the spring drive began.

The first table was reserved for the foreman and his assistant, the scaler, clerk, blacksmith, filer, and prominent visitors like the walking boss, who occasionally visited all the woods operations to monitor the jobbers' progress. Choppers, road crews, team drivers, and laborers sat at the other tables, with the non-English-speaking Frenchmen preferring to be seated separately.

At six, Isaac and Jimmy were at the horse hovel waiting for the boss to arrive. As the swamping crew stood there, they heard the teamsters inside the hovel softly talking to their horses as they adjusted them into the bulky harnesses. The horses blew and stomped at the log floor, anxious to feel the strain of their first hitch of the day.

"I didn't sign up to swamp roads," Isaac groused. "I've got a good mind to quit and go home."

"And what? Tell your father you quit the first day because you didn't like to be told what to do? I want to be there and see what he'd say about that," Jimmy said.

Isaac knew his friend was right. His father and grandfather would have no sympathy, knowing that after one day on the job, he quit for such a silly reason. He would do what he was asked to do, but that didn't mean he had to like it.

The first rays of the new day shot across the tops of the beech and maple trees surrounding the logging camp as David Daigle stepped up to the dozen swampers waiting for orders.

Daigle had worked in the woods for forty years, most of those years for the Moxie Gore Logging Company. He was a wiry Frenchman who always wore a smile, even when reprimanding a man for something he had done. This made it hard for anyone to tell if he was upset about something or just having a friendly conversation.

"Good morning, boys. Are you ready to torture a few trees today?" he asked. "For you new fellers that don't know me, I'm David D. Daigle, and I'm De Boss of De Swamp Crew. I'm one mean feller if some one of you decides to get lazy," David said with a broad grin. "So, you work hard, and I won't be so mean, maybe," he said, still sporting a smile.

"Now, the first thing we do is go to the clerk's office. He'll give you axes and saws. You won't have to pay for them unless you break the handle or lose them under the snow. Remember, your pay check not so big if you get careless with your tools."

The men paraded to the clerk's office, signing for the axes and saws that would become part of their anatomy until spring. Tools in hand, the thirteen men started the long trek up the side of Hurricane Mountain to clear a swath wide enough for the two-horse teams to drag the logs from the stump to the yard.

"Okay. We start here. Clear the road from that red rag over there on the beech to the other side where the other rag is, then to the big spruce, maybe one mile in that direction," Daigle said, pointing off into the distance. "Spread out in groups of three as we walk. You three," he said, pointing to the men who had lagged behind the others. "Stay here and work that way," Daigle said, pointing down the flagged trail.

Isaac, Jimmy, and the other men followed Daigle deeper into the woods. Every hundred yards, he'd pick three men and repeat the instructions. Jimmy, Isaac, and a third man were the last to be assigned an area.

"Everything goes. Cut trees flush to the ground. No stumps left to puncture a horse's hoof. Throw everything beyond red rags. You two listen to Emile," Daigle ordered, looking at Isaac and Jimmy. "Emile has cut more big spruce than anyone in Canada. So, Emile knows something about logging in the big woods. The cookee will bring you lunch. I'll check on you later." Daigle turned and worked his way back down the slope to check on the other crews swamping the twitch trail.

Emile tore into the small-diameter hardwood trees with a vengeance. When he came to trees too small to cut with an ax, he would grab the bucksaw and drop them faster than Isaac and Jimmy could haul them to the side.

Emile didn't stop moving. He'd run from tree to tree, drop to his knees, and cut the sapling close to the ground, leaving no nub to hinder the yarding operation. After two hours, Jimmy began to slack off, unable to keep up with Emile. Isaac wouldn't bend. No way would he let a man three times his age outdo him. The three men kept up the frantic pace until Jimmy spotted a man dressed in white pants and a red and black plaid wool coat, with a woven cedar backpack strapped onto his back, making his way toward them.

"Cookee's here!" he yelled to the others, looking for a place to sit down and eat lunch. "The beans were warm when I left," the cookee said, "but the long walk up the hill cooled them off. I'll build a fire and warm them up along with the biscuits."

"Don't bother with that. We can't wait that long. We need to get back to work," Emile said, not asking either Jimmy or Isaac if they wanted to lunch on cold beans and dry biscuits.

Each man grabbed a tin bowl from the bucket and held it out for the cookee to fill. Sitting on a fallen beech, Emile, Isaac, and Jimmy downed the beans and half a dozen cookies, not taking time to talk. After downing one more cookie and the last of the cold tea, Isaac broke the silence.

"You're a fast worker, Emile. It's hard to keep up with you."

"When I was young, I cut twice what I did this morning. Now I'm old and don't move so fast."

"How long have you worked in the woods?" Jimmy asked.

"Since I was fifteen. I left school in the tenth grade. My father got hurt really bad trying to get away from a tree that fell the wrong way. A dead limb broke as the tree fell, hitting his leg as he ran. He couldn't work in the woods for a year, so the family had no money to pay the bills. That's when I went into the woods and never left."

"Have you ever thought about giving up living in logging camps and cutting trees at twenty below zero?" Isaac asked.

"Never. I love working in the woods. I've never wanted to do anything else but cut the pine and spruce. I love cold mornings when the air is calm and you can see your breath. The forest is like a grand cathedral, and the tall spruce and pine are like hundreds of organ pipes coming out of the deep snow. I like everything about the woods: the chatter of the red squirrel warning me not to chop down his home, the Whiskey Jack trying to steal my sandwich, and the smell of the pitch that sticks to my hands and clothes. Every day is like my first day chopping wood, and every day, I learn something I never knew. How many people working in a factory can say that?

"Did you fellers see all the old men in the swamping crew? They're a bunch of old, broken-down woodsmen like me. They were at the top of their trade in their younger days. Now they're too old to cut the big spruce but still able to swamp roads. And swamping roads keeps them in the woods and alive. They'd rather jump off a cliff than sit on the porch in a rocker and rot away. Me and every one of them will work until we can't lift an ax.

"Well, time to get back to work. If I sit here too long, I stiffen up. My grandfather told me, 'Emile, if you keep moving, you'll live to be a hundred.' I plan to keep moving to prove him right."

The three wiped their bowls with pieces of moss lifted from a rock. While waiting for the others to finish, Isaac gazed at the tall hardwood. He noticed a large bump about four feet above the ground on an old maple. Curious, he walked to the tree about a hundred feet away.

"Over here!" he hollered.

While waiting for Jimmy and Emile, Isaac studied what he had found.

"Take a look at this," Isaac said, pointing at the moss-covered leather boots.

"Well, I'll be," Emile said. "So that's the tree they nailed them to."

"You know about them?" Isaac asked.

"Sure do. The boots belonged to Olaf Hakala, a Finn who worked for the old Kennebec Logging Company. I heard the story a dozen times in the past twenty years about him being killed on Hurricane Mountain. I always thought it was just a yarn somebody had made up to kill time sitting around the woodstove."

"So, what happened to him?" Jimmy asked.

"As I remember, Hakala was hauling a load of spruce logs down the mountain to Hayden Landing. The main trail had been iced during the night and was extremely slick. Usually, trail monkeys spread hay on the steep road sections to create friction under the runners and slow the load down. This way, the logs don't push the team so hard that they get run over."

Emile stopped talking and looked around the area. "There!" he said, pointing to the base of a steep pitch. "I bet there's where Hakala met his maker. Anyway, when Hakala got to the crest of the slope, he saw no hay on the road. He tried to rein in his team, but the momentum of the load of logs kept pushing them forward, and they started down the hill.

"There happened to be a team of choppers working nearby. They heard someone yell and saw Hakala pull back on the reins for all he was worth, repeatedly shouting *whoa!* The helper riding on top of the load saw what was coming and jumped off about a quarter of the way down. The choppers yelled for Hakala to jump, but he stuck with his team. All they could do was watch as the team, Hakala, and the logs went faster and faster down the hill. Olaf pulled the hand brake that forced the plow board out sideways to the tote to slow their speed. It seemed to work until it snapped under the pressure and flew into the woods. The men said he still might have made it if one of the binder chains that held the load to the sled hadn't broken. A log bolted forward, catching Olaf in the back of his head and driving him forward. The men watched him struggle to regain his balance, but he couldn't defy gravity. He fell onto the tongue, then dropped onto the road and was run over by the sled. When the men rushed to help, they found poor Olaf in two pieces, completely cut in half by the runners.

"The team stopped about two hundred feet beyond Olaf, where the haul road flattened out. Olaf could have jumped early on, but that would have meant the load would have pushed the horses so hard that they would have fallen and been sluiced by the load of spruce. Olaf saved his team, but it cost him his life.

"As for the boots, the loggers nailed them to the tree in tribute to Olaf. Most times, it's the kind of tribute that river drivers do for their own when one of them drowns during the spring drive.

"Now we better get back to work before Daigle catches us slacking off."

Isaac and Emile quickly became close friends. Foreman David D. Daigle assigned teams to work on the swamp roads each morning, and Isaac made it a point to team up with Emile. Eager to learn everything about big-time logging, Isaac would sit with Emile by the woodstove in the evenings and bombard him with questions. Emile gladly obliged, seizing the opportunity to share his stories and keep the memories of forty years of logging alive in his mind.

Stony Brook Camp was about twelve miles upriver from Dead River's junction with the Kennebec River at The Forks and about a quarter of the way down the longest continuous stretch of white water on a river in the eastern United States. It was no easy task to bring supplies to the logging camp.

Once the snow blanketed the ground, a Cletrac diesel crawler tractor towed a twelve-foot box sled to The Forks to gather supplies for the Stony Brook Camp. Moxie Gore Logging Company operated two logging camps that winter: Stony Brook Camp and Number 1 Camp, located four miles downriver. The tractor operator delivered supplies to both. Occasionally, depending on when he left Stony Brook Camp or made his return trip with supplies, the tractor driver would spend the night at Number 1 Camp and continue the following day. Below Poplar Hill Falls, the turbulent white water gave way to a somewhat slacker flow. The slower current allowed the river to freeze, and in the dead of winter, when the ice was thickest, the tractor crossed to the north side of the river for the final two miles to The Forks.

Isaac was still miffed that his job was clearing woods roads and not working with one of the chopping crews that were cutting large spruce. One morning at daybreak, Emile, Jimmy, and Isaac were making their way up Hurricane to start cutting a new twitch trail when Isaac began to complain to Emile about having to swamp roads every day.

"Have a little patience. Sometimes it takes time to get what we want," Emile told Isaac. "The company rules are that everyone who's not cut big trees starts swamping roads. Even the big boss did his share of throwing brush. Trundy did everything when he was young: cruise the timber, swamp roads, and limb the spruce. He was even one of the road monkeys long before he became the lead chopper. That's why Trundy is the boss. That man understands what must be done to deliver the wood to the mill, and he learned it by starting as a swamper. If you stick with it, you might become the big cheese someday. Although the way things are headed, logging will look a lot different than it is now."

"What does that mean?" Isaac asked.

"Changes are coming now that most of the big spruce and pine have been cut. There'll still be spruce and pine, but the trees will be fewer and smaller than what we cut now, and they won't be near the river.

"I helped log on to this side of Hurricane Mountain forty-five years ago with a crew twice the size we have now. For two winters, we worked out of Stony Brook Camp. There were so many spruce logs at Hayden that we started a new landing at The Basin. Nowadays, good spruce stands are hard to come by. If this year isn't the last long log drive on the Dead, it will likely be next."

"So what will we cut if there's no big softwood left?"

"There will always be wood to cut, and there still will be log drives, except what floats down the river won't be logs. It will be four-foot pulpwood to feed the paper mills. It's happening now. All the wood sluiced through the Dead River Dam above Grand Falls is pulpwood. A log drive on the North Branch of the Dead hasn't existed since 1931.

"And as for those spruce stands back from the river, it's a hard chance now. So if they want them, they'll have to build roads to get them out. Hollingsworth and Whitney have already built a haul road from the last house in Carrying Place Township, three miles north. One thing you can take to the bank is the company won't leave a stick standing if they think they can make a dollar cutting it.

"You know what else I think is going to change?" Emile continued without giving Isaac or Jimmy a chance to ask. "I think Stony Brook Camp is done after this winter. In case you two hadn't noticed, the bunkhouse is rotting from the ground up, and the dining room isn't much better. You almost need to get a running start to get out of the sag in the center of the floor. The logging camp has had a good run. Those buildings were practically new when I stayed there in 1925. When they finish building that road I told you about, they'll truck the crews to where they're cutting and back to Bingham at night, or maybe the roads will be so good the men will drive their own pickup trucks home. Why, hell's bells, it can't be fifteen miles from Bowtown to Bingham, and if they put a bridge across the Dead below Poplar Hill Falls, trucks could be out to the tarred road in forty minutes.

"While I'm gazing into my crystal ball, I'll tell you fellers more about what Emile Ferland has been thinking. If you two boys stick to working in the woods, you'll be the last of the men to use a crosscut saw or an ax to down a tree or a peavey to roll logs onto a pile in a yard. Take the long log river drivers; they are as good as extinct now. Once the longwood drive ends, they're finished as well. All they'll need is a crew with strong backs to follow the drive, throw the pulpwood that got stranded on the shore back into the river, and maybe a bateau or two of men to free the pulp grounded or hung up against a tree or ledge or something. In a few years, all people will have to remember how logging used to be will be an old, grainy photograph of a river driver with his pike pole riding a log through the rapids.

"The whole breed of loggers is changing. Take Ted Adams, who drives the dozer. He's good at what he does, but you can't call him a woodsman. Ted could just as well use that crawler to build a road for the State as work for the Moxie Gore Logging Company. As I said, the chopping crew days are numbered as well. Two weeks before you two showed up for work, the walking boss had a feller come in and put on a demonstration using a chainsaw. He cut wood faster than three chopping crews if he could keep the damn thing running. Between breaking down, throwing a chain, and wearing the operator to a frazzle after three or four hours of wrestling with the monster, it was down as much as it was running. But I can see that once they lick a few problems, that ear-cracking, oil-smoking contraption will cause many axes to be retired to the woodshed.

"I ain't saying change is bad. Chances are the more wood a man cuts, the more money he can take home to feed his family. All I'm saying is the old way of logging is about to die, and the new breed of logger will probably be better off for it, but he'll be a lot more boring. Anyways, that's the prediction from Emile Ferland's What It's Worth Department."

The teamsters' sleeping quarters were separate from the logging crew's bunkhouse. They needed to be close by to feed and care for the horses. They were the first to rise every morning to have their horses harnessed and ready to leave for the woods at dawn, and they often were the last to return to camp after the final haul of the day. Stony Brook Camp had six pairs of draft horses, one assigned to each chopping crew. To the men, the horses were more than 1800-pound wood-hauling machines; they were pets, and like most pet owners, each teamster believed his team was the finest in the hovel.

The other men in camp joked that the teamsters spent so much time with their animals that horse and man shared the same smell. That was not far from the truth. After a day of hauling logs in rain or snow, the teams returned to the hovel soaked. The mixture of water, manure, and sweat gave the teamsters a unique, organic smell that bonded to skin and clothes so that no amount of scrubbing could get it out.

If one of the choppers confronted a teamster about his horsey odor, he would reply that he never had as much as a cold all winter because of it. The horsemen credited the sweet smell of manure and sweat for repelling all viruses and bacteria-borne diseases. This belief allegedly produced the adage "healthy as a horse."

Trundy was constantly thinking of ways to increase production. The more logs stacked at Hayden Landing, the happier the landowner, which translated into more contracts for the Moxie Gore Timber Company. One way to stack more wood for the spring drive was for the teams to haul more. Trundy knew the teamsters were competitive, so he contrived a contest to determine which team could tote the most wood to Hayden Landing in a week. Trundy knew the pride that came with being recognized as Stony Brook Camp's most productive team was a great motivator.

The sun had set when Emile, Isaac, and Jimmy returned to camp. After leaving their axes at the filer's shack, they started back to the bunkhouse. The path led them past the horse hovel, and in the glow of a kerosene lamp hanging by the teamsters' bunkroom door, they saw a dozen men gathered as two men argued. The closer they got, the louder the commotion.

"What's going on, boys?" Emile asked, watching the exchange between the two teamsters.

"Whitten thinks Tylander cheated on the amount of wood he hauled to the landing," said the man standing next to Emile.

"How's that?" Emile asked.

"Last Sunday night, Trundy showed up at the bunkhouse saying the team that hauled the most wood this week would get a two-pound can of Bugler cigarette tobacco. He tacked a piece of cardboard to the back of the door, listing each team and the days of the week. About fifteen minutes ago, Trundy showed up, wrote the daily scale for each team, and totaled them up. He asked Tylander to come up and presented him with the tobacco. That's when the shit hit the fan.

"As soon as Trundy was out of earshot, Whitten commenced his tirade, saying the only way Tylander could have won was to cheat. He said there was no way his team could have hauled that much wood, and accused him of bribing the scaler. At first, Tylander laughed it off and went outside for a smoke. Whitten followed him and kept at him. Since then, it's been one insult after another between them."

Emile, Isaac, and Jimmy listened as the two continued to argue.

"There's no way your nags could haul that much wood!" said Whitten.

"Nags, are they? Well, those *nags*, as you call them, outclass those lightweights of yours. I'm surprised Trundy even took on a pair of 1400-pounders unless he figured the rest of us would make up for what logs you couldn't haul!" Tylander shouted.

Whitten shot back. "We all know you whip your team, trying to make them pull a load they just plain can't pull."

"You take that back! I've never whipped my team!"

"You damn well have!" Whitten turned to the others. "You boys have seen him, haven't ya?"

No one spoke to back up Whitten's claim.

"Well, I have! And it ain't right. Only a man with no respect for his animals would whip 'em."

"Why you…" Tylander lunged at Whitten.

He'd probably have killed him if Emile hadn't stepped between the two.

"Whoa, there, boys! Let's not get into a brawl over bragging rights and two pounds of tobacco. Seems to me there are too many variables to have a fair contest on who hauls the most wood. Why, sometimes the trees are smaller in one place than another, and it takes longer to make up a load than with big spruce. How do you fellers feel about me talking to Trundy to see if I can't get him to stop the contest? He knows every one of you put in a full day and haul your fair share of logs."

Everyone spoke in favor except Tylander and Whitten, who continued to glare at each other. Emile took their silence as a yes. "Well, it appears to be unanimous. I'll talk to Trundy and see what he'll do."

That evening, Emile visited Trundy's cabin. He convinced him that having a winner each week would cause more rancor among the teamsters than it would be worth, and if he didn't end it now, Trundy might not have *any* team to haul wood. Trundy agreed. There would be no second week of the competition.

Late winter, Isaac caught a break. Trundy asked if he'd be willing to take over for the limber who had severely sliced his leg swinging his ax and needed to go downriver to have it tended to. Isaac jumped at the chance. The new job put him one step closer to cutting trees.

A chopping crew included the head chopper, two sawyers, a limber, a sled tender, and sometimes a swamper to clear a pathway for a tree to fall.

Ten hours a day, Isaac whacked the whorls of branches off the fallen spruce. Starting at the tree's lower end, he worked to the point where the diameter was too small for a log. An ax flying among the thick branches was an accident waiting to happen. An unnoticed limb could easily deflect an ax from its intended target to a leg or ankle. Sometimes, it penetrated the flesh clear to the bone.

Jimmy also got a promotion of sorts. He gave up his swamper's job for one with the road monkeys, who iced the roads at night so the steel runners of the sleds carrying tons of softwood logs would glide more easily.

To ice a road, the road monkeys filled a five-hundred-gallon wooden tank at the river. Two peeled cedar poles leaning against the tank served as a track to slide an empty bucket to the ground and to hoist the full one to the top of the barrel, where one of the men used a push pole to tip the bucket for the water to run into the tank. The raising and lowering of the bucket were accomplished by a rope connected to the bucket's handle, then threaded through a pulley with the other end attached to the horse. Jimmy's job was to walk the horse away from the tote, raising the bucket, and then walk him back to lower it. Once loaded, the single horse pulled the sled up the main haul road between Hayden Landing and the yard where the logs had been collected. There, Jimmy and another man pulled the two plugs on the rear of the tank, spilling the water into the tracks of the haul sleds to freeze. The road monkeys' other job was placing hay on critical grades to slow down the loaded sleds. Except for having to work most of the night in the bitter cold, it was a much less demanding job than cutting trees and hauling brush ten hours a day.

As Christmas approached, Isaac became homesick. The men would have Christmas Day off from work. However, because the holiday was on a Wednesday, there wasn't enough time for Isaac to go home to visit and be at work at five the following morning.

Saturday night before Christmas, while most of the men congregated around the woodstove, swapping stories and playing cards, Isaac lay on his bunk, wondering what was happening at home. He remembered this was the Saturday before Christmas, the night of the town Christmas party above Leavitt's Store. The Christmas party and the 4th of July celebration were the two main social events of the year in the Dead River Valley. The entire town would be there, he thought. There would be stews and chowders, loaves of homemade bread and rolls, and more pies and cakes than could be eaten. The hall would be lavishly decorated with boughs, red bows, winterberries, and miles of green garland draped around the windows and doors. In the center of the room, a monster Christmas tree would be covered with dozens of colorful paper ornaments made by the younger children.

Isaac knew his grandfather and half a dozen older men would grab their winter coats and disappear for a time. When they reappeared, their faces would have taken on the glow of the Christmas season.

After the meal, the men would stack the tables against the wall, and the piano would be rolled into position. Miss Savage, Isaac's third-grade teacher, and Mrs. Taylor would take turns playing. Isaac knew from previous Christmas parties a waltz, a foxtrot, and Lady of the Lake and Boston Fancy, two dances he never understood and avoided like the plague. The list of songs would repeat until the evening ended. Oh, how he wished he could put on his dancing shoes.

In the middle of it all, Santa would burst into the hall with a bag of gifts for all the children. After giving out the toys and dancing with Mrs. Claus, he would disappear out the door and leave in his sleigh—the youngest children would assume. At ten, someone would flick the lights, the sign for everyone to gather around the tree. The lights were shut off, and all sang along as Miss Savage played "Silent Night."

After the music stopped, the lights snapped on, and in unison, everyone shouted a Merry Christmas and headed for the coat rack. Isaac remembered standing outside the store, seeing the beam from a dozen flashlights waving back and forth, guiding the families home, as others got into their sedans and trucks and drove back to Dead River or some distant farmhouse at the end of a dirt road.

Isaac could see it all in his mind. In high school, he couldn't wait to leave the backwater settlement of Dead River, and now, what he wouldn't give to be back there, even if it were only for Christmas.

Sunday was the one day of the week when the loggers weren't cutting or hauling wood. The time was their own, and most of the men spent it around camp playing cards and repeating the stories they had told during the week. A couple of the men ran traplines to make a few extra dollars, and Sunday was the day they checked them. Others spent the day on Hurricane Mountain, hoping to catch a big buck feeding on the fresh cedar the swampers had cut during the week.

Sunday was also the time to wash clothes. Last week's work clothes were tossed into large kettles of hot water along with a healthy amount of Tide, a new powder detergent that the logging company furnished to improve the sanitation at its winter operations. While clothes simmered on the woodstove, men waited for their turn at one of the bunkhouse sinks to shave, and then, with a basin of hot water, each man found a vacant corner to give themselves a quick going over to get rid of last week's grime and sweat. Washed clothes were strung up to dry on a rope that stretched from one end of the bunkhouse to the other.

After Isaac hung his clothes on the line, he lay on his bunk, flipping through last summer's Sears Roebuck catalog.

He was studying the latest in women's undergarments when Jimmy rushed up to his bunk.

"Isaac! You need to come see this!"

"See what," Isacc said, his eyes glued to page 128.

"Tim Ford is going after a Christmas tree for the dining room, and a bunch of us are going with him."

Isaac dropped the open catalog on his chest. "Jimmy, I know what a fir tree looks like. I don't need to go traipsing around the woods to watch Tim cut one."

"He's not going to cut it. He's going to shoot it!"

"Jimmy, someone's pulling a joke on you."

"No, really. A couple of the guys have seen him do it. Come on, Isaac. It'll be fun to watch!"

Grudgingly, Isaac pulled on his half-dry leather boots, grabbed his Mackinaw jacket, and followed Jimmy outside. At least a dozen men were gathered around Tim Ford, who was holding the butt of a double-barreled, twelve-gauge shotgun resting on his shoulder.

"Timmy, how about a little wager that you can't bring down a six-foot Christmas tree with a single shot," a man standing off to the side hollered.

"I'll do more than that. I'll make it a seven-footer," Ford said, spitting his chew into the snow.

"So that we understand one another. You're going to shoot down a seven-foot balsam fir with one shot," the logger said.

"That's right. It's a nice full one, too. You'll have to drag it back to camp and set it up."

"I've got a dollar says you can't do it."

"I'd be honored to take that dollar. Any more of you want to lose a dollar?"

Four other men said they were in.

"Jimmy, you hold everyone's money. Here's my five dollars," Tim said.

Fifteen men followed Ford up a haul road. Five minutes later, he stopped and looked at the tops of a stand of thirty-foot fir trees.

"Do you boys see that one fir that's kind of off to the side of the others?" Tim said, pointing to the top of the solitary tree. "That one's going to be the dining room Christmas tree."

Tim knew he might have gotten a little ahead of himself when he told the others he could shoot down a seven-foot tree. The tallest he'd ever brought down was six feet. He paced back and forth, sizing up the tall fir for a clear shot.

Tim played his audience for all it was worth. He rubbed his chin and flexed his body as if studying the best angle for a shot. Then he leaned his shotgun against a nearby tree and took out a plug of chewing tobacco, still staring at his victim.

"Quit stalling, Ford!" one man yelled. "You know you can't blow the top off that tree. Save yourself a load of buckshot and pay up."

Tim was buying time, wondering how he could ever shoot the top off that tree with one gun blast. The largest tree he had ever blown the top off was about four inches in diameter. This tree looked closer to five inches. His back to the spectators, Tim opened the gun's breech and dropped two double 00 shells into the chamber. He did a little more pacing and a little more looking. Finally, he found the perfect spot and dropped to one knee. He raised his weapon, took aim, and pulled both triggers so fast that everyone heard only one blast from the gun.

The top of the tree dropped until its top pointed down, but it did not fall. A sliver of wood held it to the tree. A round of catcalls rang out from the other loggers.

"Pay up, Ford! You didn't do it."

Tim didn't say a word. He approached a dead red maple and rocked it until it broke.

Then Tim walked back to the fir. Holding the maple like a baseball batter going for the fence, he whacked the tree for all he was worth, sending shock waves reverberating to the top of the tree. Two seconds later, the hinge let go, and the Stony Brook Logging Camp's Christmas tree fell onto the snow.

"Hey! That's cheating!" Roger yelled. "The deal was you would knock it to the ground with one shot."

"I did," Tim said, "and it's a seven-footer, too," he said, holding the tree next to him. "Jimmy, would you be so kind as to bring me my money?"

Christmas passed, and Isaac recovered from missing Christmas with his family. It was the middle of March when the operation was starting to wind down. A series of late winter snowstorms made it nearly impossible to get around in the woods and even harder to limb the spruce that buried themselves in the deep snow when they fell. There was one stand of spruce still left to cut before the season ended.

"Hey, Greenie!" Camille, the lead chopper, called to Isaac, whaling away at the limbs of a downed tree. Greenie was the nickname the Frenchman called all the first-season woodsmen. "Come over here, and I teach you something."

Isaac wallowed through the snow to see what the man had to say.

Camille walked up to the next spruce to be cut. "You want to chop the spruce? Then you need to learn how. Here, you notch the tree," the Frenchman said, giving the chopping ax to Isaac.

The two sawyers watched, grinning as Isaac approached the large spruce.

"First thing you do is walk around the tree and pack the snow. You waste a lot of good wood if you cut too high. Then you see which way the tree wants to fall. Look up and see which way it leans."

Isaac did what he was told and pointed to where he thought the tree would land.

"Okay. Now, you take the chopping ax and make a face cut the way it wants to go, like this."

Camille used his finger to draw an imaginary notch in the direction the tree would fall, telling Isaac the cut needed to go a third of the way through the spruce.

Isaac began to cut the notch. After five minutes of swinging the ax, Isaac needed to stop and rest his arms. The men laughed.

"If you're going to be the lead chopper, you put some meat on those bones this summer," Camille said.

Hearing Camille say he might be a lead chopper next year caused Isaac to tear into the tree for all he was worth.

"Okay, that's deep enough. Now you listen to me. You need to tell Jacques and Louis where to place the saw on the back of the tree. Remember, they can't see through wood, so you tell them where to start the cut. The line of the cut follows the deepest part of the notch. You follow with your eye to make everything line up."

Jacque and Louis moved into position and held the five-foot saw blade against the tree. Isaac motioned to move it up an inch.

"Okay. Now you watch them cut. Make sure the saw goes through the tree even. Don't let one man get ahead of the other, or the tree will swing and not go where you want it to. Also, if you want to live to be an old woodsman, once you see the tree start to fall, you get out of the way, *fast*. In case the wind decides it should go someplace else."

The crosscut saw flew through the thirty-inch spruce. Moments later, a faint snap. The tree shifted slightly toward the west, the direction Isaac had told the swampers to make a bed for the behemoth. Jacques and Louis backed the saw out of the cut and ran away from the falling tree with Isaac close behind. The hinge on the stump broke, and the tree's fall accelerated. It landed with a hollow *woof* exactly where Isaac had predicted.

"Not bad for a Greenie," Camille told Isaac, smiling.

Isaac was on his way to becoming a lead chopper, something he had wanted since arriving at Stony Brook Camp. The following two weeks, Camille taught him everything he knew about felling a big spruce.

In mid-April, the cutting operation was finished, and most of the logging crew had left for home. The remaining ones would follow once the logs at Hayden Landing were rolled into the river and on their way to the sawmills in Madison, Skowhegan, and smaller towns along the water route. A dozen or so men who wanted to earn extra money would follow the drive and relaunch logs grounded by the dropping water or hung up on a snag or behind one of the car-sized boulders.

Camille, Jacques, and Louis hitched a ride on the tote sled going out to The Forks with supplies the camp no longer needed. At The Forks, they planned to flag down a trucker for a ride back to Canada.

The day after the French crew left Stony Brook, Isaac threw his belongings into his rucksack and began the long walk home. At Hayden Landing, he saw Jimmy pushing logs into the current using a pike pole as other men stood on top of the pile of logs, rolling more logs into the river. Isaac had said goodbye to Jimmy the night before and didn't intend to stop. However, Jimmy spotted Isaac walking past and hollered for his friend to come down to the river.

"I wanted to tell you Trundy asked me if I wanted to stay on a while longer and follow the drive to The Forks."

"What did you tell him?"

"I said sure. He's paying three dollars a day. Depending on how many logs are hung up, it should take about two weeks. That's forty-two bucks! With what I earned swamping and icing the roads, I'll have enough for a down payment on a car when I get out of the navy.

"Of course, I'll give my mother some, too. She can use it now that Father is gone."

"You're going to be rolling in dough," Isaac joked. "I'll see you back home in a couple of weeks."

Walking back to the tote road, Isaac heard the straw boss holler to Jimmy to grab a peavey and free the log blocking others on the pile from rolling into the river.

Isaac happened to glance toward the far end of the landing, where he saw Emile putting the company's mark on each log's face using the stamping hammer.

"Emile!" he said, walking toward his friend.

"Are you heading home?" Emile asked.

"Yes. It's a long walk. It'll be dark by the time I get there."

"Camille told me before he left that he thinks you will make a fine chopper next year."

"You were right, Emile."

"About what?"

"Telling me to have patience. That a man doesn't get everything he wants when he wants it; you have to earn it."

"Oh, I think you would have figured that out for yourself after a time. I just sped the process up a bit."

"It was more than that. I was ready to say hell with it and head home. Anyway, thanks for all your advice. Will you be working for Moxie Gore next winter?"

"I think so. I still have a few good swings of the ax left in me. How about you?"

"I sure will. You know something I've been thinking about, Emile?"

"What's that?"

"One day, I will own my own logging company."

"I wouldn't bet against you, Isaac. And when you do, maybe you'll be in the market to hire an old broken-down logger to swamp your roads."

Just then, a thunderous crash came from the river, followed by a chorus of frantic shouts. Isaac ran toward the commotion with Emile close behind.

Half the log pile had collapsed. One man was standing next to the river holding a coil of rope as several others paced the shoreline, looking at the tangled mess of logs clogging the water. As Isaac ran toward the scene, he scanned the landing, looking for Jimmy. When he didn't see him, Isaac knew that it was his friend the men were looking for.

"What happened? Where's Jimmy?" he asked frantically, stepping up to the man holding the rope.

"Out there. Under the logs. Nathan is out there as well," the man said, still poised to throw the rope if one of them surfaced between the logs.

Isaac ran along the shore, looking for his friend. In a panic to find him, he started to leap onto the floating logs.

"Isaac, don't do it!" Emile yelled. He knew that if Isaac misstepped or a log rolled, he would go into the water and become trapped by the raft of spruce logs.

Isaac rushed up to Emile. "We need to save Jimmy! We have to do something before he drowns!"

"It's too late. There's nothing we can do to save Jimmy. He's gone," Emile said, having witnessed the same tragic scene play out several times over his years of logging.

Isaac returned to the shore and continued to scan the river, hoping for a miracle. Then he turned around, looking for the landing crew boss. He found him with a few other men discussing what had caused the pile of logs to let loose and roll into the water.

"What happened?" he asked, interrupting the conversation.

The straw boss recognized Isaac and knew Isaac and Jimmy had been friends.

"There was a log near the bottom of the pile that got crossed sideways, preventing the pile from rolling into the river. Three men rolling logs on the top of the pile yelled that there was a problem. I saw the log that had jammed everything up and asked Jimmy to take the peavey and move it enough to get the logs rolling again. I'd just called Dead River Dam to have them open the gates a quarter to release more water before the logs got hung up on the rocks, so we didn't have a jam to blow. When I turned to see how Jimmy was doing, I saw him starting to crawl among the logs—to get better leverage on the crossed log, I supposed. I yelled not to go in there. He heard me and was nearly out when the pile let go. Half the logs rolled. It all happened so fast.

"When the logs began to roll, the men on top of the pile lost their balance and fell. Ralph and Tuna scrambled back up the pile, but Nathan's leg got caught between two logs and he was dragged toward the river. He took a god-awful pounding by the logs rolling over him. I think Nathan was dead before he hit the water. It was terrible. I've never seen that much wood collapse at one time."

"We need to find Jimmy before he's dragged downriver," Isaac said.

"I called the dam and told them to close the gates. We'll put two bateaux at the head of the jam and have the men use their pick poles and picaroons to clear the area of logs. We'll find Jimmy and Nathan before the current grabs them."

Isaac paced the shore, watching the men guide one log after another into the current. The nest of spruce logs was half cleared when one of the men yelled, "We've got one of them!"

Isaac prayed it was Jimmy. He wanted his friend's body out of the water before it slipped by the men. Once the current grabbed it, it could travel miles through the rapids before it washed ashore or got snagged by a tree that had toppled into the water.

"Looks like Nathan!" the man called out, working the body toward the bateau with his pike pole.

Isaac's heart sank.

The shore was nearly free of logs with no sign of Jimmy. Dark thoughts ran through Isaac's head. What if they don't find him? What if he did get carried down the Dead, and his body wasn't found until summer after the water level dropped? Worse, how would he tell Jimmy's mother that her only son had drowned, but his body could not be found? Isaac felt sick to his stomach.

"Over here!" yelled a man walking along the bank looking for the body. "Over here! He's about ten feet from shore, fetched up on a tree limb."

Isaac ran to where the man was standing and looked down at the familiar face. Without hesitating, Isaac jumped into the water to retrieve his friend.

⁂

Jimmy Parson's body would be taken out to The Forks that afternoon. The company would pay to have the body moved to the funeral home in Skowhegan. After that, the family was responsible for the funeral and burial.

Isaac wanted to be back in Dead River to tell Jimmy's mother what had happened before she learned of the accident by way of a stranger. He accompanied the body back to Stony Brook Camp. Once Jimmy was secured to a tote sled, Isaac left for home.

Walking past Hayden Landing, he tried not to look down to where Jimmy had been killed only an hour earlier. He didn't notice the three men standing near the water watching him, knowing that Isaac and Jimmy were best friends. When Isaac passed from view, the men resumed pushing the floating logs into the current. Life went on.

Isaac found the hike to Grand Falls much longer than he remembered. Already, the sun had begun its downward way toward the west. He would never be home before dark. The best he could hope for was making it to Long Falls in the daylight, where he would spend the night and finish the last twelve miles in the morning.

Isaac stood on the ledge, staring at the water as it disappeared over the falls. His thoughts were locked on his friend's sudden death. Perhaps Jimmy's death was only a nightmare and Isaac would soon awaken and find everything as it should be. A sudden chill from the cold mist hitting the rocks below snapped him back to reality. He needed to start a fire and find a place to sleep.

The night sky was cloudy; there was not even a silhouette of the forest around him, just blackness. Jimmy lay on his bed of fir boughs, listening to the never-ending roar of water going over the falls. Then it hit him, and his heart began to pound. He was sleeping on the same wedge of ledge that Jimmy and he had camped on in the eighth grade. That was the first time the two friends had spent a night away from home, their first adventure tenting out and exploring. Now, their time together at Long Falls meant more than ever to him, a memory that he swore he would never forget. The thought was almost more than Isaac could take. A sudden breeze swept up from the falls. Isaac shivered, pulled his wool blanket up tight under his chin, and drifted into a restless sleep.

He awoke to the snort of a startled deer in the woods behind him. It was still dark, but the eastern sky had a soft reddish glow. Isaac was too anxious to be home to wait for sunrise. He stuffed his blanket into his rucksack and continued to Dead River.

As Isaac was making his way home, his father stopped at Leavitt's Store to pick up the mail. The mail delivery driver watched Leavitt finish postmarking the letters for the outgoing mail.

"Did you hear about the accident over on the Dead yesterday?" the driver asked Leavitt.

"No. What happened?"

"When I stopped to pick up the mail at the Solon Post Office yesterday afternoon, a woodsman from Moxie Gore's logging operation at the Stony Brook Camp came in to pick up his mail. He said two men drowned earlier in the day at Hayden Landing."

Time stopped for Harry Blanchard. All he could hear was his heart thumping in his chest, with the words *drowned* and *Hayden Landing* reverberating in his head. Harry walked to the post office window.

"Sorry to have eavesdropped. I heard you say that there was an accident at Hayden Landing. Do you know who drowned?" Harry asked, dreading to hear the mailman's answer.

"No names. Only that both were rolling logs into the Dead when the pile gave away."

Harry didn't wait for his mail; he needed to go home. If it was Isaac who had been killed, he didn't want his wife to be alone in case someone stopped at the farm to deliver the bad news to the family.

Sarah was standing at the cookstove when Harry entered the house.

"Sarah, why don't you sit down a minute? There's something I need to tell you," Harry said, pulling the kitchen table chair out for her.

Sarah looked at her husband. The expression on Harry's face told her it was about their son.

"It's Isaac, isn't it?"

"I honestly don't know. The mail delivery driver at Leavitt's Store said there was a bad accident at Hayden Landing yesterday. Two men were killed on the rollway. That's all I know."

Sarah looked at Harry for several seconds and then returned to the stove. She picked up the spoon and slowly stirred the stew she had made for their lunch.

"Did you hear what I said?"

"I heard you. Now wash your hands; it's time for lunch." Growing up, Sarah had been taught that a woman needed to remain strong in times of trouble and not give in to her emotions. However, inside, Sarah was being torn apart by the fear that her only child might be dead.

On his way to the kitchen sink, Harry glanced at his father sitting on the couch. Elwin's concerned look and a slow shake of his head told him what both of them feared had happened to Isaac.

No one spoke during the meal. Only the sound of the wall clock ticking away the seconds and the family cat meowing under the table for a scrap of food interrupted the deafening silence. Harry attempted to ease the tension.

"On the way home, I stopped at Bill Oliver's place. He has a cousin who lives in The Forks. Bill tried to call him to see if he knew more about what happened, but he couldn't get through. The operator said there was a problem with the phone line between Solon and Bingham. She said they had sent a man to fix it. Bill will stop by once he's talked to his cousin."

"We told him Hayden Landing was cursed," Sarah said barely above a whisper, staring at the table. "We told him not to go near that place. He promised he wouldn't."

"Sarah, we don't know if it was Isaac. All we know is that there was a bad accident at the Landing. We need to wait until we hear the details before jumping to conclusions," Elwin said in a comforting tone.

In the distance, the neighbor's dog barked. A few minutes later, footsteps could be heard on the back porch.

"That's Bill. He must have talked to his cousin," Harry said, going to the door.

As Harry reached for the doorknob, the door opened.

"Hello, Father."

"Isaac! Sarah, Isaac's home!"

Sarah closed her eyes and gave a barely audible "Thank you." Her prayers had been answered.

"We're glad you're home, son," she said, then hugged Isaac. "You must be starved, walking all that way. You sit down, and I'll warm the stew."

While Isaac ate, his grandfather asked about working the winter at Stony Brook Camp. Whatever Isaac told him, Elwin would interject with his own experiences working in the woods as a young man.

Sarah stood at the kitchen sink doing dishes, smiling as she listened to the men talk. Her son was home, and all was good.

Later, Sarah went to the living room to read. Elwin, Harry, and Isaac stayed at the kitchen table, discussing Isaac's winter at the logging camp. Eventually, the questions faded. It was time for Isaac to tell his father and grandfather what had happened at Hayden Landing.

"Did you and Gramps hear about the accident at Hayden Landing?"

"We heard. Although we don't know the details," Isaac's father said.

Isaac glanced at his mother sitting in the rocker reading. "Jimmy Parsons was one of the men killed," he said, his voice cracking with emotion. Saying aloud that his friend had died was almost too much for Isaac.

Isaac needed to recount the tragedy. Since Jimmy's body had been secured to the sled, he hadn't talked to anyone. He'd replayed it over and over in his mind: his last conversation with Jimmy, the terrible sound of the logs crashing down, and seeing his friend's body underwater looking up at him—all of it.

"That's going to be hard for Mary. What with Harold passing two years ago of influenza. To lose a child is bad enough, but her husband and only child so close together will tear her apart," Harry said.

"Does she know?" Elwin asked.

"I don't think so. I want to be the one to tell her, not a stranger from the company who didn't know Jimmy. I was going to stop when I walked past her house, but I decided to come home first and tell you. I'm going now. I can't put it off any longer."

"Do you want me to go with you, son?" Harry asked.

"No. This is something I need to do myself."

Isaac walked out the kitchen door, slowly pulling it shut behind him. His father and mother watched through the kitchen window as their seventeen-year-old son walked along the road to deliver Jimmy's mother the worst message a mother could hear.

4.

"Nobody likes to be forced out of their home."

—Evan Leavitt, postmaster and proprietor
of Leavitt's Store, Flagstaff, Maine

Augusta, Maine
Central Maine Power Headquarters
December 9, 1923

As daily life played out for the residents of the Dead River Valley, the leadership of Central Maine Power Company continued to gather information necessary to design and secure the State's approval to construct a dam at Long Falls.

"The Engineering Department has the numbers you asked for, Walter," Everett Buckingham said, walking into Wyman's office.

"Good. Let's hear it," Wyman said.

"The preliminary engineering cost for the design and construction of Long Falls Dam is three point eight million. A reasonable cost considering the dam at The Forks would be ten times as much."

"What about buying out the properties that will be flooded?"

"Engineering inventoried seventy-three houses located within the flood zone. Nine are in Bigelow Township, eighteen in Dead River, and forty-six in Flagstaff, along with several businesses. Additionally, there are twenty-three barns and dozens of small outbuildings, including woodsheds and chicken coops. Using the State's property evaluations and an adjustment factor, considering that people will expect high prices for their properties, it would cost the company approximately two hundred thousand to purchase them all, including eighteen thousand acres of farmland and woodland."

"I'll ask the same question I did last time we discussed this. There are nearly two hundred people who live in those three towns. And there's bound to be a few that won't agree to sell no matter what we offer," Buckingham said.

"Everett, you're a lawyer. We'll take it by eminent domain if we have to. I've already planted the seed with some of our friends at the State House. They're a little reluctant to slip into the proposed Charter Bill right now, but they'll be in our corner when the time is right. The one person that we do have to worry about is Percival Baxter. The Governor has been vocal about the water belonging to the people of Maine. And using his bully pulpit as Governor, he's been getting plenty of free press about it as well."

Fog can form in the Dead River Valley at any time, particularly in early fall when the crisp autumn air flows down Mount Bigelow over the river's warmer waters. Often, the mist lingers over the river long after it has been "burned off" over the land warmed by the penetrating rays of the morning sun.

Such was a morning in early October. Seth Wright had spent the night curled up in the small, crude shanty he had built in a narrow strip of woods separating two hayfields near the Dead River. The land wasn't his, but Joe Viles, the landowner, didn't mind. He and Seth were cousins, and Joe knew Seth had his problems—alcohol and drinking too much of it. Besides, Seth helped Joe hay in the summer if he could keep Seth sober long enough to get the last bale into the barn. What Joe saved on labor was more than he'd make charging Seth a few dollars for squatting on his land.

Seth stayed in the shack during the times he went on a bender. When sober, he lived with his sister on Parsons Road, near Flagstaff Cemetery. Seth was smart enough to avoid going there while drunk to avoid her wrath as soon as he staggered through the door. "Come into my house drunk one more time," Phyllis warned Seth, "and you'll need to find somewhere else to stay." A decent Christian widow would be the talk of the town if anyone found out she was harboring a drunk, even if Seth was her brother. Knowing Phyllis meant it, Seth had built the tarpaper shack on his cousin's land. He used it as a refuge until he sobered up after having a rendezvous with a fifth of Seagram's 7. Seth not only had a drinking problem but was also a bit slow, never finishing the eighth grade. He made enough money to support his alcohol and cigarette habits by doing chores for several farmers in Flagstaff and Dead River. The shack would likely have been his permanent home if his sister hadn't felt sorry for him and taken him in after both their parents died, leaving Seth with nowhere to live.

Seth stepped out of the windowless hovel. The sudden light of day forced him to use his forearm to shield his eyes from the sun, struggling to break through the morning haze. He could barely make out the narrow row of maple trees lining the river, obscured by a thick fog hovering over the river's still-warm water. Seth's head throbbed with each heartbeat, a not-so-friendly reminder of last night's bender. A brisk walk around the field's perimeter would ease his headache and clear the remaining cobwebs clouding his mind before he slithered home to face his sister.

As he walked along the narrow grassy headland that separated the corn rows from the pencil-thin strip of woods next to the river, Seth stopped. He heard voices from the river, or at least he thought he did. He squared up to the river and listened, peering into the fog to catch a glimpse of whoever was on the water. Only the hammering of a pileated woodpecker latched onto the rotting trunk of a dead maple broke the early-morning calm. Perhaps what he thought were people talking had been the sound of the hungry woodpecker attacking the tree looking for breakfast.

Once again, he heard muffled voices. Now, he was certain it was real. Seth carefully made his way down the wooded bank to get closer to the river and listen to what was being said. One man appeared to do all the talking, with only an occasional word of agreement from the second person.

Sound travels a long way in pea-soup fog on a calm day. Seth heard the steady rhythm of the canoe paddles as the bow parted the still water with each stroke. He sat by the water, his back against a large red maple tree, waiting for the canoe to come by. There was no need to hide. The fog was so thick that he could barely see the river, and there was no chance the two men in the canoe would spot him.

"Just think, Walt. It won't be long before there will be fifty feet of water over this very spot," Seth thought he heard the man in the canoe's stern tell the one seated in the bow.

"You got that right. The bid proposal for the dam construction will go out next week. Dirt will be flying before year's end," the man in the front replied.

Seth was shaken. The two men were talking about flooding the Valley! He listened to what else they might say. All he heard was the even strokes of the paddles breaking the water as the canoe continued up the Dead.

Seth jumped to his feet. He needed to tell someone what he had overheard. His first thought was to run home to tell Phyllis, but that wouldn't work, he thought. She would call him crazy and then rip him apart for being out all night. He'd tell Jim at Leavitt's Store. Jim would know what to do. Seth scrambled up the steep bank, grabbing small saplings to prevent himself from slipping on the frost-covered leaves.

He ran the mile and a half to town, stopping in front of Leavitt's Store just long enough to catch his wind. Still pumped on adrenaline, he ran up the four steps and into the store. Leavitt was in the post office sorting mail when Seth darted through the aisles, yelling for him.

"In the mailroom," Jim hollered, sliding letters into the slots in the bank of post office boxes.

Seth ran up to the cage that separated the mailroom from the rest of the store.

"Jim, I just saw him! He said they would flood the Valley with fifty feet of water! We'll all drown!" Seth shouted, still hyperventilating from his run.

"What in tarnation are you talking about, Seth? Hold on a minute; let me finish sorting the mail, and then we'll talk," Jim said, calmly pushing letters and newspapers into the post office boxes.

"Now, what's this about someone talking about flooding the valley?" Jim said, stepping around the corner from the post office.

"I heard them talking not fifteen minutes ago. It was Walter Wyman himself and another guy. They canoed right by me."

"You mean you saw the President of Central Maine Power Company canoeing on the Dead?" Jim said, glancing at the clock over the cash register. "He must be an early riser because it's only quarter past seven."

"Well, I didn't actually see him. It was too foggy. But I know it was him."

"How can you be sure if you didn't see him?"

"Because of what he said. He said there would be fifty feet of water on top of Flagstaff. And the other guy said they were going to build the dam real soon."

"Wait a minute, Seth. Let's back up and start again. What exactly did you see? Did you see the men in the canoe?"

"No," Seth said sheepishly.

"Did you see the canoe?"

"No."

"But you knew it was Walter Wyman?"

"Sort of."

By this time, two customers had come into the store. Hearing Seth and Jim's conversation, they walked to the back of the store to listen.

"Sort of? Seth, have you been drinking?"

"Not since the sun came up."

Jim glanced at the customers, trying to keep a straight face.

"I tell you what, Seth. Why don't you head home and get a little rest? I'm not saying you didn't hear Walter Wyman, but I'd hold off on telling folks you did until we confirm that's who it was. Does that make sense to you, Seth?"

"I guess. But he said he was going to flood the Valley," Seth protested.

"Seth, there have been rumors for years that the power company will build a dam. And it may happen yet. But I guarantee that no dam will be built and flood out the Valley until the folks in Augusta agree that Walter Wyman and his sidekicks can build that dam at Long Falls. So, in the meantime, I suggest we all go on with our lives, live in the present, and not worry about what might happen down the road. What I'm saying, Seth, is to live for today. That's the best any of us in the Valley can do."

Jim and the others watched Seth leave the store and walk toward his sister's place.

"Poor Seth," Jim said. "That man can be such a dunderhead. I probably shouldn't tell you, being I'm the postmaster, but this is not the first time Seth has gone off the deep end."

"You can tell us. We won't repeat a word of it," one of the customers said, grinning at the man beside him.

"Well, about two years ago, Seth came into the store all excited, much as he just did now, thinking it was Walter Wyman canoeing on the river. At that time, he was waving an envelope saying the letter needed to go out in the afternoon mail. It must be important, Seth,' I said.

"He told me he'd seen an ad in *Grit*[4] about becoming an intellectual. Seth said he was tired of people thinking he wasn't very bright, and by becoming an intellectual, he'd show them how smart he really was. All he needed to do to get his Intellectual Certificate was to take a quiz after sending one dollar and twenty-five cents to the Albert Einstein School of Correspondence.

---

4. *Grit* started as a newspaper targeting families in small rural towns.

"I tried to reason with him by saying you can't become an intellectual by taking a quiz. However, nothing I said was going to stop him from getting that certificate. Every day for a month, Seth stopped to see if the quiz had arrived from the correspondence school. Eventually, he stopped checking. It must have sunk in that there wouldn't be any intellectual quiz in the mail for Seth Wright."

Seth continued to drink himself into a stupor, and when he did, to avoid his sister's wrath, he'd sober up in his tarpapered shack on his cousin's land next to the Dead River. If Seth continued to hear voices from the river, he kept it to himself.

Burleigh Crockett of Bigelow Township waited for Jim Leavitt to finish with a customer, anxious to tell him about the latest news about the construction of Long Falls Dam. Burleigh stood there marking time as the traveler rattled on about the great deal he'd gotten on his new Studebaker Land Cruiser. He told Leavitt he'd get ten dollars if he went to the dealership in Portland and mentioned his name to the salesman. Jim nodded politely, not wanting to encourage the man to continue talking. Finally, the man grabbed his pack of smokes and left the store.

"What can I get for you, Burleigh?" Leavitt asked as soon as the door closed.

"I stopped to tell you former Governor Baxter is giving a radio address Sunday night at seven. He's going to talk about damming the Dead. It's going to be carried by WCSH in Portland. Maybe he will announce that he's against CMP flooding the Valley and drowning out the towns."

"I wouldn't get your hopes up on him saying that. But then again, anything is possible."

Every radio in the Dead River Valley was tuned in to Percival Baxter's address on Sunday evening. At Eben Storey's home, several like-minded neighbors gathered to listen to the ex-governor's remarks. WCSH's station manager was introducing Baxter when Eben glanced toward the kitchen and saw Austin Titcomb standing in the doorway. Austin owned a small farm in Dead River and was not particularly sociable.

"Hello, Austin. I'm glad you could join us. Come in and take a seat," Eben said, surprised that Austin would join a meeting of his neighbors.

"I prefer to stand."

"Suit yourself," Eben said, turning back to the radio as Baxter began to speak.

> "On the first of January this year, at the Bryant's Pond Grange, I made a New Year's resolution, which I am keeping by giving this address to the radio audience tonight. I told the Grangers that I should speak out openly and fearlessly on public matters, should give the people of Maine the benefit of my experience and do what I could to interest them in public affairs. This never has been done before by an ex-governor. I am seeking nothing, am not a candidate for any public office, have nothing to sell, and am able to pay my own expenses, including the expense of broadcasting these talks. As a rule, the people at large are not allowed 'behind the scenes' in politics and government. They see only surface currents. There are certain things they ought to know, things which help them form opinions on matters that concern their welfare and that of their descendants. I wish to do what I can to protect the interests of the men and women of Maine, who in the past have so highly honored me, and I now propose to take my fellow citizens into my confidence."

"Come on, Percy," someone said. "Get to the point. I've got better things to do with my time than sit here and listen to you pat yourself on the back."

> "In 1917, a few members of the Legislature and myself took up the Water Power fight in the interest of the public. My associates looked to me as leader. We were opposed by a group of corporations with the Central Maine Power Company at its head. The organization against us was the most powerful that had been in Augusta up to that time. We stood by the Fernald Law, passed in 1909 when the late Senator Fernald was governor, and which says that Maine's hydroelectricity shall not be taken out of the State; we strengthened that law and kept Maine's waterpower in Maine for Maine people."

"So, when is he going to talk about flooding the Valley?" said a voice from the back of the room.

"Give him time. He has to get through the preliminaries first," Eben said.

As the talk continued, it became apparent that Baxter would not address the plight of the citizens of the Dead River Valley.

> "I would grant no rights whatsoever in the Dead River or Fish River region or elsewhere until the Wyman-Insull[5] people cease their political activities, cease their campaign to repeal the Fernald Law, enter into a binding agreement never to EXPORT power and accept the Carter Bill.[6] With these assurances of good behavior, I should be glad to see a proper lease made of the Dead River and other projects,

---

5. At the time, Insull was the parent company of Central Maine Power. See Part 2 for details.

6. The Carter Act allowed the export of surplus power, but it was defeated in a referendum.

the State retaining title and receiving adequate rental. The development of storage at Dead River and Bingham, with the public interest adequately protected would increase the productive value of the Kennebec River basin, an object greatly to be desired…"

Eben turned off the radio. "Well, that was twenty minutes of a whole lot of nothing."

"Actually, he said a lot," Horace Smith said.

"Like what?"

"For one thing, Baxter is all for building the dam. He only wants the Central Maine Power Company to lease the dam site from the State and not give them the land and the privilege of using the people's water for profit. And for another, he wants all the power to stay within the state and not be sent to someplace like Massachusetts. If the Central Maine Power Company agrees to those conditions and keeps their corporate nose out of politics, he's a happy man."

Another man spoke up. "So, you're saying he doesn't give two cents about the people in the Valley having to pull up roots and leave so the CMP shareholders can receive a bigger dividend? That leaves us in the same place we were twenty minutes ago—on our own. I guess we know what he thinks of us."

"Nobody's going to stop them building the dam. We either take matters into our own hands or go with the flow, sell out to CMP, and start fresh somewhere else. Keep in mind that half the folks in the Valley support the dam, and another quarter don't like it but believe it's the patriotic thing to do. So, the chances of us convincing Augusta to halt the project are slim to none."

"Well, I ain't done trying to stop it. It will be a cold day in hell when that money-hungry company steals my farm," Austin Titcomb said, and abruptly left the meeting.

"On the bright side, CMP can't build the dam until the legislature says they can. So for now, we're safe," a man from Bigelow Plantation said.

"We all know how that works," someone said. "Once enough hands get greased, they'll find the votes they need to pass a law that says they can build it. Baxter said the power lobby is already spending big bucks to convince the public that the dam is in their best interest."

"So, boys, what will we do, fish or cut bait?" Eben asked.

"It looks to me like we're screwed. Between three-quarters of the town accepting the idea of being flooded out and the power company putting on a full-court press on the legislature, we might as well start packing," Smith said.

5.

"The pupils are fortunate to have a mountain [Bigelow] to look at. City people would give a great deal to have a mountain to climb."

—Arthur Irish, Superintendent of Schools
Dead River, Maine, 1940

Leavitt's Store
Flagstaff village
April 30, 1927

"Mrs. Leavitt, did you see this morning's paper?" Justin Harris asked, hardly able to contain his excitement.

"Read the paper! I haven't had a chance to eat breakfast, with Jim leaving for Farmington before sunrise. He promised Ed Barker he'd have his grain order ready by noon today. What has you all excited, Justin?"

Justin picked a copy of the daily paper from the shelf. "Read this!" he said, pointing to a headline on the front page.

Mrs. Leavitt silently read the headline: *Legislature Passes the Kennebec River Reservoir Charter Clearing the Way for Dam.*

"I hoped this would never happen. I guess if there's anything good about it, it's knowing that it will be built. At least we can start planning to leave, knowing for sure we're going to be flooded out."

"Not only that, the paper also says CMP can take people's land if they refuse to sell. The entire agreement is inside the paper. It also says they're going to dig up the dead in the town cemetery and move the bodies out of the Valley, too."

Others drifted into the store after learning about the new law.

"Have you heard the news?" Franklin Pierce asked, bursting into the store with a rolled newspaper.

"Yeah, we know," Justin said, holding up a copy of the newspaper.

"For one, I'm glad the wait's over. Not knowing if it's going to be built is worse than knowing. Now I can plan on leaving here and trying something different. I'm tired of leaving home every fall to work in the woods, leaving my wife to care for the livestock, keep the fires going, and oversee the three kids," Pierce said.

"That makes two of us," said another landowner. "I'm not getting any younger. I've been eyeing a place in North Anson, right next to the Carrabassett River. With the money I'll get for my ninety acres, I'm going to buy it and spend my mornings fishing and sitting on the porch rocking myself silly every afternoon."

"You fellers might be happy about the news, but I ain't," said Pearly Stevens. "I'm older than you, and Maude and me don't want to move. I planned on dying here. I'm sitting tight until CMP tells me to leave. And when push comes to shove, I'll go. The only way I can look at and accept the situation is that all of us living in the Valley are indirectly helping those in the state to get power to their homes, which will make for a better life for them."

"My God! Flagstaff and Dead River are nothing but widenings in the road. There's nothing here!" Frank told the others. "It's not like the power company will wash out Farmington or Skowhegan. Most people in Maine couldn't point to the Dead River Valley on a map if their lives depended on it, let alone ever have driven here."

Two aisles away, Florence Cotton was going about her grocery shopping while listening to the men talk. Florence was dead set against flooding the Valley and was never shy about telling everyone she met what she thought of the Central Maine

Power Company. Hearing Franklin Pierce say her hometown was nothing but a widening in the road was more than she could stand.

"Well, it's not a widening in the road to me!" she said, stepping out from one of the grocery aisles.

The men were surprised to see Florence, unaware she was in the store.

"It's *home*! And I don't want to leave it. Flagstaff is my heritage—and yours, too, for that matter—and no one, including the Governor himself, should be allowed to steal it from us. Think about all the work that went into clearing the land. Hundreds of acres of good interval land have provided every one of you with a decent livelihood. And the woods that's provided us with lumber and firewood for generations. None of that should be allowed to be taken from us.

"Can you think of a better place to raise a family? I can't. Children have the Dead River to fish, Flagstaff Pond to skate upon, and Jim Eaton Hill to slide down in the winter. They can go off exploring alone without their parents, knowing they'll be safe if they use a little common sense. No one in the Valley even locks their doors at night or when they go downriver for a day to shop or see the doctor. Try that in a big city and see how you make out.

"How many places in Maine can a child walk to school each morning and see a mountain as grand as Bigelow? It's a sight I never tire of seeing. That mountain is a part of our lives, so much a part that it tells us if it will rain or snow or be crisp and clear. I can't imagine looking out my living room window and not seeing the mountain looking back at me. It's like a friend that is always there.

"So you see, Franklin Pierce, Flagstaff and Dead River are more than just widenings in the road, and you should know better than to say they are.

"Now I must leave. I'm going to pick fiddleheads this morning with *your* wife," Florence said, her eyes glaring at Pierce.

Despite having the authority to construct Long Falls Dam, CMP's priority was to build a hydroelectric dam on the Kennebec River, a mile north of Bingham. Meanwhile, the newly authorized Kennebec River Reservoir Company quietly bought property in the three townships as it came onto the market. The threat of using eminent domain would be kept in the company's back pocket as an insurance policy, which could be used if a selling price was not reached or a property owner refused to sell.

Flagstaff High School
Flagstaff, Maine
May 15, 1927

"Okay. Everyone take a seat," Jim Leavitt told the hundred Dead River Valley residents gathered at the Flagstaff High School gymnasium. "The Senator just arrived, so we'll start the meeting. He will update us on the new law the legislature passed last month in Augusta. It's going to affect every family in the Dead River Valley. I'm sure there will be many questions for Senator Holley, so we need to be organized about it. So, the first order of business is to elect a moderator. Nominations are open. Remember, this is not a town meeting, so it can be anyone from Bigelow, Dead River, or Flagstaff."

"How about Ralph Cline of Bigelow Plantation," someone shouted from the back of the room.

"Not Ralph! We need someone that can hear. No offense, Ralph, but you can't hear worth beans," another person yelled.

"I heard that, Bradford. The next time you stop to buy a dozen of my eggs, they'll cost you fifty cents extra."

"Okay. Let's all settle down," Leavitt said. "I know some of you are in the middle of planting, so we want to get this meeting over as quickly as possible. Nominations for a moderator are what we're after."

"I nominate Ralph Cline. His hearing isn't too bad as long as you folks speak up," Ralph's cousin Bart Cline said.

"Do I hear a second?" Leavitt asked. Silence. "I need a second to nominate Ralph Cline as moderator."

"I'll second it. Anything to get the show on the road," Sonny Whitman said, checking his watch.

"Are there any more nominations?"

"How about you, Ken? You run a pretty good School Board meeting," said Leroy Hammond, a farmer from Dead River.

"For God's sake, Leroy. He has to be nominated. I'll do it. I nominate Ken Taylor as moderator."

"I second it, then," Leroy said.

"Seeing there are no more nominations, we'll vote by a show of hands for each candidate," Leavitt said, anxious to move the meeting along.

"I oppose!" shouted Ralph Cline, causing a rash of friendly boos and jeers from the crowd.

"Why do you oppose, Ralph?" Leavitt asked.

"'Cause it has to be done by secret ballot. That's the only fair way."

More moans and condemnation from the citizens.

"Come on, Ralph. I've got chores to do. Why drag the process out? We're not voting for the next chairman of the Ford Motor Company, for gosh sake," someone was heard to say.

"We can't do it, Ralph. We don't have a ballot box. When the town office storage room was painted last year, the selectmen moved everything to Larry Roberts's house for safekeeping. Nobody has gone to bring everything back. We didn't want to seem pushy with Mary, being she's still mourning over Larry's sudden passing."

"It ain't there," the third selectman shouted. "I went over last week to bring everything back, and the ballot box ain't there. Neither are the town records from 1918 to 1921."

"Hold on!" cried Cyrus Bailey. "My grandfather built that ballot box from a cherry log he cut up behind the home place. He didn't charge the town a cent for it. It was his gift to the town. Now you tell me it's missing. How can you lose a two-by-three-foot cherry ballot box?"

"It's not lost. We just can't find it," the third selectman said. "It has to be somewhere in Larry's house."

A hand went up in the front row.

"Go ahead, Winnona," Leavitt said.

"It's in Larry's study. I saw it there when I helped Mary clear out Larry's desk. Mary said he didn't want the ballot box to warp in the shed because of moisture, so he brought it inside for safekeeping. So's the box of records. Larry was working on Robert's family genealogy at the time he passed. He was going through the box of town papers looking for the dates his second cousin, Silas Roberts, served as road commissioner."

"I still want a vote by secret ballot," Ralph demanded.

"All right. Bill, run over to the store and grab one of the empty boxes that oranges come in," Leavitt said. "Bring the box top, too."

Bill returned in a few minutes with the Florida orange crate, and the election process began. Twenty minutes later, Leavitt announced the results.

69 votes for Ken Taylor

1 vote for Ralph Cline

1 vote for Charles Lindbergh

"Ralph demands a recount!" somebody in the room yelled.

"So does Charles Lindbergh! He can't believe that he didn't get more votes than Ralph."

"Looks like Ken's the moderator," Leavitt said and sat down beside his wife.

"Thanks. I'll do my best to move the meeting along. Now, Senator Holley drove up from Anson to tell us about the latest developments in Augusta concerning the legislation to grant the Kennebec River Reservoir Company the authority to begin buying our land for the Long Falls Dam project. Go ahead, Senator Holley."

"Just a minute. Forget saying 'the Kennebec Reservoir Company.' Everyone in this room knows that's just a dummy corporation. The Central Maine Power Company is pulling all the strings," Charlie Evans said.

While Holley made his way to the front, someone yelled to Ralph that he might want to move up front to hear what the Senator had to say. After the crowd stopped laughing, the Senator began his talk.

"Folks, I'll get right to the point. Last month, the Eighty-third Legislature approved and Governor Brewster signed a bill to form the Kennebec River Reservoir Company, led by the Central Maine Power Company. The new company has the authority to negotiate to buy all properties in the Valley. Now, I know this news is no surprise to most of you. There's been talk about a dam at Long Falls for the last twenty years. However, the passage of this bill makes it official. Rather than going into all the vagaries of the bill, I will try to answer any questions you might have."

A dozen hands went up.

"Go ahead, Betty, you go first," Ken said.

"When will they begin buying our land?"

"It's going to be a while. The new corporation has to get organized first, and staff must be hired. I'm only guessing, but it will probably be another year before any contracts are signed," Holley said.

"How do we know we're getting a fair price?" another person asked.

"It's going to be based on market value. The company appraiser will evaluate each property in the Valley. As landowners, each of you will get a price for the acres you own and the market value of those acres. It is the same with the structures. You'll get a written appraisal from hen coops to the home place, which will be the basis for what CMP will pay you for your property."

"Market value? If they're going to flood us out, then our property has *no* market value."

A wave of discontent moved through the crowd.

"It will be a cold day in hell before they steal my land," one of the farmers from Dead River said, with others agreeing.

The Senator went on the defensive. "I'm sure there is more to setting a value than just market value. I don't have all the particulars memorized. I'll check into that the next time I'm in Augusta."

"What if some of us don't want to sell, no matter the price? My relatives have owned land in the Valley since 1850. They faced floods from the Dead River, fires that destroyed barns, and droughts that ruined their crops. But they stayed. They didn't sell and run. I'm of the same mind. I'm looking for no check from the power company. All my family and I want is to be left alone so we can live the life we want. As far as I'm concerned, they can stick the dam where it does them the most good."

"You tell 'em, Eben. We're with you," said a half dozen others supporting Eben's stand.

"The Lewiston paper said that Central Maine Power can take our property. I want to know if that's true," Merton Prescott said.

This was the question that the Senator had hoped he wouldn't be asked. Holley had voted in favor of the Kennebec River Reservoir Charter, which included granting the power of eminent domain. To openly support taking people's homes would be political suicide, at least in the eyes of the residents of the three towns in his district. He sidestepped the issue as best he could.

"Yes. There is a clause in the charter that could cause this to happen. However, it would only be used in extreme cases. I'm certain Central Maine Power Company will treat everyone fairly when they do their appraisals. Even though the power company is in business to make a profit, you'll find their people are dedicated to the welfare of the Valley's citizens and will make this process as painless as possible."

A sarcastic, "Yeah, right!" came from the back of the room.

Another hand went up. "Go ahead, Darcy," Taylor said.

"Well, I can't speak for the others, but as far as I'm concerned, selling to CMP is the right thing to do. Sure, we all want a fair price for our property. But selling and moving is in the best interest of the people of Maine. Imagine the thousands of homes in our state having electricity delivered right to their doors, thanks to us.

It's called progress, and we should feel proud of doing our part to make it happen."

A few people in attendance nodded in agreement with Darcy. Most sat passively, more concerned about whether CMP's buyout offer would be fair and when they would be told to move.

The Senator answered questions until they started to repeat themselves. At that point, Taylor ended the meeting.

Leavitt's Store
Flagstaff, Maine
September 16, 1933

Flagstaff's population swelled 170 when the 178th Company of the Civilian Conservation Corps (CCC) arrived in 1933. The CCC camp was one of twenty-eight established across Maine, authorized as part of Franklin Delano Roosevelt's New Deal to provide jobs for young men aged 18 to 26 who were unemployed due to the Depression. This group of paid volunteers planted trees, constructed fire roads and hiking trails, remedied years of erosion, and more. In Maine, approximately 16,000 men served in the CCC.

"That will be three cents," Leavitt said, applying the stamp to the letter. "I see you're from Portland," he continued, attempting to make small talk with the young CCC corpsman.

"I am. I really miss the coast. I hope to go back soon as the Depression ends and businesses start to hire again. Then I'll make some real money," the young man said.

"I read the government pays thirty dollars a month. You should be able to salt a little away, since you would be hard put to spend that much around here."

"You've got that right. Other than playing pool at Hazen Ames Pool Hall, there's nothing in Flagstaff to spend money on.

We get thirty a month but must send twenty-five of that home. That's CCC rules. The idea is to help families who don't have much money."

The bell above the door jingled.

"Hello, Erwin. Did you stop in to pick something up for your mother?" Leavitt asked, looking down at the boy from behind the counter.

"My mother told me to ask you for a piece of nutmeg the size of a hen's egg and a red string about eighteen inches long," Erwin said, dropping a nickel on the counter.

"Sure, Erwin, but what does she plan to do with the nutmeg and string?"

"It's not for my mother. It's for me. The nutmeg I have now is falling apart. See," Erwin said, tugging a red string around his neck until a rotted nutmeg popped out from under his shirt.

The CCC corpsman approached the counter to see what Erwin was showing Leavitt.

"Why do you have a nutmeg under your shirt?" the corpsman asked.

"To stop nosebleeds," Erwin said as if everyone knew that. "I haven't had a nosebleed since I was five, other than the time my sister hit me in the nose with a rock by accident."

"How old are you now?" the corpsman asked.

"Six."

"Well, it seems to work," said Leavitt. "I'll see if I can find a nutmeg the size of a chicken egg. I know I have the red string." And he went to the far end of the store in search of the perfectly sized nutmeg.

The corpsman started conversing with the boy while Leavitt was away from the counter.

"Erwin, do you have a dog?"

"Yes. Blackie. He likes to chase cars."

"I'll tell you what, Erwin. You always want to have good luck, don't you?"

"Sure."

"Not many people know this, but stepping in dog doo-doo brings a feller good luck."

"Really?" the boy giggled.

"Really. But you must step in it with your left foot. If you step in dog doo-doo with your right foot, something terrible will happen to you. Do you know what foot your left foot is?"

Erwin pointed to his foot.

"No, Erwin, that's your right foot."

Erwin pointed at his other foot.

"Yep. Make sure you step in the dog poop with that foot. Now sometimes, when you and your mother are in the yard, you go around to all of Blackie's poops, and you step in them with your left foot. The more of them you step in, the better luck you will have. Do you understand?"

Erwin nodded.

Soon, Leavitt returned with a fresh nutmeg and an eighteen-inch red string. Erwin took both and ran toward the door.

"Hold up, Erwin, you forgot your change."

Erwin ran back, grabbed the penny from Leavitt's hand, and ran out of the store.

"That boy is quite the character. His mother and father are some old proud of him."

"I bet they are," the corpsman said, smiling. "Well, I've got to get going myself. I've got the second watch tonight and need to hit the hay early."

On the way out the door, the CCC corpsman passed the Holman brothers coming up the steps. Enoch and Ivan were nice enough, ready to drop everything to help a neighbor. That is, if the neighbor in need had roots that could be traced back two generations living in the Valley. Enoch and Ivan had it in their heads that only true natives should have a say in town affairs. The Holman clan boasted that their ancestors were one of the original families to join Miles Standish when he settled in the Valley in 1845. A new arrival in the Valley was considered an interloper and not included on the Holman brother's very short list of friends.

"Hello, boys. How's things in Bigelow Plantation?"

"Everything's fine as far as I know. Although I'm not so sure what's going on over by the Safford Place," Enoch said.

"How so?" Leavitt asked.

"When Ivan and me drove back from the Ledge House after getting gas, we saw two cars with Maryland plates parked next to the Fire Warden's Trail. We slowed down and did a little rubbernecking to see what was happening. Eleven of them gathered around the hood of one of the cars, looking at a map of some sort. I think one of them was a woman."

"There's no law against looking at a map," Leavitt said.

"No, there isn't. However, I'm just a tad concerned about what eleven people are doing so far from home studying a map at the base of Mount Bigelow. You don't suppose they're up here to buy land, do you? The last thing we locals need is to be told how to live by a bunch of city transplants."

"Well, Enoch, why don't you ask them," Leavitt said, motioning to the two vehicles stopped in front of the store.

The door opened, and a parade of ten men and one woman entered the store. Ivan and Enoch melted into the background, watching the strangers make their way to the soda cooler.

"How much do we owe you for the drinks?" one of the men asked.

"Eleven Coke's come to one dollar and ten cents," Leavitt said. "If you don't mind me asking, where are you folks from?" Leavitt asked, giving the man his change.

"We're all from Maryland. Most of us live in Annapolis or Bethesda and work in Washington. We're members of the Potomac Appalachian Trail Club. We're staying at the West Carry Pond Sporting Camps for a few days to do a little hiking."

The man glanced at Enoch and Ivan, standing beside him, sizing him up. He knew the locals might not be too impressed that a group of government bureaucrats had enough free time to drive to Maine to walk in the woods. "Although I'm originally from Lubec, Maine," he added, hoping to regain a degree of credibility.

Enoch couldn't help himself and walked up to the stranger. "Don't they have hiking trails in Maryland?"

"Oh, yes. Some great walks around the shore of Chesapeake Bay."

"Then why drive all the way up here to go for a walk?" Enoch asked, fishing for answers as to why these strangers were in the area.

"Well, actually, we're in Maine to locate a route for a trail that will run from Mount Katahdin to Springer Mountain in Georgia."

"Now, why would you want to do that?" Enoch pressed. "Seems to me people have better things to do with their time than to walk halfway to Florida."

The man knew he would be wasting his time trying to convince this local man of the value of the long-distance trail, but he kept swinging, hoping to get through to him.

"Times are changing. More people live in cities and need a place to experience the wilderness before it disappears."

"Well, folks don't have time to commune with nature around here. We're too busy trying to survive than waste time staring up at the trees philosophizing," Enoch said, reaching for the pack of Luckys in his shirt pocket. "I still don't see why a person would want to walk from Georgia to Maine unless they needed something to do."

"Some people would do it for the challenge. Some to breathe the fresh air. Others to see the natural beauty."

The woman broke in and told the group's leader they needed to leave if they expected to be back at the West Carry Pond Camps in time for supper. As the group walked toward the door, Enoch called after them.

"Mister. What's your name?"

"Myron Avery," he said.

"Well, Mr. Avery, here's an idea. Tell your hiking friends if they want to breathe fresh air and have a challenge, they can help Ivan and me cut and split ten cords of firewood so we don't freeze to death next winter," Enoch said, grinning and looking at his brother.

"Thanks. I'll give it some thought," Avery said, closing the door behind him.

"I guess you told them where the bear shits in the buckwheat, Enoch," Leavitt said once the door closed, shaking his head.

"I think they got my point."

6.

"I guess it's a good thing in the end, probably. But I kind of hate to leave. It's just hard to tell where we're going and what we're going to do."

—"Captain" Cliff Wing
March 8, 1949
Waterville Sentinel

Flagstaff village
Flagstaff High School gymnasium.
December 3, 1938

Twelve years had elapsed since legislation authorized the construction of the Long Falls Dam. Still, Central Maine Power Company had not indicated when or whether the project would begin. The uncertainty was just as frustrating as the dam's construction itself. Nearly a quarter of the residents had sold their places to CMP and relocated to start a new life. The remaining residents of Dead River Valley planned to stay in their homes until the company told them they had to move.

The years of not knowing the company's intentions took their toll. Money needed to be raised to run Dead River and Flagstaff. Parents wanted to know if their children would graduate from Flagstaff High School or be sent to a neighboring town to complete their public education. Residents couldn't plan their future and were unsure when or if they would be forced out of their homes. The Dead River and Flagstaff selectmen had their own dilemma: when the State would require both plantations to surrender their organizational status. To address the uncertainties, a special meeting was called with the two plantations and Bigelow Township to discuss what could be done to get a straight answer from CMP as to their intentions for building the dam.

Ken Taylor was again elected to moderate the meeting.

"Welcome, everyone. Let the minutes show that ninety-five citizens of Dead River, Flagstaff, and Bigelow are in attendance to determine Central Maine Power Company's intentions as to when they're going to build Long Falls Dam."

"More than that!" said a man in the front row. "We want a straight answer as to whether they *will* build it. And if they *are* going to build it, a firm date for when they will start construction."

"And when they say we will have to leave our homes! No more keeping us in the dark. We want to know the valley's expiration date," said another.

"We've put up with their indecision for twelve years, and we're all sick of it!" another Flagstaff resident hollered.

"I want to know when CMP is going to buy our property. I can't buy another home without my money," Ethel Pease said.

Taylor wrote each question on a chalkboard. "Okay, are there any others you want to be listed before we decide what we need to do to get them answered?"

"I don't have a question; it's more of an observation," said Jim Mitchell. "Central Maine Power started buying up properties when they came on the market in 1921, when they first got the bright idea about building the dam, and they've been doing so ever since. I drove around the Valley last week and counted nineteen properties now owned by CMP. Every one of them is abandoned, dilapidated, or both. The lawns have grown up to weeds and brush, and in some cases, alders. The entire Valley is beginning to look like one of those bombed-out European villages during World War I. It's no incentive for a person to keep their property in good repair when half the town looks like a town dump. Folks have asked me why they should spend good money to paint or reshingle their roofs, knowing at some point the company will buy them out and let them rot into the ground.

"The problem is that most of us left take pride in our homes, and it goes against the grain not to maintain them. As foolish as it sounds, I just ordered enough paint from Leavitt's Store to repaint my house. Carol even sent away to Burpee's for a bunch of perennial flower seeds, hoping for a miracle the dam wouldn't happen."

Mitchell's commentary brought a round of applause from some.

After thoroughly discussing each question and concern on the board, Taylor asked for a motion.

"I move the selectmen meet with Walter Wyman and get the answers to our questions," Ethel Pease said, jabbing her husband with her elbow.

"I second Ethel's motion," he shouted.

"Okay, the motion to meet with the president of CMP has been seconded. Discussion on the motion?" Taylor asked. "Go ahead, Jim, your hand was first to go up."

"You folks have got it all wrong. Walter Wyman isn't going to listen to us. He never has, and he won't now. Sending the selectmen to Augusta would be as effective as sending my eight-year-old daughter. Wyman's New York lawyers will chew them up and spit them out. I say we hire an attorney. Let *him* go to the State Legislature and tell them what we want. Put them on notice that we want answers from the company. They'll do it. There is one thing a politician doesn't want, and that's to piss off the voter. Sorry, ladies, for being a bit blunt. But I know how they operate down there in Augusta."

Ethel withdrew her motion. The towns unanimously decided to hire an attorney to represent the citizens before the Judicial Committee at the State House.

The selectmen hired Augusta attorney John Wilson to represent the towns. Wilson testified before the Judiciary Committee on February 14, 1939. He let it be known that the townspeople were not opposed to the project but only wanted to see when the company would build the Long Falls Dam so they could plan what they would do. A Central Maine Power Company spokesperson said it would be built when business conditions warranted such a move. Neither the committee nor the attorney representing the towns tried to pin the company down further.

"Well," Eben Storey said to Leavitt when he stopped in to pick up his mail, "so much for hiring a fancy lawyer to determine when they'll start building the dam. Maybe we should have sent Jim's daughter. She couldn't have done any worse and would have saved us taxpayers four hundred dollars in legal fees." It was a sentiment shared by most residents.

January 23, 1939
Leavitt's Store
Flagstaff, Maine

The door opened, and a gust of wind blew a dozen copies of the weekly sale flyer off the counter.

"Holy cow, Everett, shut the door, or I'll pick up paper off the floor for the next three days!"

"I guess the weatherman down in Portland was right. He said it would begin to blow early afternoon."

"Let's hope he's wrong about the rest of the forecast. The last thing we need is another two feet of snow on top of the eighteen inches we got from last week's storm," Leavitt said. "I was stuck twice trying to get to Stratton to pick up an order the wholesaler refused to deliver to Flagstaff because of all the snow, and that was two days after it stopped snowing."

"You can thank that moron, Charlie Ferguson. I'll never understand how he got a job driving truck for the State Highway Department of Transportation. He can't even back it up without someone directing him. Worse, Ferguson waits until there are two-foot drifts before plowing."

"I'll tell you how he got that job," came a voice from the direction of the woodstove. "His cousin's the foreman for the Stratton Division for the State Highway Department. Half the men that work there have the last name Ferguson, and the other half are married to one," said Ralph Morin, known more for his frugality than his ambition. Each day, Ralph made it a point to show up at Leavitt's Store to read yesterday's paper for free before Leavitt tossed them in the garbage.

"Come on, Ralph. You're just miffed because you didn't get hired," Everett said.

"And do you know why I didn't get that job.? I'll tell you why. My last name isn't Ferguson."

Leavitt and Everett looked at each other and shook their heads.

"Uh-oh."

"What is it, Everett?" Leavitt asked.

"It's Hattie Pearson, and she's headed this way."

"She said she would stop in today with eggs," Leavitt said.

"God! That woman talks so damn loud, I can hardly think. She thinks that because she's as deaf as a rock, everyone else is, too," Ralph said, standing up to see Hattie coming up the steps.

"Good morning, boys," she bellowed, pushing through the door carrying a cardboard box.

"Hello, Hattie. How many dozen eggs have you got for me today?" Leavitt asked.

"Eight dozen, and they are all extra-large and fresh. Six were laid not an hour ago."

"Hold on, and I'll get my ledger. I want to be sure you get the proper credit for them."

Hattie kept talking while Leavitt went to look for the account book. "Make it fast, Jim. My water pipes are frozen again, and I need to get back to melt snow for the chickens before they die from thirst. This is the third time this winter they've froze," Hattie said so loudly that Everett stepped back to cut down on the volume.

"Here you go, Hattie," Leavitt said, passing her a receipt for a three-dollar credit for the eggs. "You've got a total of eight dollars built up. Do you want to use any of it today?"

"Not today, Jim. I need to get home and make water," Hattie said at the top of her lungs and headed for the door.

Once the door shut, the men just looked at one another. "You know," Ralph said, "any other woman in the Valley would have said I need to get home and melt snow." The men laughed.

"Well, it'll be dark in an hour, and I want the wood box full before it snows. If there's one thing I hate doing, it's wading through knee-deep snow in the dark carrying an armload of wood," Everett said, starting toward the door.

As Everett opened the door, the store phone rang.

"That's probably Ethylene wanting to know what's taking me so long to get home. I swear, I can't go anywhere without her tracking me down. I should never have let her talk me into putting in a phone."

"You're safe, Everett. That wasn't Ethylene. It was Mrs. Martin. It seems the two schoolteachers who board at her place hitched a ride downriver for the weekend to visit friends. She's all concerned that they won't make it back before the storm hits and wondered if they had stopped at the store on their way home."

"Whereabouts did they go?" Everett asked.

"Skowhegan."

"If they haven't started back, they'd be smart to stay there and wait out the storm."

"Well, I wouldn't count on that happening," Ralph said. "Most teachers I've known have plenty of book smarts but lack the common sense to come in out of the rain," he continued, still sitting by the woodstove flipping through the paper.

Miss Mable Day and Miss Martha Fletcher had heard about an approaching storm but were confident they could return to Martin's Boarding House before it started to snow. Besides, they needed to be back for the start of school the next day. Before accepting their teaching positions, Mable and Martha had learned that Dead River and Flagstaff were not known for closing schools due to bad weather. As dedicated young teachers, they were determined not to disappoint their students.

Martha convinced a family friend to drive her and Mable back to the boardinghouse, which was an easy sell. Wally Coburn, a junior in high school, had a crush on the twenty-one-year-old teacher and eagerly jumped at the chance to sit next to her for the two-and-a-half-hour ride to Flagstaff. The challenge for Wally was persuading his father to let him borrow the family's car, a 1931 Model A Ford, the family's first automobile.

Mid-Sunday afternoon, Martha and Mable tossed their luggage in the rumble seat and squeezed into the front of the Model A for what they hoped would be an uneventful ride back to Flagstaff. Before Wally pulled away from the curb, Martha and Mable's friends made one more attempt to convince them to spend the night in Skowhegan and leave early the following day. They thanked them for the offer but were confident the storm would hold off until they got home.

An hour later, they were in Madison, and there was still no sign of the storm. Now Martha and Mable were sure they had made the right decision to beat the storm back to Flagstaff.

Mable joked that no matter the weather, she would be toasty warm and dry in the oversized raccoon coat her brother gave her when he learned she would teach in northern Somerset County.

They had planned to grab something for a late lunch at the local grocery store. However, Madison's markets closed early due to the warning about the approaching storm. Unfazed, the Model A rumbled through the nearly deserted downtown, and the three continued toward North Anson as the late afternoon dipped below the tree line.

A mile north of Madison, snow began to fall. Fluffy, cotton-ball-sized flakes drifted down, coating the road with a veneer of snow that was quickly whisked away by the car's draft as it traveled north. It was an idyllic winter scene: a Model A passing through the countryside, its yellowish headlights cutting a path through the gently falling snow.

Once past the village of North Anson, as if the car had crossed an invisible line, the tree limbs began to rock, and the wind-driven snow blew horizontally across the road. Wally struggled to see the road ahead as the storm intensified. Martha and Mable stared into the whiteout, sharing the same thought: keep the car on the road. Fifteen minutes passed, then a half hour, and the storm showed no sign of slackening.

"Look!" Mable shouted.

Wally slammed on the brakes, not knowing what Mable might have seen. The women screamed as the car skidded toward the edge of the road. Fortunately, the tires grabbed the gravel shoulder, stopping the vehicle just before it struck a telephone pole. After a few seconds, the three regained their wits.

"Why did you yell 'look,' Mable? Did you see an animal in the road?" Wally gasped.

"No. I only wanted to tell you that I saw the Lexington Town line marker. Sorry."

"Oh. The town line marker. Mable, the next time you see a town marker, please tell us using a complete sentence so I know we're not about to hit a nine-hundred-pound moose.

"I think with a little nudge, we can get the car back on the tar. Mable, you and Martha push, and I'll steer it back onto the road."

"I've got a better idea. Why don't you and I push the car and let Martha drive."

"I can't do that. I promised my father that I would drive. It's the family car."

"You're right, Wally. Your father is probably watching us from behind a tree, making sure you don't let one of us drive it fifty feet," Mable said, slamming the car door.

Five minutes later, the Model A was again on the road north.

"I don't know about continuing, Wally. Let's turn back. It's snowing harder than ever," Martha said, staring into the darkness.

"I think we should keep going," Wally said. "We're closer to Flagstaff than we are to Skowhegan. Besides, we should meet the plow truck at any time. Then it will be easier going."

"I agree with Wally," Mable said. "I don't want to miss a day of school. The last thing I want is to be known as the teacher who caused the Flagstaff School to close for the first time in fifty years. Let's keep going. All we need to do is drive through Lexington and Highland, and we're there."

"I suppose," Martha said, still thinking that spending the night with friends in Skowhegan made more sense.

Twenty minutes later, they left Lexington behind and entered Highland Plantation.

"Where is that plow truck?" Mable asked.

"You've got me," said Wally. "I thought for sure we would meet it by now. Maybe he's broken down. Flagstaff can't be that much further. We'll be fine." He was holding onto the steering wheel with a steel grip with one hand, wiping the moisture off the windshield with the other.

The tires slipped as the grade steepened. The road appeared as a winding white ribbon delineated by the silhouettes of large maple and beech trees on each side. Conditions were deteriorating, and everyone knew it was only a matter of time before the Model A ground to a halt in the deepening snow.

"Hang on!" Wally warned. Coming up fast was a two-foot-high snowdrift. Wally's only chance was to floor the accelerator and power through it. He almost made it. The rear tires lost traction just as the front wheels broke out of the drift.

The three just sat there as the wind rocked the tiny automobile. Martha was the first to speak.

"What are we going to do? We can't just sit here and wait for the plow truck. We'll freeze to death."

"How far do you think it is to Flagstaff?" Mable asked.

"I have no idea," Wally admitted. "The last time I was in Flagstaff, I was nine. My father took the family to watch the log drive on the Dead River."

"That's not what I wanted to hear, Wally," Mable said.

"What about the Ledge House?" Martha asked.

"Yes! The Ledge House. It can't be that far. I'm sure they would put us up for the night," Mable said.

"I don't know," Wally said. "I think we should stay here and wait for the plow. At least we'd be out of the wind."

"Wally, it could be days before they break out the road," Martha said, pulling her hood up over her head. "We have nothing to eat and no way to keep warm. The three of us can't fit inside Mable's raccoon coat. We need to leave *now* and find help. I've read too many stories of people dying in their cars thinking someone would find them, and all along, there was a farmhouse right around the corner. We'll take the flashlight that's in the glove compartment."

Wally relented, and the three left the car stuck in the snowdrift. They had gone just a short distance when Wally looked back. The wind had slackened enough to see the outline of his father's car before it disappeared in the storm. He worried the plowman wouldn't see it and would drive it into the ditch, totaling his father's pride and joy.

Heads down, hands covering their faces, they leaned into the wind to begin the snowy slog to the Ledge House. Martha led the procession, lighting the way with the flashlight. Fifteen minutes later, she stopped.

"Someone else take the lead. My legs are killing me breaking trail," she hollered over the howling wind.

"Martha! I can't take much more of this. Maybe Wally was right. We'd be better off waiting in the car. What do you say we go back?"

"Go back? We can't go back. We need to keep going. We must be near the Ledge House by now."

"Martha," Wally said, pointing to the side of the road. "Shine the flashlight on those trees. It looks like a sign nailed to one of them."

Martha waved the flashlight around the trees until she locked onto what seemed to be a snow-covered board nailed to a maple tree. The three wallowed through the nearly knee-deep snow to investigate. Wally cleared the snow off the sign.

"Keep Out," Martha read aloud.

"Keep out of what?" Mable said. "All I see is a forest of snow-covered trees."

"This road, I guess," Wally said, stepping into the opening. "There's another No Trespassing sign on the other side of the woods road. Look! There are footprints in the snow. Someone was just here!"

"Maybe a moose made them," Mable said.

"I don't think it was an animal. The tracks appear to be going in both directions. You can see who or whatever it was walked to the middle of the road, turned, and went back up the road," Wally said, studying the track half-filled with blowing snow.

"I bet someone was checking to see if the plow had gone by. Someone must live there. Let's see if they will help us," Mable said, starting up the road.

"Hold up a minute, Mable. We have no idea who lives up there. I remember overhearing the men talking at the store that some backwoods people had moved to the area. They said they were a strange lot. Maybe it's them."

"I don't care if it's Count Dracula that lives there. I need to get out of the storm. I'm wet, and I'm cold. All I want to do is sit by the fire and dry out."

Martha considered asking Mable how she could possibly be colder than Wally and herself, being wrapped in her brother's heavyweight coonskin coat while they only wore lightweight button-up wool coats. Then she thought better of it. Mable was her friend as well as a fellow teacher. Their situation was too dire to cause an argument over something as silly as who had the warmest coat. "All right. We'll see if whoever lives here will take us in. Let's get going before the storm gets worse, if that's possible."

"My God. How far back do these people live? It feels like I've been walking for an hour."

"Mable, it's been less than ten minutes since we left the Flagstaff Road."

"Well. My legs feel like it's been an hour. What if Wally is wrong and an animal did make the tracks, and it's taking us deeper and deeper into the woods until we're totally lost," Mable said.

"No," said Wally. "They're human tracks. I'm sure of it. I needed to learn to tell the difference to get my Track Identification Merit Badge in Boy Scouts."

"I'm sure if you learned it in Boy Scouts, you must be right," Mable said. Mable viewed Wally Coburn as a seventeen-year-old twit who only offered to drive them to Flagstaff so he could be near Martha.

The trio continued walking toward what they hoped would be shelter from the storm.

"I see a light!" Wally said.

Martha and Mable peered into the wind-driven snow.

"I don't see anything," Martha said, using her hand to protect her face from the sting of the snow.

"Neither do I. Wally, I think you're hallucinating. The storm has you seeing things. Let's keep going before we freeze to death," Mable said.

"There it is again!" Wally repeated a few minutes later.

Again, the two women gazed into the darkness.

"Now I see it!" Martha said, spotting an intermittent yellow glow each time the wind slackened.

The surroundings suddenly turned to black. "Damn! The batteries died," Martha said.

"Try wrapping the flashlight against your other hand. That might bring them back to life," Wally said.

"It's no use. They're done for."

"It doesn't matter. All we need to do is walk toward the light. It can't be more than a couple hundred yards," Mable said, walking past Martha to lead the way to what they presumed to be a cabin.

"Hold up," Wally said just as Mable was about to step onto the porch.

"Why? We want to get out of the storm, don't we?"

"Of course we do. But if we start pounding on the door, who knows what the people inside might think? Maybe they're old people living alone. They might be so scared they won't answer the door."

"So, what do we propose we do? Write them a letter and see if we get an invite to come in the next time we're in the neighborhood?" Mable said.

"I think we call to them instead of knocking on the door. It's a lot less threatening," Wally said.

"That's ridiculous," Mable said, stepping onto the cabin's deck and marching to the door. She hesitated momentarily and gave the door three hard blows with her fist.

All hell broke loose. Roscoe had been sleeping curled up next to the woodstove. Hearing the banging, the dog snapped to life and charged the door. He stood on his hind legs, bouncing up and down, trying to see out the glass to get a look at the intruders. All the time, he gave out a half bark and a half deafening whine, begging his owner to let him at them.

As Mable placed her face close to the glass to see if she could see anyone inside, Jake put his face against the window to see who or what was on the other side of the door. All Mable saw were two eyes and hair.

At the sight of Jake Barton's scraggly, full-face beard, Mable was so startled that she backpedaled away from the door and stepped off the edge of the deck, landing in a heap in the snow.

"Who's out there, Jake?" Dolly asked.

"Looks like two women and a man. I'll let Roscoe out to chase them back down the road."

"Don't you let him out! He'll attack them. Let me look," Dolly told her husband, pushing him away from the window.

"They look harmless enough. They must be lost or something. Let them in so they can get warm."

"I'm not letting three strangers into our house. They can keep walking to the Ledge House if they need help."

"Jesus, Jake, that's another three miles in a snowstorm! Let them in, for God's sake."

"Not me, Dolly. If you're so goddamn interested in being a good Samaritan, you let them in."

"Why are you being such a shithead? Go put Roscoe in the spare room."

Once Roscoe was isolated from the rest of the Bartons, Dolly opened the door and stepped outside.

"What do you three want?" Dolly asked, peering into the darkness.

"Our car is stuck about two miles from here. We hoped you would let us in so we can warm up," Martha said.

"Get in here and be quick about it before all the heat goes out the door," Dolly said.

Wally, Martha, and Mable did a quick huddle.

"These people seem a little weird. Do we go in or keep walking?' Martha asked.

"I vote to go back to the car and wait for the plow," Wally said.

"I say we go in. I'm frozen. If I go any farther, I'll collapse," Mable said.

"I'm with Mable. We'll go in and warm up. Then we'll tell them we left something in the car that we must return and get. That will be our excuse to leave."

"What?" Wally asked.

"I don't know, something."

"I know," Mable said. "We'll tell them Wally forgot his medication, which he needs to take as soon as possible."

"What kind of medication?' Wally asked.

"Damn it, Wally, what difference does it make?" Mable said.

"What if one of them asks?"

"Tell them it's your hemorrhoid cream. That fits you perfectly, as you are becoming one big pain in the ass," Mable said in a loud whisper.

"Are you three coming in or not? I'm offering you a chance to get out of the storm. If you don't want to take it, there's no skin off my ass," Dolly said, growing impatient, holding the door open.

"Let's go," Martha told the others.

Once they stepped inside the cabin, all three began to cough. The stench of unwashed bodies and dirty diapers, intensified by the heat from the woodstove, was overwhelming.

"I don't want any of you near the children if you have colds," Dolly told them, oblivious to the cabin's pungent odor.

Martha told Dolly they wouldn't go near the children and managed, between coughs, to say thank you for allowing them into the cabin.

The entire Barton clan gathered in the living room, staring at the three strangers: Ken and his wife Molly, Tim and Lolly, and their half dozen children. In the background, Roscoe frantically scratched at the door, whining to join the group.

It was clear that the adults looked a bit peculiar. Not that the men were ugly, although it was hard to know for sure, not being able to see their faces. The three men were the same build: short and slender, and they sported the same scraggly salt-and-pepper beard and hair. The three women were blond and slim, with similar facial features, and wearing the same-colored dresses that appeared homemade. Martha theorized that the men were brothers and the wives, sisters.

"Mind if we step closer to the woodstove?" Mable asked, still wearing her raccoon coat.

The twelve family members parted to give the unannounced visitors space to gather around the wood heater.

"What are you doing out in the middle of a blizzard? Seems to me that's not the smartest thing to be doing," Jake remarked, studying the three crowded around the stove, rubbing their hands together.

"We left Skowhegan about two o'clock trying to beat the storm back to Flagstaff. Everything was going fine until we reached Lexington, when it started snowing and blowing. Our friend's car got stuck in a drift a couple of miles back down the mountain," Martha said.

"Do you live in Flagstaff?" Jake asked.

"We teach there. At least Mable and I do. Wally offered to drive us."

Jake smiled. "Teachers? I would have thought that if anyone wouldn't be caught out in a blizzard, it would be two smart teachers like yourselves. Apparently, neither of you studied weather when you got your schooling," Jake said, still grinning.

Martha gave Jake a questioning look. Mable returned fire.

"We're teachers, not God."

"I had a couple of teachers in Westbrook who thought they were God. They were the reason I lost all faith in public education and told the bunch of them to take a flying leap. Same for all of us. We had better things to do than sit in class and diagram sentences or memorize some idiotic formula that you'd never use in ten lifetimes unless you happen to be some kind of budding genius. Which we're not, in case you hadn't noticed."

Mable was about to make a caustic remark about their raw intelligence but fortunately thought better of it.

Martha tried to change the subject, seeing that their host seemed sensitive about education.

"We want to thank you again for allowing Mable, Wally, and I to warm up inside. We won't stay long. We need to return to our vehicle and pick up a few things we left behind."

"What would that be? Perhaps we have them here, and you won't have to go back out into the storm," Dolly asked.

"It's Wally's hem—"

Martha cut Mable off.

"Pills. Wally left his prescription in the vehicle."

"Oh, we can't help you there," Dolly said. "We don't take pills. If one of us gets a cut or an infection of some kind, we rub Balm of Gilead ointment on it. We make it ourselves. It works every time."

"Are you sure you won't spend the night? You three can stay in the spare room with Roscoe. He's not so bad once he gets to know you," Lolly said, sitting in an overstuffed chair and breastfeeding her youngest.

"Now, Lolly, these folks have made up their mind about leaving, so there's no sense trying to convince them otherwise," Jake told his sister-in-law, anxious to have the strangers gone so the extended Barton family could continue their lives free of outsiders.

"Quiet!" Ken Barton ordered. "Do you hear that?"

Everyone listened. Even Roscoe stopped whining—briefly.

"I hear it. What is it?" Molly asked.

"It's the plow truck. He's heading south."

"Then we must leave," Martha said, grabbing her coat off the back of a chair. "If we hurry, we can make it back to the car before he plows his way back up the mountain. He can pull us out of the drift!"

"We don't have a flashlight," Wally said.

"Dolly, can we borrow a light to see our way back to the car?" Martha asked.

"We don't have any spares to loan out," Jake said.

"Of course we do, Jake," Dolly said, glaring at her husband. "They can take mine."

"Thanks. I'll leave it at Leavitt's Store. You can pick it up when you go to town to get your mail."

"We go to town once a month. We'll need that light before then," said Jake.

"Then, after school is dismissed tomorrow afternoon, I'll wrap it in a bread bag and place it under the Keep Out sign at the end of the driveway."

"See that you do. I don't want to have to come looking for it."

Martha, Mable, and Wally hurried out the door and disappeared into the blowing snow.

◆

An hour later, the plow truck returned. Charlie Ferguson used a chain to pull the Model A out of the snowdrift, and Martha, Mable, and Wally continued to Hazel Martin's Boarding House. The next day, school started on time for the Flagstaff and Dead River children. Martha and Mable's lesson focused on winter storms and how to prepare for them. They both swore that teaching the crash course in weather had nothing to do with Jake Barton's assessment of their college education.

Wally also spent the night at the boardinghouse, sleeping on Mrs. Martin's living room sofa. On his way back to Skowhegan, Wally left the flashlight in a bread wrapper beneath the Keep Out sign.

Martha Fletcher taught one year at the Flagstaff school before taking a teaching position in Rutland, Vermont. Mable Day remained in Flagstaff until 1945, when she moved to Norridgewock to teach. Mable and Wally became reacquainted, and they began dating. In 1947, Mable married the former immature twit from Skowhegan.

7.

"As far as wins go, our basketball team has shown little promise, but the team should not be judged by this. The girls' team, coached by Ken Taylor, had only four high school girls on it; the rest of the team is made up of girls from the fifth grade and up. But while even though these girls are small, they have the will to play."

—Elwood Allen, Principal
Flagstaff High School, 1942

Leavitt's Store
Flagstaff village
August 1942

Sid Morton was an odd duck. No one in the Valley knew where Sid had come from. He just showed up on a hot, stifling day in August when he walked into Leavitt's store asking to rent a post office box. After Leavitt told him the monthly rent was twenty-five cents, payable in advance, Sid decided to receive his mail via General Delivery.

Few people in town knew where Sid lived until a boy fishing at Mill Pond needed to relieve himself and wandered into the woods for privacy. Just as he was about to do his business, he heard a door open.

Through the trees, he saw Sid step out of his house, toss a basin of water onto the ground, and then go back inside. Sid had taken up residence in an abandoned two-room house on land owned by Jack Morris. Morris had died a few years earlier, and, having no descendants, the cabin fell into disrepair and was forgotten by the townspeople.

Sid was small-framed, only slightly larger than an average teenage ballet dancer. A long, jagged scar on his right cheek pulled his eye to the side, giving him a rather frightening appearance to both children and some adults. The absence of two middle fingers on his right hand added to his mystique as a recluse. Some had heard he lost them in a train accident when he slipped while trying to jump onto a rail car at the Chicago stockyards, his hand landing in front of the steel wheels as he fell. Others, mostly children, claimed Sid had told them he had lost them while fighting off a saber-toothed tiger trying to enter his tent during a trip to the Grand Canyon. Despite his unusual appearance, Sid seemed harmless enough and kept to himself, and, over time, everyone in Flagstaff accepted him for the oddity he was.

Each week, Sid strolled to town, picked up some groceries at Leavitt's, and checked for mail. In the eight years he'd spent in his shack by Mill Pond, Sid had not received even a single Christmas card, according to Postmaster Leavitt.

Slowly, Sid's appearance changed. One summer day, he appeared in Flagstaff wearing a faded Boston Braves baseball cap covered with a dozen spruce cones stitched to the cap's visor and a cluster of bunchberries pinned to each shoulder of his ragged shirt.

Even with his decorative hat, people paid Sid no mind. However, before long, his appearance slipped another notch. Sid always looked a little scruffy, with his long, matted hair sticking out in all directions of the compass and his gray-and-black beard in dire need of a trim, but he did appear to bathe regularly. However, people noticed that he was becoming downright filthy. He started showing up at Leavitt's Store with his jacket covered with safety pins. Just the pins with nothing attached. Between his distorted eye, missing fingers, the decorated hat, his jacket covered in pins, and his grubby appearance, Sid had turned into one wild and woolly-looking character.

Occasionally, Sid worked long enough to earn a few dollars for groceries, mostly cleaning out the tie-up at Fred Hardy's farm. Slight of build and not exceptionally rugged, it was all Sid could do to push the wheelbarrows of fresh manure from the barn to the nearby manure pile. He'd last a few days, then quit, only to reappear several weeks later when his supplies ran low. Fred always rehired him, feeling sorry for Sid, and each time Sid quit, Fred cleaned the barn himself.

Come fall, Sid hadn't been seen in town for two weeks, and people feared something might have happened to the hermit. Fred Hardy volunteered to visit Mill Pond to check on him. It was deathly quiet when he stepped into the clearing. Everywhere there was junk. Car parts lay scattered around the yard, even though no vehicle was in sight. A broken wringer washing machine sat next to the porch steps, and a pile of scrap metal blocked the path to the outhouse. The handle of a rusted push mower leaned against the porch rail, its reel overrun with weeds.

Fred gingerly walked across the spongy porch floor, rapped on the door, and waited, but no one came. He cracked the door open and called for Sid but got no answer. Fred stepped inside and was immediately overwhelmed by the stench of stale air. He shouted to Sid between coughs while taking quick, shallow breaths to avoid inhaling deeply whatever nastiness might be lurking in the stagnant air. Fred expected the worst. He picked his way through heaps of newspapers, baskets of pinecones, birch bark, and cardboard boxes filled with items he couldn't identify. Fred stopped abruptly at the sight of a leg blocking the doorway, its owner hidden by the partition between the rooms. Fearful of what might be around the corner, he hesitated.

"Sid?" He said, barely above a whisper, not expecting an answer.

"What!" a voice snapped back.

Sid lay on the floor, his back pressed against one of a half dozen boxes of used books.

"Didn't you hear me holler?"

"I was reading and don't hear nothing when I read. What do you want, anyway?" Sid said, looking up at Fred at such a sharp angle that his bad eye was stretched to the limit.

"We hadn't seen you in town for a while and were worried something might have happened to you."

"Well, I'm fine. Now, if you don't mind, I'll get back to my book."

Fred reported that there was no need to worry; Sid was well.

Maine newspapers renewed their interest in the plight of the Valley's two hundred residents now that the dam's construction was certain. Nearly every major paper in the state had, at one time or another, sent reporters to interview locals about their communities' pending demise.

In the spring of 1947, a reporter from the *Lewiston Journal*, working on a human-interest story about the flooding of the Valley, stopped at Leavitt's Store to talk to folks. Nearly everyone in town had spoken to a newspaper reporter at least once, and the questions were always the same: How do you feel about your town being flooded? How long have you lived here? Where are you going to go? This reporter was no different until he concluded his interview with the half dozen people gathered around the store's woodstove.

"That answers the questions I had about the dam. I have just one more, and then I'll let you folks get back to your business. How do people in the Valley feel about leaving their homes, knowing that Long Falls Dam isn't going to produce electricity?"

Norris Jones was the first to respond after a long silence.

"I believe you are mistaken, Mr. Roberts. Of course, the dam will make electricity. Why else would they build it?"

"Not according to the cover letter of a solicitation for bids document I obtained from a CMP employee," Roberts said, opening a thick manila folder crammed with paper. "Here it is. Let me read you the first paragraph of CMP's Request for Bids package:

> Central Maine Power Company, doing business as the Kennebec River Storage Company, is requesting bids for the construction of the earthen and concrete structure to be built on the Dead River at Long Falls, Spring Lake Township, Somerset County, Maine. The resulting impoundment will be a twenty thousand-acre fluctuating pool designed to provide low-flow augmentation to downstream hydroelectric facilities and to control flooding along the Kennebec River.

"I swear, I remember reading in the newspaper that the State authorized up to five thousand horsepower of hydropower could be included in the dam," Norris said.

"It did, in the old Dead River Charter that was withdrawn from consideration. The charter that became law in 1927 doesn't say that. It does say that the Kennebec River Reservoir Company may allow water drawn from the dam to develop power and construct canals, penstocks, power plants, and transmission lines. However, according to my source at CMP, they elected not to do that and to use the reservoir to supply water to other hydro dams downriver. There is no mention of the use of turbines. It is strictly a water storage reservoir. Certainly, the power company told the people affected by the dam that it wouldn't be used to produce electricity."

"We just assumed it was going to be a hydroelectric dam," Jones said, looking at the others.

Ed Haley joined in. "So, from what you read, I take this to mean that the lake will be drawn down whenever they need more water at Wyman Dam. Does that mean they could drain it dry during a drought?"

"I'm not an engineer, but I believe that is correct. They will send as much water as possible to Wyman Dam to keep the turbines spinning and making power."

"So, what they tell us is going to be a lake, could, at times, be a mud flat?" one of the men asked.

"Well, a mud flat might not be the proper term. However, if CMP did drain the lake to pre-dam conditions, it would likely look like a barren wasteland with the old Dead River channel flowing through it as it does today."

"I don't mind telling the rest of you boys that I am pissed," Jones said. "I thought the dam was going to produce electricity. Also, what we all thought would be a beautiful lake after the dam was built could disappear each time they draw down the water!"

"It sounds to me that we were sold a bill of goods," Virgil Harris said.

"You've got that right," another man said.

"So what are we going to do about it?" Jones asked.

"Absolutely nothing, except bitch," Cyrus said. "What's done is done. We can't stop the project just because of a misunderstanding on our part. At the time, we should have asked more questions."

"Do you think that's true, Mr. Roberts? I mean, about being unable to stop them now that we know the truth about what they're going to do?" Harris asked.

"Cyrus is right. CMP might not have been straightforward with the town about the dam's purpose. However, legally, they can build the dam, flood the Valley, and lower the lake level as they want."

"Now fellers, it's not all that bad. I bet that lake will make some of the best duck hunting in the state. Why, flocks of Canada geese coming down from Canada in the fall will love stopping to feed in the marshy backwaters. People from all over New England will flock here to get a whack at them. We could make a ton of money guiding them."

"For crying out loud, Jacob. Who, other than you, is willing to give up their home so they can go duck hunting?"

"Hey. Don't get all upset with me about it. I was trying to put a good face on a bad situation. Guides make good money guiding flatlanders."

8.

"...I would like to tell you a little more about the most pleasant and generous people I ever knew. I don't remember a house in Flagstaff ever being locked... I don't remember any remuneration given to Monty Young, Perley Stevens, or Harry Bryant for making their trucks available for us kids to go to the movies in Stratton almost every Saturday night... I don't think we paid Harry Bryant for edgings [firewood] he supplied for years... Perley [sic] came around and plowed gardens for all that wanted him to. He never stopped long enough to get paid, nor did he expect it. We kids, used to ask Harold Flint or Dutchie [Leavitt] to open their store after hours and on Sundays to get candy or ice cream. They never refused..."

—Duluth Wing
Flagstaff resident
There Was a Land, page 312

Leavitt's Store
Flagstaff, Maine
March 16, 1943

"Come over here for a minute, Larry," Leavitt said, seeing Larry enter the store. "You've met Pearly Haley, haven't you? He inherited the old Hiram Stevens farm just beyond the School House Hill Road."

"We met at the town dump last Saturday."

"I was telling Pearly that today is the seventh anniversary of the big flood we had back in '36. Pearly doesn't believe the entire town was flooded."

"Believe Jim, it flooded. There wasn't a building on this side of the river that didn't have water two feet inside. The only building that didn't was the high school, since it sits thirty feet higher than any other building in town."

"Take a look at this," Leavitt said, motioning Pearly to follow him. "See this pencil mark on the door casing with 1936 written next to it? The water reached a depth of thirty inches during the flood. Thank God I didn't own the store back then. Harry Flint did and lost nearly all his merchandise. To make matters worse, he made a trip to Farmington the day before the flood to pick up a load of supplies for the spring log drive and stored them in the back room. That night, the river rose ten feet and destroyed everything. Fortunately for Harry, the Stratton Bank lent him enough money to repair the damage and restock the shelves."

"I remember Ralph and Kenny Cline paddling a canoe inside Hazen Ames's Pool Hall across the street and asking Hazen if they could play a game of eightball," Harry said.

"That's right. Ralph and Kenny tried to paddle into the store, too, but they could only poke the bow through the door, being the beam on the canoe was too wide to fit through the door jamb," Leavitt said.

"Even though it was the worst disaster since the Pumpkin Freshet of 1922, nearly everyone took it in stride. The kids only missed a day or two from school. Flint used his motorboat to ferry the kids and the teachers to the foot of School House Hill and back home after school ended. Most of the homes in Dead River didn't get flooded so badly as on this side of the river. The water never flooded the first floor of our house, but you could hear the water slosh between the pine boards walking across the kitchen floor," Larry said.

"The scariest time for most people was when both bridges washed out. First, Big Bridge, then a day later, Little Bridge.

Massive slabs of ice piled against the iron stringers until they came unhinged from the piers and collapsed into the river. Flagstaff was isolated for nearly a week. Mail and supplies came by motorboat from the Ledge House," Leavitt said, then hesitated.

"Pearly, you know when I said everyone took the flood in stride?" Leavitt went on.

"Yes."

"Well, that wasn't completely the case. A tragic accident occurred during the flood."

"I don't think Pearly needs to know about that, Jim. It's something most of us want to forget. Marshall and Howard were close relatives on my wife's side of the family."

"If Pearly is going to live here until all of us are permanently flooded out, he might as well know some of the town's history. We better sit next to the woodstove. This will take a while. I will tell you precisely what Ed Parsons said about the accident.

"The winter of 1935 and '36 was wicked cold and snowy. Three days before the rain began in March, the weather started to warm up. With the rising water and runoff, the river quickly became ice-free. Then, on the seventh, Marshall Brown and his son left their home in Dead River to check their trapline. The weather was fine, with a blue sky and slightly warmer than average for the second week in March. Marshall told his wife they would be gone for four days and be home Sunday for their daughter's fourth birthday. Marshall and Howard mostly trapped up the tributaries of the North Branch of the Dead River. As near as anyone can figure, they were somewhere on Alder Stream when it commenced to rain. Of course, neither they nor anyone else knew the rain would last for days.

"The Dead began to spill over its banks on the third day. Mrs. Brown was certain that her husband and son were in trouble. Late that afternoon, she was startled by someone pounding on the kitchen door. Ed Marquis, a family friend and a trapper himself, had been in the same area as Marshall and Howard. Upon returning to Dead River, he met Marshall and Howard a short distance above Sarampus Falls. Marshall asked him to stop by and tell Lucy they were fine and would start home after checking out a new area to trap next winter. For a while, Lucy stopped worrying about her husband and son.

"That night, Lucy heard a strange sound coming from downstairs. Thinking it was Marshall and Howard, she went downstairs to greet them. About halfway down the stairs, she shined her flashlight ahead. It was then she saw water up to the second step. A piece of firewood lifted by the rising water tapped against the step's riser. Lucy retreated upstairs, unsure if the house would lift off its foundation and be carried downriver.

"The following morning, the floodwater began to recede. Lucy heard someone hollering her name and opened the bedroom window to see Ed and his nephew backpaddling while trying to get her attention. Ed asked if she wanted to stay at the high school until the water receded. Lucy refused the offer, not wanting to be away when her husband and son returned. Ed convinced her to take the food they had brought and told her to go to the kitchen door, and he'd paddle the canoe onto the porch so he could hand it to her.

"After Lucy took the food, she told him she had a bad feeling about Marshall and Howard and sensed they were in danger. She didn't come out and ask Ed to look for them; asking for favors wasn't Lucy's style. But she planted the seed.

"Ed took the hint and told Lucy that if they were not back by tomorrow morning, Adam and he would go looking for them.

"Conditions improved the following day. The flood water had withdrawn from the homes and upper fields, leaving only the bottomland flooded. Ed and Adam stopped to tell Lucy they were on their way to look for Marshall and Howard.

"After paddling for an hour, it started to rain. At first, it was light, hardly more than an annoying drizzle. As the morning wore on, the light, intermittent rain turned into a torrential downpour that Ed figured was the last band of rain before the sky began to clear. Before long, the river started to rise once more. Ed and Adam kept going, unaware that the flooding would soon be more severe than before. Just after noon, through the rain and fog, they could see Sarampus Falls, nearly washed out by the immense amount of water pouring over it. Ed had expected to meet up with Marshall and his son by now. The two paddled to shore to rest and decide what to do, now that they were back where Ed had left the Browns two days earlier.

"With the canoe's bow tied to a tree limb overhanging the bank, the two climbed up the bank and sat on the trunk of a fallen tree in the downpour, eating their lunch. Adam was about to ask his father what they would do next when something in the water caught his eye. It was the bow of a canoe sticking out of the water near the shore, about fifty yards beyond where they were sitting.

"They hurriedly finished eating and floated to the sunken canoe. A rope still attached to the bow stretched downriver, whipped back and forth by the current's pull. Adam grabbed the rope, hoping to free the canoe, and, in the process, nearly upset their own canoe.

"Ed used his paddle to recover from the near-fatal roll while yelling to Adam to drop the rope, or they would both be in the water. They retreated to shore to contemplate what they were going to do. They agreed that Marshall and Howard must have flipped their canoe trying to shoot the falls. They needed to find them, whether alive or dead, for Lucy's sake. The two decided to sweep the shoreline to see if they could find any evidence of them.

"They paddled toward the base of the falls, crossed to the west side of the river, and rode the current downstream as they continued their search. It wasn't long before they spotted a stack of beaver pelts bound with a cotton cord caught in an eddy behind a large boulder.

"Five minutes later, Adam spotted Howard's body close to shore, caught on a tree limb. Ed put Adam ashore with a rope while he maneuvered the canoe next to Howard's body and tied the other end under Howard's arms. Once ashore, they pulled Howard's body free of the tree and then over the bank.

"Howard and Adam were the same age and had remained close friends since high school. Seeing Howard's pale skin and wide-open eyes overwhelmed Adam. Until now, he had believed that death only happened to old people, not to someone who was just eighteen. Watching his friend lying in the wet snow, looking up at him, was more than Adam could bear. Feeling nauseous, Adam walked away and retched. Upon his return, his uncle had covered Howard's corpse with fir branches.

"Adam and Ed returned to the canoe and continued along the bank, searching for Marshall. After traveling half a mile downstream, they crossed to the other side and paddled back toward the falls. The two agreed if they didn't find Mashall by the time they reached Sarampus, they would load Howard's body and return home. Once the water level receded, they would attempt to locate Marshall again, hopefully before a pack of wolves discovered the corpse. An hour later, they loaded Howard's body into the canoe and commenced the long journey back to Dead River.

"Two miles below the falls, Ed and Adam spotted Marshall's body pinned against a half-sunken log in the middle of the river. They managed to pull the body into the canoe and took father and son home, dreading having to tell Lucy that her husband and son had drowned.

"So that's the tragic story that came from the 1936 flood. Other than Lucy being so heartbroken by her loss, she sold the farm just two months after the deaths of Marshall and Howard and left the Valley. Supposedly, Lucy moved in with her sister somewhere along the coast. The Valley lost three good people, all due to that flood," Leavitt said.

In late September 1946, the Central Maine Power Company finally announced that construction of the dam at Long Falls would begin in 1949. The residents read the news in the daily newspapers. Some complained that the company should have had the common decency to send each landowner a letter informing them of the decision to move forward with the dam. After all, it was their lives that CMP was turning upside down. However, knowing that the dam would be built came as a relief to residents who had lived under uncertainty for eighteen years. Regardless of their feelings about being displaced, families could now plan where to go before the Valley was flooded.

9.

"Residents of the little town of Flagstaff need no longer wonder where they will go when the waters of the Dead River are backed up over their homes by the storage dam project underway. Today, authorities of Canaan [Maine] informed them that they would not only be welcome here, but to show the sincerity of their invitation, they offered three years of tax exemption to any person who comes here and builds a home or business."

—*Waterville Sentinel*
March 8, 1949

Long Falls on the Dead River
Spring Lake Township
June 7, 1948

Nearly a hundred people gathered at the site of the long-awaited dam on the Dead River. Today marked the ceremonial start of building the 1,300-foot-long structure of concrete and earth. County, state, and federal politicians and other dignitaries were present to praise the project and take credit for the achievement whenever they found an opportunity. Selectmen representing Dead River Plantation and Flagstaff, along with a dozen or so residents, were also in attendance. If there was any sadness about losing their homes, it was well suppressed. The list of speakers was long, as were their remarks. Former Governor Baxter chose not to attend. Some attendees speculated that he wasn't invited to the ceremony, while others said he was preparing for another overseas trip.

Governor Horace Hildreth began the ceremony by reflecting on the twenty-five years of negotiation that had led to this day. The older politicians in attendance remembered it as twenty-five years of nonstop wrangling. Hildreth requested a moment of silence for Walter Wyman, who had passed away before he could see his vision for Long Falls Dam come to fruition. He then delivered a fifteen-minute oratory on the dam's importance to Maine's economic future. Now, turbines in the hydroelectric dams along the Kennebec would spin efficiently through droughts and summers when runoff is at its lowest, thanks, he said, to the new reservoir named Flagstaff Lake.

Frederick Payson, Central Maine Powers Company's Chief Engineer, reeled off facts and figures about the project. The dam would stand 45 feet high and stretch 1,329 feet between abutments. Thousands of cubic yards of concrete and compacted gravel were required to hold back 300,000 acre-feet of water. Payson informed the guests that the gates would be closed during the winter of 1949. Over the following year, the reservoir would gradually fill, eventually creating a twenty-one-mile-long lake that covered 20,000 acres, offering wonderful recreational opportunities for everyone to enjoy. However, he neglected to mention that two hundred people had sacrificed their way of life for the project to proceed.

After the speeches, a large Caterpillar D7 bulldozer roared to life, releasing a cloud of blue smoke. The overweight operator, puffing on a cigar, inched the machine forward and lowered the blade, scraping away a ceremonial layer of topsoil as the spectators applauded politely. Twenty-six years of uncertainty and anxiety for the people of the Dead River Valley was officially over. The construction of Long Falls Dam had commenced.

The following day, work began in earnest. Men with transits shot elevations for the cuts and fill needed to prepare the site for the dam's footing. At the same time, half a dozen bulldozers and dump trucks worked nonstop, pushing and hauling material from one location to another.

Amid the organized chaos, the foreman stood on a bulldozer track, giving instructions to the same operator who had performed at yesterday's groundbreaking. He had just jumped to the ground and started walking away when he heard the machine operator yell. The boss looked back to see the man clutching his right arm.

"I've been shot!"

An hour later, the construction site was ablaze with flashing red and blue lights. An ambulance, three Somerset County Sheriff vehicles, two Forest Service pickups, and the District Game Warden had descended on the scene. Even a reporter from Skowhegan's *Independent-Reporter* newspaper, who happened to be at the sheriff's office when the call came in, joined the parade of vehicles that sped up the newly constructed Long Falls Dam Road.

Once loaded into the ambulance, the dozer operator was transported to a Skowhegan hospital.

"Does anyone know what happened?" Sheriff Sheridan Smith asked, glancing at each of the construction workers gathered around the ambulance to see their coworker off.

"That would be me, Sheriff. I'm Clifford Bell, the foreman for Mid-Maine Construction Company, the primary contractor for the project. I spoke to Bruce just before he was shot."

Sheriff Smith led Bell away from the other men. "So, what happened before the shooting?" the sheriff asked, opening his notepad.

"Nothing, really. I was standing on the dozer's track telling Bruce how much soil to scalp off that knoll over there," Smith said, pointing over his shoulder. "I got off the dozer and walked about fifty feet when I heard Bruce holler that he'd been shot. I quickly checked his arm, then ran to the construction shack to call an ambulance. As soon as I hung up, I called you."

"Did you hear the shot?"

"No. There was so much noise from all the equipment that I had to yell for Bruce to hear me, even though I was only two feet away from him."

Smith studied the scene. "Is that the way the bulldozer was facing at the time of the shooting?"

"Yes. I shut the machine off before some of us helped Bruce down to the ground."

"Then the shot had to come from the north side of the river. Somewhere in those woods, I guess. Whoever pulled the trigger made a hell of a shot. That has to be at least three hundred yards."

"Maybe he wasn't so good," Bell said.

"What do you mean?"

"Maybe he was aiming at the heart and missed."

Jim Leavitt was ringing up a customer when Harry Flint's youngest boy rushed into the store, all excited.

"Mr. Leavitt! Mr. Leavitt! Someone killed the bulldozer man at the dam!"

"What're you talking about, Billy?"

"Timmy Sampson told me. He said he was riding his bicycle up the Long Falls Dam Road to watch the equipment when a long line of cars with lights flashing passed him. When he got there, he heard some men talking. They said a man driving a bulldozer had been shot!"

Just then, Tim Hardy, a farmer on the east side of town, entered the store. "Did you hear the news about the shooting at the construction site?"

"Billy Flint just told me a man was shot and killed."

"Well, he was shot, all right. But he wasn't killed. Someone shot him in the right arm, just below the elbow."

"You mean a gun went off accidentally?"

"No. Someone shot him intentionally. The sheriff thinks it might have been someone in the woods with a rifle."

Soon, half a dozen others came into the store after hearing about the shooting at Long Falls, all of them having an opinion as to who might have shot the construction worker.

"I bet it was Arapaho Nell. I wouldn't put anything by her after her run-in with those surveyors," one man said.

"Nah, it couldn't have been her. She lives ten miles from Long Falls. I doubt an eighty-year-old woman would trek that far through the woods to take a potshot at a guy operating a bulldozer," said another man, standing off to the side, sucking on his pipe.

"Well, several folks at the town meetings got pretty heated about the dam being built."

"For God's sake, Bill! You know those fellers as well as I do," said Seth Jackson, Flagstaff's second selectman. "There isn't one of them men going to shoot someone over that dam. They were just telling their feelings about the Valley being flooded. All of us have fretted over it, one time or another."

"I don't think Bill is that far off in his thinking," Phil Roy said. "On the way over here, I wondered about who might have done it. Then I remembered a while back when Eben Storey held a meeting at his house with half a dozen other men from Dead River conniving on how to stop the dam from being built. Who knows what went on at that meeting. I counted seven cars in Eben's driveway when I happened to go by."

"*Happened* to go by?" Seth said as the others tried not to laugh. Phil was the closest thing to a town gossip in the Valley. If someone wanted to know about the latest happenings, Phil Roy was the person to ask.

"Yes, I happened to go by. My wife had told me to go do something constructive, so I decided to drive down to Hurricane Falls to catch a few trout. Anyways, I'm just saying we don't know what was discussed. Maybe they were plotting to sabotage the dam. Perhaps they thought if they shot one of the workers, the company would see they weren't welcome here in the Valley and leave."

"God, Phil! You have way too much time to think," Jim Leavitt said. "Do you actually believe that if one of our neighbors shot someone at the dam site, it would cause Central Maine Power to cower and not build a three-million-dollar dam? I guarantee you the only thing that would come out of that stupidity would be spending the next thirty years in the State Insane Asylum for the nut case who pulled the trigger."

"Now, hold on a minute. I'm not saying any of them did the shooting, but I'm sure they've been scheming to block CMP from flooding the Valley. You know how vocal Eben was at the town meeting, saying the power company had no right to take someone's land if they didn't want to sell," Phil said. "Maybe Eben and the rest of them plan to blow up the dam before the water starts backing up behind it. I know that when Maurice Cormier worked on river drives, his job was to dynamite the log jams. He's still got a bunch of the stuff stored in the barn and uses it occasionally to blow an old stump or boulder to smithereens in one of his fields."

"Wait just a minute, boys," jumped in Charlie Rand. "Let's not drift off into fantasy land. Why do all of you assume it was someone from Flagstaff or Dead River who shot that guy? It could have been one of those backwoods families that squatted on the old Frank Watts farm south of the Ledge House. Dunn tells me there's quite a tribe living there—at least three families with a raft of young ones. Dunn said that once or twice a week, he hears rifle shots behind his place from around midnight to four in the morning. Night hunting is what they're doing. They get Dunn's hound all worked up so that his howling wakes the guests in the cabins. A few tourists told him it would be the last time they'd spend a night at the Ledge House. Said there was no way they would pay three dollars for a cabin and have to put up with that racket."

"So why doesn't he call the warden? Let him go up there and read them the riot act. That's why he gets paid the big bucks for enforcing the fish and game laws."

"That's what I asked Dunn. He said he was afraid they might retaliate. They're bound to know he ratted on them since he's the only one living within two miles of their compound. Anyhow, what I was getting at was that one of those characters might be just foolish enough to have taken that shot. Maybe they don't like being disturbed by all those dump trucks downshifting going by their place, so one of them thought he'd send CMP a message."

After the men tossed around a few more possibilities, almost bordering on the ridiculous, they began filtering out of the store to go about their business.

Leavitt's Store
Flagstaff, Maine
November 14, 1948

Five months had passed since the shooting at Long Falls. The incident, once the only topic of conversation in the Dead River Valley, was replaced by more pressing concerns, such as whether the Flagstaff Boys Basketball Team would make the State Finals and if there would be tracking snow for deer season. Still, someone stopping at Leavitt's Store occasionally offered their unsolicited opinion about the shooting.

"I don't think the State Police ever will find the person that shot that dozer operator," Neal Roberts said, watching Leavitt sort through the morning mail.

"The last thing I heard about the investigation was a few days after the shooting, when the State Police found an empty casing just inside the woods on the north side of the river," Leavitt said. "The newspaper said it matched the caliber of the bullet the doctors dug out of the man's arm."

"Yeah, for a few days after they found the casing, cops were around every tree looking for clues. I haven't seen hide nor hair of the law since. It's like they've given up trying to find out who did it."

"How'd the guy that got shot make out?"

"He's fine. He's back at work, driving the crawler. It seems that he's become quite a celebrity. Half the kids in Dead River and Flagstaff have ridden their bikes to Long Falls just to get his autograph. I've heard they wait until the crew breaks for lunch, then shove pencil and paper at him while he eats."

"Speaking of being shot," Leavitt said, seeing Lenwood Andrews pull up in front of the store. "Maybe we can find out what happened at Frank Moody's Camp on Saturday.

"Hello, Lenwood," Leavitt said as soon as Lenwood entered the store.

"Hello, Jim. I just walked into Frank's camp to pick up a few things I had forgotten when I left after the accident. Also, before I forget, Frank wanted me to stop by and ask if you knew someone who would shovel the snow off his camp this winter. He and his wife are working at a Fort Lauderdale hotel in Florida for the winter. I'd do it myself if it weren't for my wife having hip surgery. She could be laid up most of the winter, so getting away to do it would be tough."

"I think I can find someone. How's your friend who got shot doing?"

"Doug's kind of down. The doctors want to remove his right arm. They said the bullet tore the nerves and muscles all to hell."

"Is he going to have it done?"

"I don't think he is. He figures he'd rather have limited use of the arm than no arm at all."

"What exactly happened, anyway? About all we heard was his rifle went off, and the bullet hit him in the shoulder."

"I'll tell you exactly what happened. That is one day I'll never forget.

"Up until the accident, we were having a grand old time. Six of us stayed at Frank's camp at Jerome Brook for a week of deer hunting. We shot two nice bucks on Roundtop Mountain. The plan was to hunt until noon on Saturday and then head home.

"Harold and me had a date to play at a social at the Dead River School on Friday evening. Everyone wanted to go except for Butch, who was a little under the weather. The place was packed with young and old, all dancing in their stocking feet while Harold and I played the fiddle and harmonica. After it was over, we headed back to camp. Doug, Harold, and Smitty walked back the way we came, following the West Carry Pond Tote Road to Jerome Brook and up the brook to Frankie's hunting camp.

"Frank said he'd hitch a ride back to the Ledge House and follow the spotted trail to camp. I went with him. That turned out to be one long walk in the dark. Frank had a flashlight but refused to use it. It was darker than the inside of a boot, yet he still wouldn't turn it on. He claimed the batteries were too expensive to waste. We worked our way along the base of a hill next to the bog. I asked Frank if he knew where he was. All I got was a grunt or an 'I don't know.' I told Frank to fire his rifle to let people know where we were. He said not yet, and we continued plodding along. I was exhausted. I must have walked into half a dozen trees and fallen into just as many brush piles. I told him that if he wasn't going to shoot, at least turn on the light before I drove a spruce branch into my eyeball. All he said was, 'Follow me.'

"What felt like two hours later, even though it was probably only twenty minutes, we stepped into a small clearing. Frank aimed his rifle at the sky and fired a shot. Instantly, four flashlights began scanning the woods to investigate what was happening. We weren't fifty feet from the camp. Well, don't you think everyone didn't have a good laugh when Frank told the guys about our jaunt through the woods? As it turned out, that would be the last laugh we had on that trip.

"The following day started out all right. Around five o'clock, Ralph Wing showed up. He had a hunting party cancel at the last minute, so he decided to hunt with us until noon. We didn't realize it at the time, but having the best deer hunting guide in Somerset County along proved to be a stroke of luck.

"After overdosing on pancakes and molasses donuts, we struck out. The six of us walked about a half mile up the west side of Roundtop and then spread out about seventy yards apart. Ralph was going to wait about a half hour, then make a sweep toward us from the north, hoping to drive a big buck our way.

"Frank was the first man, then Smitty, Harold, me, Doug, and Butch, the furthest uphill. I sat on the ground with my back against a half-rotted maple.

"I had just put my rifle across my knees, looking in the direction a deer would come if Ralph kicked one out to us. Then someone shot. *Pow!* I must have lifted three feet off the ground, it surprised me so. For two or three seconds, there was dead silence. Then Doug yelled, '*I shot my arm off!*' I'll never forget those words as long as I live.

"I shouted to Frank, Smitty, and Harold to get up here fast. Butch was talking to Doug, trying to keep him calm when we got to him. Doug lay on the ground in agony, saying, 'I can't believe it, I can't believe it.'

"Harold took the handkerchief from his hunting coat and stuffed it inside Doug's shirt, attempting to control the bleeding. No luck. Instantly, it was soaked with blood.

"The boys asked me to try to stop the bleeding since I was the only one with some first-aid knowledge. As a former funeral director, I knew where the major arteries are in an arm, so I got to work. I told Hank and Smitty to head to the small brook nearby and collect a half dozen rocks the size of walnuts. I placed the stones under Doug's arm and secured them with a trifold handkerchief tied over his shoulder. Then, I pushed a small stick through just below the knot and twisted it until the bleeding slowed to a trickle.

"Amidst it all, Ralph found us working on Doug. He took one look at him and told the rest of us to construct a stretcher to carry Doug off the mountain while he went to find a doctor. Ralph dashed down the mountain and made for the Dead River Post Office, four miles away, to call the osteopathic doctor in Stratton.

"While I stayed with Doug, Hank and Smitty started to cut a path wide enough to carry the stretcher. Frank and Butch rushed back to camp for blankets, a fistful of spikes, and an ax to build the stretcher. It needed to be rugged enough to accommodate Doug's two-hundred-pound frame. We used our cartridge belts to hold the maple saplings together and pounded the spikes into the sides of the frame to carry Doug. Hank cut fir boughs to lay across the belts to make it more comfortable for Doug. The mile back to camp proved to be a rough ride for him.

"We were about three-quarters of the way to camp when Ralph and the doctor intercepted us. The only light moment of the whole ordeal came when the doctor said, 'He's out now,' after giving Doug a shot. Doug responded clearly and loudly, 'Like hell I am!'

"Game wardens met us at Frank's camp. They took over transporting Doug to the waiting ambulance at Bog Brook and brought him to the Skowhegan Hospital. Hank and Smitty followed the ambulance in case Doug needed blood. Frank, Butch, and I went back to camp. We didn't say much while cleaning up the camp. I think the three of us were lost in thought about Doug getting shot and how close he came to bleeding to death.

"That was one hunting trip I'll never forget."

Once construction began on Long Falls Dam, reality set in for the Valley's residents. Now that it was happening, there would be no turning back. Flagstaff, Dead River, and Bigelow had one year left before they would fade into memory. However, not everyone had accepted that they needed to move on with their lives.

"I ain't selling!" Ralph Cline told the others gathered at the counter of Leavitt's Store.

"Don't. The power company doesn't care if you sell or not. They will take it anyway, now that our illustrious state legislature has granted them the power of eminent domain."

"That's right. Central Maine Power knew there would be obstinate old coots like you, Ralph, that would try to stop the project by not selling out."

"Well, I may be an old coot, but them land grabbers have no right to kick me out of my house. My grandfather didn't build that place ninety years ago to have it burned down and flooded out by some corporation. If he knew what was happening, Grampa Ted would be rolling over in his grave."

"Well, your Grampa Ted might not find out yet. Walter Hinds and a couple of others are going to start digging up the bodies at the town cemetery in about a week and moving them to Eustis to be reburied."

"And that's another thing that sticks in my craw, digging everyone's relatives up and moving them. It's sacrilegious doing stuff like that. And what's more, it ain't natural. Those people died expecting to be planted in one place until the end of time. Why, poor Mildred Sawyer only died a year ago, and now she's being uprooted and driven twenty miles to be reburied in a place she ain't the least bit familiar with."

"They can have my place as long as they pay me for what it's worth," Wilber Warner said. "I'm sick of jacking and leveling, replacing sills, and everything else that goes with trying to keep a hundred-year-old farmhouse from falling around my ears. I'd take the money, move to Connecticut, and work at Pratt and Whitney building planes for the Air Force. No business in the state of Maine pays those kinds of wages unless it's one of those high-end law firms in Portland."

"They're not getting my place without a fight. They'll have to get by me and my Remington 81 Woodmaster first," Robert Biner told the others. "My house is the oldest place in Dead River. My great-grandfather built it in 1850, and the ridgeline is as straight as the day he built it. They're wrong if the power company believes it can just throw a bunch of money on the table and expect me to pick it up. All the Biner men were born and died in my place, and when my final bacon is curled, I plan to die there myself, one way or another," Biner said, storming out of the store.

The others watched through the store window as Biner drove toward Big Bridge. "I hope he can swim," one of the men said, setting off a round of laughter.

10.

"No Sir, we're not cry babying. We admit the advance of progress, and the necessity for industrial development in the State of Maine—and by heavens, we're carrying our own burden without asking for any sympathy from the outside world!"

—Anonymous
Lewiston Daily Sun, July 2, 1949

Construction on the dam continued through the summer and into the winter of 1949, with the shooting incident unsolved. While nearly everyone in the Valley regretted the shooting of the dozer operator, it soon faded into the background of everyday life. CMP wasn't quite ready to move on from the episode, so they increased security to prevent it from happening again. The company ringed the construction site with an eight-foot-high chain-link fence and hired a private security firm to monitor the area around the clock.

Sub-zero temperatures and unrelenting howling winds during the third week of January forced the general contractor to halt operations until working conditions improved. The workers were informed that the pause on construction would last until February 1. A week off allowed the workers to be home with their families, leaving only two security guards to monitor the site.

"Damn, ain't it cold out there!" Fred Stevens said, slamming the door of the construction trailer used to house the security company personnel.

"Tell me about it," Barry Dubord said. "On my way to the outhouse, the wind ripped my hat off. I chased it for a mile before I finally caught up with it. I thought my ears would drop off, they were so cold. Anyway, we've got two hours before we have to make the rounds again. Just enough time to crawl into the sack and take a snooze."

At four fifteen, the alarm went off, and both men began to dress for another inspection of the perimeter fence. Fred glanced at the thermometer fastened to the outside window casing.

"You've got to be kidding me! Eight below zero, and the wind is blowing a gale. I bet it feels like fifty below out there." Fred stared out the window, thinking.

"You know, Barry, it doesn't make much sense for us to go out in these frigid temperatures. No one in his right mind would attempt to break into the construction site with it this cold."

"So, what are you saying, Fred?"

"I'm saying we ought to skip the four thirty rounds."

"What about the log? We can't leave a blank entry. It's the first thing the superintendent checks each morning."

"We don't leave it blank. We'll write, 'Nothing to report,' just like we've done for every other log entry for the past four months. What do you think? Wouldn't you like to get another hour of shuteye instead of freezing your ass off for nothing?"

Fred and Barry turned off the gas light and went back to bed. They didn't make the four thirty or the six thirty perimeter check. They were awakened at seven o'clock by a vehicle pulling up to the construction trailer. Barry looked out the window.

"Holly shit! It's Clark! He wasn't supposed to be here till noon. Get dressed before he comes in!"

The door swung open, and Ralph Clark, the Long Falls Dam Project Superintendent, stepped inside. He glanced at Fred and Barry and asked, "You boys just getting up?"

"Oh no, we just got in from doing the rounds," Barry told him.

Clark didn't believe their story for a second. Barry's hair was matted from lying on the pillow, and Fred's eyes looked as if he had just woken from a long winter nap. Clark went along with the two to see what else they might come up with.

Clark picked up the security log off the desk. "There are no entries for the four thirty or six thirty rounds."

"Really? I guess we forgot to write it in the log. Although there was nothing unusual to report," Barry said as he finished buttoning his shirt.

Fred and Barry glanced at each other uneasy about what might happen next.

"You two might be interested to know that while driving on the access road, I came across two fresh sets of tracks in the dusting of snow we got last night. I thought they belonged to you, so I set out to catch up, thinking I'd tag along while you made your rounds. Do you boys know what I found when I came to the end of those tracks?"

Fred and Barry shook their heads.

"I found a hole about three feet wide by two feet high cut in the bottom of the fence. It appears someone broke into the construction site during the night.

"Now, the three of us are going over the site with a fine-tooth comb to see what they might have been up to."

Fred glanced at Barry with a subtle smile, thinking they were off the hook for neglecting to make their security rounds.

The men scanned the snow for tracks left by the intruders. If there had been any, they were long buried by the blowing snow. Clark, Fred, and Barry checked the two equipment sheds for missing tools. Then, using their flashlights, they examined the construction equipment for signs of vandalism. The search came up empty. There was no indication of any mischief, and the three returned to the trailer.

Clark wasted no time telling the two security guards they were fired. "I want you two to pack what's yours and get the hell out of here. Hendrick Security can deal with you two."

"Nothing was stolen. The only damage was to the fence," Fred fumed, thinking Clark was overreacting to the break-in.

"Lucky for you that there wasn't, or CMP would sue you and the security company for damages caused by your negligence. Now move!"

Fred glared at Clark while he and Barry stuffed their belongings into their bags. As he began to close the trailer door, Fred made a snide remark and released the doorknob, allowing a gust of wind to violently slam the door against the trailer.

Clark watched the men get into the car and drive off. As soon as their vehicle passed through the perimeter gate, he called the Somerset County Sheriff's office in Skowhegan. The dispatcher informed him that Sheriff Smith was out sick but would call him once he returned to work.

The construction crew returned two days later, and work on Long Falls Dam resumed. The same day, the county sheriff interviewed Clark about the break-in three days earlier.

"At this point, it appears nothing was taken, and no damage was done except to the fence," Clark told the sheriff.

"Could have been just kids looking for something to do," the sheriff said.

"In the middle of the night and the frigid cold? They must have been really bored," Clark replied.

Clark accompanied the sheriff back to his car. Sheriff Smith told Cark he would write up the incident, but he doubted anything could be done other than documenting that a break-in had occurred, and he drove off.

Above the din of the working machinery, a loud crash could be heard at the far end of the dam. A dozen workers ran toward the commotion. Even the men operating dozers and cranes jumped from their rigs and followed the others.

Clark raced after them. When he got there, a group of workers stood atop the partially constructed earthen dike, gazing at the river as a dozen men made their way down the steep slope to the scene of the accident.

"What happened?" Clark demanded.

"McAllister was pushing fill down the embankment. About a quarter of the way down, the dozer stalled. I saw the whole thing. He dropped the blade, but the dozer just kept on rolling. I could hear gears grinding, trying to put the transmission into low gear. They wouldn't mesh at the speed he was going. All he could do was ride the machine to the bottom. The impact of striking the boulders threw him out of his seat. He slid across the tractor's hood and bounced off the top of the blade, landing in the river."

"The brakes should have stopped him," Clark said.

"They should have, but they didn't," the worker said, watching four men pull McAllister from the river.

Several workers assisted McAllister in reaching the top of the embankment. Clark urged him to visit the hospital to be checked out. McAllister declined, informing his boss that he was okay, apart from being sore and bruised. Clark's attention turned to the cause of the accident. He ordered one of the men to find the lead mechanic to inspect the disabled machine.

The mechanic inspected the bulldozer for mechanical issues that could have caused it to stall. After twenty minutes, he crawled out from under the machine and motioned for Clark to join him.

"I found your answer as to why it stalled. Someone put sand in the fuel tank," the mechanic said, holding a fistful of diesel fuel-saturated sand. "I emptied this mess from the sediment bowl. We'd be lucky if it didn't ruin the engine."

"That explains why it stalled, but it doesn't explain why the brakes didn't stop the machine."

"Come over here," the mechanic said to Clark. "Look between the track and the engine. See that copper line running along the frame? You can see the stain where the brake fluid leaked out. That brake line was cut. I'm willing to bet we'll find a puddle of brake fluid if we check where the dozer sat last night."

"That cut line means someone intended for the dozer operator to get hurt or killed. I need to get the sheriff back here before things spiral completely out of control."

After interviewing Clark and the heavy equipment mechanic, Smith drove to Flagstaff to talk

with Jim Leavitt. If there was any scuttlebutt about what had happened at the construction site,

it was bound to have been mentioned at the store.

"Hello, Sheriff, what brings you to Flagstaff this cold winter day?" Leavitt asked.

"Hello, Jim. I'm afraid this isn't a social call. I need to find some answers about what happened at the Long Falls Dam."

"I heard there was some kind of accident there this morning. What happened?"

"It seems that someone sabotaged a piece of equipment, and a man was nearly killed. Knowing that everyone in the Valley comes into your store at one time or another, I thought you might have heard talk about what happened. Perhaps a name of who might have done it?"

"Sheridan, many people are unhappy about being forced to leave their homes, but none are so upset that they would want to see someone hurt out of revenge. Besides, there's no reason to take their frustrations out on a man just doing his job to provide for his family."

"That may well be. But it makes more sense that a local did it rather than some stranger driving up from Farmington or Skowhegan in the middle of the night to cut a brake line."

"I don't know anyone who would stoop so low as to sabotage a bulldozer, let alone want to hurt a construction worker…unless…"

"Unless what?"

"Well, there are several families living together in the woods just below the Ledge House. Most people around here think they're a strange bunch. I'd have to agree after seeing how they acted when they came into the store."

"How so?" The sheriff asked, taking a notebook from his shirt pocket.

"The first time they came in, it was only the father and what I assumed to be his two boys. They just went up one aisle and down the other looking. Finally, the father set a quart of milk on the counter. As I made the change, he noticed the morning paper next to the cash register. There was a front-page story about breaking ground for the dam at Long Falls. He stood there, read the article, and put the paper back on the counter."

"Is that it? There's nothing unusual about reading the paper besides being too cheap to buy it."

"That's it, except for what he said before he left the store."

"Which was?"

"He said he didn't move up here to live next to a dam, and someone should put a stop to it."

"Sounds like I need to visit those people and hear what they have to say."

"I'd take reinforcements if I were you. Cliff Dunn at the Ledge House had a run-in with them a while ago. According to Cliff, when he visited their cabin to politely ask them not to practice shooting at all hours of the day and night, one of the three men told Cliff where he could stick it and ran him off their property. He suspects they're poaching deer, as well, and there's a nest of them living in one cabin."

"I'll do that, Jim. There's always safety in numbers. Also, you mentioned something about the first time they came in. Did something happen another time?"

"You might say that. About a month after their first visit, they returned to the store. This time, twelve of them—six adults and six kids. They scattered all over the store like ants looking for sugar.

June and I were working that day. Between us, we couldn't keep track of them all. Eventually, one of the women bought a couple of loaves of bread, and they left. Later that day, June noticed we were out of bacon and only had one bag of chocolate chips on the shelf. I did inventory the day before, so I was certain plenty of both were in stock. Thinking back, I figured they stole it while June and I were distracted. Two of the men kept asking me about fishing in the area and where to go, and at the same time, June was tied up with three of the kids trying to decide what kind of candy they wanted."

"They sound like a fine addition to the community. Do you know their names?"

"Only that their last name is Barton. They don't receive mail, and they don't send any, at least from here. That seems a little strange to me."

"How do I find the Bartons?"

"As I said, they live in the woods about three miles south of the Ledge House. Look for a sign nailed to a tree by the road that says 'Backwoods Haven.' You can't miss it. A dozen no-trespassing signs are plastered to the trees on both sides of the entrance as well."

The sheriff slipped the notebook into his pocket and left Leavitt's Store.

Somerset County Sheriff Smith and Deputy Dennis Pike drove to Dead River the following day to interview the Bartons. Sheriff Smith turned onto the narrow dirt road that presumably led to the homes of the three families Leavitt had mentioned.

"I've seen tote roads in better shape. We'd better walk. I don't want to explain to the County Commissioners how a hole got in the Plymouth's oil pan," Smith said.

After walking for five minutes, Smith and Pike had still not reached the family compound.

"Judging by the no-trespassing signs on about every tree and how far we've walked, I don't think these people want to be found," Pike told his boss.

Before Smith could answer, a dog barked.

"By the sound of that bark, let's hope that dog is chained," Smith said.

"Apparently not. Here he comes!"

The giant German shepherd charged down the road on a mission to thwart the interlopers. Stopping a few feet in front of Smith and Pike, his bark transformed into a menacing snarl, revealing a mouthful of exceptionally large teeth. The dog circled Smith and Pike and made repeated lunges toward them, looking for an opportunity to plant his incisors deep into a leg.

Pike unsnapped the strap that secured the revolver to the holster. "If that son of a bitch even sniffs a hair on my leg, he's as good as dead."

"Roscoe! Get your hairy ass back here!"

Smith and Pike turned to see a man stepping out from behind a spruce tree. They waited for him to approach them.

"Didn't you two see the no-trespassing signs?" the man said, not impressed that Smith and Pike were dressed in police uniforms.

"We're looking for the Bartons. We heard they live on this road," Smith said.

"I'm Jake Barton. Suppose I don't want to talk to *you*." the man said, holding a determined Roscoe back by the collar.

"That's quite the dog," Smith said, ignoring the man's comment.

"He serves the purpose. I wanted a dog that hated outsiders as much as I do, and Roscoe here hates everyone except family. Isn't that right, Roscoe?" Hearing his name, the shepherd snarled and made another lunge at Smith and Pike. Roscoe would have torn into them if Jake had let go of his collar.

"What are you two doing here? I don't recollect calling the police."

"I'm the Somerset County Sheriff, Sheridan Smith, and this is Deputy Sheriff Dennis Pike."

"I don't care if you're God Almighty. I'll ask you one more time: What do you want?"

"There was an incident at Long Falls yesterday, and we wanted to see if you might know something about it," Smith said.

"What kind of *incident*?"

"It appears someone cut the brake lines on a bulldozer, and a man was nearly killed."

"And you thought I did it."

"No. We thought you might know something to help us find who did it."

"Sheriff, I might not have finished high school, and maybe I'm not the sharpest pencil in the pencil box, but I'm smart enough to know that the only reason you two walked up here is to find out if I cut those brake lines. So don't try to bullshit me. Unless you have a warrant, I suggest you head back to your car."

"We just had a few questions to ask you," the sheriff said.

"You heard my brother. Leave!" bellowed someone behind Smith and Pike.

Smith and Pike spun around to find a bearded man standing barely an arm's length away, a revolver strapped to his waist. Another man stood a hundred feet behind him, cradling a rifle and observing everyone.

"Okay. If you hear something that might help our investigation, we'd appreciate you calling us," Smith said, holding out his card.

"You keep your business card, sheriff. You'd just be wasting paper. You see, there's no way in hell I'm going to call you about anything. If I have a problem, I'll solve it myself. That's what being self-sufficient is all about."

Smith and Pike started back to their car. Pike glanced back to be sure they weren't being followed—by either man or dog.

"What do you think, Sheriff? Do you think they're the ones who did it?"

"Hard telling. All three seem to have a hair across their ass about something. We know one of them told Leavitt someone needed to stop the dam from being built. Maybe he and the others decided it would be them. Then again, perhaps they're all social outcasts, and moving to the woods was a way to escape society, and that what one of them told Leavitt wasn't any more than bitching about the dam being built and upsetting their backwoods lifestyle."

"It would be nice to find out who these characters are," Pike said

"We can. We'll check the Registry of Deeds and see whose names are on the deed."

Now, the Somerset County Sheriff had two cases to solve: finding the person who'd shot the construction worker and identifying the individual who'd sabotaged the bulldozer. Smith was confident that the same person had committed both crimes. The motive also seemed clear. Someone was determined to prevent the Valley from being flooded and was doing everything possible to stop the dam from being built.

"What's our next move, Sheriff?" Pike asked, driving back to Skowhegan.

"For starters, we'll interview every last resident in Dead River and Flagstaff if we have to. Someone must know about what happened at the dam. Why, the combined population of both towns can't be two hundred, and likely everyone knows everyone else's business."

"Maybe it wasn't a local that did it." Deputy Pike said.

"Not a local? That doesn't make sense. Who else would have the motive to shoot one construction worker and nearly kill another by tampering with the bulldozer?"

"It could be someone who works for the construction company or has it in for Central Maine Power Company."

"Now, that's a stretch. I'm not ready to investigate if a ratepayer thought his electric bill was too high, so he took a potshot at a dozer operator. I think we'll stick with the obvious suspects.

"Tomorrow morning, I'm going back to Flagstaff to see what I can find out. I want you to go to the Registry of Deeds and get the names of those birds living in the woods. Once you do, run them through the State Police in Augusta and see if they have a record. I should be back in the office late afternoon. You can fill me in on what you found out."

"Here's an idea," Pike said.

"I hope it's better than your last one. Go ahead."

"Instead of knocking on doors, why don't you ask the selectmen of Dead River and Flagstaff to hold a joint public meeting? You can frame it as an informational meeting to inform the two towns about the investigation's status."

"Dennis, that is one brilliant idea! I'll call the first selectmen in both towns as soon as we
return to the office."

Three days later, Flagstaff's First Selectman Barnie Flint introduced the County Sheriff to a packed Flagstaff High School gymnasium. Nearly everyone in the Valley had heard rumors about someone vandalizing the construction equipment and wanted to know about the latest developments.

Sheriff Smith reviewed the shooting and vandalism at the dam site. Finally, he got to the point of the meeting. However, he never imagined what he said next would spark such an uproar.

"In conclusion, I would invite anyone here with information that could help my department solve these two incidents to call me." Smith stepped up to the portable chalkboard and wrote as large as possible: **896R**. "That number will ring at my desk. Anything you tell me will remain confidential. Now, are there any questions?"

A rush of mumbling spread through the crowd. Then, a man at the front of the room stood up.

"I don't have a question, but I have something to say, Sheriff. It seems you're suggesting that one of us here is either the person who committed these crimes or that we know who did it. And I, for one, don't appreciate what you're insinuating."

The crowd clapped. "You tell him, Simon!" someone standing against the wall yelled.

Before Smith could respond, Martha Priest of Bigelow Township stood up. "Simon's right. You're not talking to people who live in some crime-ridden city like Boston or New York.

You're speaking to folks who take pride in how they live and act. I know everyone in this room to one degree or another, and there is not one of them who would be so perverted as to shoot someone or vandalize another person's property."

Another round of applause. Smith was stunned by the people's reaction to his asking for their help.

"Now, folks, don't take me wrong. I wasn't saying that one of you did it."

"Then what *were* you saying? It seems to me you wouldn't ask for our help if you didn't think one of us knew something about it," a man called out from the audience.

At this point, Smith wished he'd never listened to his deputy. Worse, he was coming up for election in the fall, and judging by the crowd's reaction, he had just lost two hundred votes. Smith struggled to restate his comment, although he still believed that someone in the town was responsible for what had happened at Long Falls.

"What I meant to say is that when you're downriver shopping and happen to hear about something that might help me figure out who's causing the trouble at Long Falls, please let me know."

Smith's weak response did little to alter the citizens' collective opinion that he suspected one of them was behind the trouble at the construction site. Nonetheless, there was nothing more to discuss, and the meeting ended.

Sheriff Smith began to leave, too, but Jim Leavitt stopped him at the door.

"Don't take what was said in the meeting personally, Sheridan. Since construction began, people's attitudes have changed, realizing that in just over a year, the gates will close and the Valley will be flooded. Between now and then, people need to know how much the power company is going to give them for their property, pack their belongings, and find a new place to call home. Everyone is under a lot of stress. Even folks who initially thought the flooding of the Valley was a chance to start somewhere where there were more and better opportunities for work and schooling for their kids are having second thoughts. It all sounded like a good idea to give up their land and move somewhere else until you start packing scrapbooks and old family photo albums. Worse yet is driving through the Valley, knowing that everything you ever knew and cared for will soon be at the bottom of a lake. All we'll have for a lifetime of living in the Valley are memories of how life used to be. Nope. It isn't easy, even if you feel you will likely be better off financially in the long run. In my estimation, most people will look back on living in Flagstaff, Dead River, and Bigelow as some of the happiest times of their lives. And I suspect I'll be one of them. So people are a little tense right now, and it doesn't take much to set them off."

"Understood. However, I still have to do my job and figure out who's causing all the trouble at Long Falls."

"I'll level with you, Sheridan. Even with what I just said about a lot of upheaval, with the dam and moving, those people who spoke up at the meeting are right. My store is pretty much the clearinghouse for gossip and facts about what goes on in the Valley. If there was a hint that someone was going to do something crazy, sooner or later, I'd hear about it. Sure, some folks are dead set against the dam and being forced to leave. However, these individuals merely sent letters to the legislature and the governor expressing their opinions. Every one of them is a good person and a patriotic Mainer."

"Are you saying you've never heard anyone say anything threatening against the power company?"

Leavitt began to backtrack. "Sure, some of the old-timers who've lived in the Valley their entire lives were upset about the dam, and a few of them said some foolish things, but they didn't mean anything by it."

"Like what?"

"Oh, I heard a couple of them say the only way CMP would get their land would be over their dead body."

"That sounds like a threat to me."

"It was just talk. There was nothing meant by it. I know the boys who made those ridiculous claims. That's just how they talk. All bluster, trying to sound tough, but every one of them is a law-abiding citizen who wouldn't hurt a fly. If I thought they were serious, I'd tell you."

"Why don't you tell me their names and let me talk to them."

"I can't do that, Sheridan. I'd be giving you the names of innocent people."

"If you're not going to tell me, then I'll have to question everyone in the Valley."

"Then go ahead and interview people. However, I'm telling you right now, you'll come up empty."

"What did you learn about our friends at the Registry of Deeds?" Smith asked the following day at the office, still smarting from the drumming he took at the meeting.

"Plenty," Pike said. "For starters, three brothers, Jake, Ken, and Tim Barton, own the land. According to the deed, they lived in Leeds, Maine, when they bought two hundred acres from a Martin Savage of Wilton. I checked with the State Police in Augusta to see if they had records. All three have convictions for breaking and entering, burglary, and night hunting. They did two months in the Androscoggin County Jail for the theft and suspended sentences for breaking and entering and night hunting."

"Did you call the police chief in Leeds?"

"Yes. He said he had so many run-ins with them that everyone was on a first-name basis. According to him, the three brothers hooked up with the Popp sisters, Molly, Dolly and Lolly, about three years ago."

"Hold on a minute. Are you serious? Molly, Dolly and Lolly Popp? That sounds like the name of an act in a burlesque show at the Old Howard Theater in Boston's Scully Square."

"I wouldn't know anything about that. Have you been there?"

"Seldom. So, what else did the chief tell you?"

"The six of them lived together on a farm belonging to a cousin of the Bartons. After that, things seemed to quiet down.

The chief said they disappeared sometime last year, and no one seemed to know or care where they went. Do you think we should make another trip to Backwoods Haven and talk to the Bartons?"

"Not yet. Even though they're prime candidates, we have nothing to connect them to what happened at Long Falls. Let's wait till we have a reason to talk to them."

The dam's construction continued, as did life for the inhabitants of the Dead River Valley. Each day, the haunting wail of the siren, followed by the dull thud of a dynamite blast, reminded those who stayed in their homes that their days in Dead River and Flagstaff were numbered.

Leavitt's Store remained the gathering place to trade news on the dam's progress and who would be the next family to leave the Valley. Instead of discussing how the Red Sox were doing and the weather, they now focused on losing their homes, finding jobs, and wondering where the children would go to school in the fall.

Sometimes, construction workers stopped at Leavitt's to get cigarettes or soda for their ride home after a day working on the dam. Most locals in the store would converse with them, curious about how the work was progressing and whether the job was on schedule, and other small talk. However, some of those who had opposed the dam from the beginning weren't very friendly.

Florence Peters had just exited Leavitt's Store with her groceries when a pickup truck pulled up in front of the store. As she was about to walk past the vehicle on her way home, she noticed *Central Maine Power Company* painted on the door. Florence stopped in her tracks and waited for the driver to come around the truck to go into the store. Then she pounced.

"Why do you think you have the right to flood us out of our homes?" she asked.

The man stopped and looked around, unsure who Florence was addressing. "Excuse me," he said, "were you talking to me?"

"You work for the power company, don't you?"

"Yes. I work for Central Maine Power."

"Then I was talking to you. I want to know why your company is pushing us out of our homes," Florence said, her voice rising with each word.

"Ma'am, I work for CMP as a timekeeper at the construction site. My job is to record the hours the employees work each day."

"You are still part of the problem. Don't you realize that dam will ruin the lives of hundreds of people? Families with deep roots in the Valley for generations are being forced to move, leaving children uncertain about where they will go to school next fall. All the fields cleared of trees a century and a half ago will be at the bottom of that damn lake. Even the dead are paying the price of your stupid dam. The shame of it all, digging up bodies and reburying them in Eustis."

"Like I said, I only work for the company. I had no part in approving the project. I only want to provide for my family and pay my bills. You need to talk to someone else about how you feel about the dam. Now I have to go." The man hurried up the steps and into the store, anxious to escape Florence's wrath as quickly as possible.

"Who's that woman that just read me the riot act?" the man asked Leavitt.

"Oh, that's Florence Peters," Leavitt said, seeing her cross to the other side of Main Street.

"She just gave me an earful about the dam flooding the Valley. She seemed to think I was responsible for building it, for some reason."

"That sounds like Florence. She's been on a mission to stop the dam from being built for the past fifteen years."

"Has anyone told her she needs to get over it? Nothing will stop the dam's construction short of divine intervention."

"She's working on that, too."

11.

To All Citizens of Dead River:

The report of (my) inspection is as follows: Number of children examined, 14; Defective teeth, 11; Defective throats, 11; Poor posture, 4; Defective vision, 2. Reports of defects have been sent to parents.

Respectfully submitted,
Ruby G. Bennett
Public Health Nurse

Before the Central Maine Power Company could set the purchase price for a property, an appraisal was necessary for all residences and their associated outbuildings, including barns, sheds, and chicken coops—more than two hundred structures. The Real Estate Appraisal Division of Central Maine Power Company assessed all properties within the reservoir's footprint. The company's chief appraiser, Don Brann, started buying properties in 1927, anticipating the construction of Long Falls Dam. Although not everybody held CMP in high esteem, everyone liked Don. He was easygoing and personable. Though his evaluations were fair, they were generally on the conservative side. During his twenty-one years in the Dead River Valley, he got to know most families by name and watched babies grow into young adults. No matter the locals' feelings about the power company taking their land, Don was considered one of them.

"Back in town again, Don. What does this make it? Three times this week?" Leavitt said, seeing Brann step into the store.

"That's right. Perhaps I should consider renting one of your apartments to save myself from always being on the road. Actually, the higher-ups in Augusta are putting pressure on me to wrap up the appraisals. They want all properties in the flood zone bought before the gates are closed."

"Can you do it?"

"I think so. There are only another twenty or so properties I need to look at, and most of them are in Dead River. So far, everyone has agreed to sell except for three property owners holding out for more money."

"I heard that from the rumor mill. Personally, I don't see any advantage in waiting. What bargaining power does someone have when the water is lapping at the eaves of a house?"

"Exactly. I try to explain that to anyone considering waiting until the last minute, hoping to get a better deal. Some landowners believe they have the company cornered by refusing to sell. They think CMP can't flood the Valley until they agree, which would compel CMP to pay more for their land. They don't realize that my evaluation is the basis for CMP's offer. If a landowner refuses the company's price, the company could seize their property through eminent domain, leaving the landowner with nothing—or, at most, the initial offer. The other kicker is that the property is worth less as the time approaches for flooding the Valley. I've got to get going. I need to deliver Austin Titcomb his appraisal at nine and appraise the Sam Decker property at eleven."

"Sam Decker, you say?"

"Yes. Is there anything I should know about the man?"

"Oh, Sam's all right."

"That doesn't sound like a ringing endorsement."

"Don, are you a patient man?"

"I like to think so. Why do you ask?"

"Well, you'll need the patience of Job when conversing with Sam. Sometimes, that man will not give you a straight answer even if his life depended on it. Every so often, you need to pull him back on track. I swear, if that man's house ever caught fire, and he called the fire department, it would burn flat before he spit out the name of the road he lived on."

"Thanks for the heads-up," Brann said.

Brann had met with Austin Titcomb two weeks earlier to assess his property. Although Austin didn't seem overly friendly at the time, he did take him around the farm so that he could complete the appraisal forms. Austin, a widower, lived alone in the same house his parents and grandparents once lived in. His home had fallen into disrepair since his wife passed away three years ago. Although the homestead was modest, Titcomb owned one of Dead River Valley's largest and most productive parcels. The sixty acres of cropland would be highly valuable along the Sandy or Kennebec Rivers.

Brann drove into the driveway and saw Titcomb splitting firewood beside the woodshed.

"Hello, Austin," Brann called, stepping out of the car.

Austin looked up. Seeing Brann, he continued splitting wood. Brann patiently waited for him to split the last piece of ash. Done, Titcomb gave the ax a final swing, burying the head firmly into the hardwood chopping block.

"I suppose you want to go over the property evaluation," Titcomb said.

"Yes. We had an appointment for me to stop by at nine."

Austin didn't let on that he had forgotten. "Let's go inside. We might as well sit at the kitchen table and be comfortable."

Brann unrolled a map of Austin's property and reviewed his evaluation and the calculations used to generate the figures.

"So, summarizing my figures, the house and the attached barn have an appraised value of eighteen hundred dollars, the chicken coop fifty, and the storage shed thirty."

"What about the land?" Austin said.

"Land is challenging to evaluate. The standard practice is to assign distinct values for cropland, pastureland, woodland, and hayland. I calculated that you have sixty acres of cropland valued at sixty dollars per acre, fifty acres of pasture valued thirty dollars per acre, thirty-five acres of hayland at forty-two dollars per acre, and a hundred and ten acres of woodland valued at twenty dollars per acre."

"What's the total?"

Brann pointed to the figure at the bottom of the calculation sheet. "The company's calculated value for all the property—houses, outbuildings, and land—is ten thousand six hundred seventy dollars."

"That's not much money for someone who doesn't want to sell."

Brann didn't answer. Austin stared at the map, thinking. A full minute passed before he finally spoke.

"I'm not interested in selling for that kind of money. You've got to do better if you want my property."

"I can't. I need to apply the same method to all properties in the Dead River Valley to ensure everyone is treated equally."

"As far as I'm concerned, you're trying to steal my land. I know full well that a good bottomland like mine goes for twice what you're offering. My cousin bought a farm on the Sandy River in Farmington last year and thought he stole it at ninety dollars an acre."

"I don't doubt for a second that he did, Austin. However, Farmington is a significant agricultural area in the state, and the demand for class-one farmland drives up the price. I'm required to look at what similar land sells for around here. Land like yours would be used to grow high-value crops along the Sandy. Here in the Valley, it's used for cow corn, a lower-value crop than sweet corn, peas, and beans, intended to feed the local canneries."

"I still say you're a crook. Just like Central Maine Power Company trying to hoodwink us locals out of our homes. Why, I bet you get a big fat commission each time a property owner signs a sales agreement for some lowball price."

"Austin, I resent you accusing me of doing something illegal and immoral. I follow the appraisal rules set by the State of Maine. If I did what you suggested, I'd lose my appraiser's license."

"I ain't *suggesting* you're a crook. I'm telling you straight out you're one. If my wife was still alive, she'd tell you the same. Now roll up your map and leave! You're lucky that no one has taken a potshot at you, or worse."

Brann hurriedly tossed Titcomb's appraisal in his briefcase and left. Backing out of the driveway, he saw Titcomb standing in the open kitchen door, glaring at him.

Brann was shaken by what Austin had said. None of the eighty other landowners he'd visited had ever been confrontational or made veiled threats toward him. Brann was so upset that he decided to return to his Skowhegan office until he remembered he had an eleven o'clock appointment with Sam Decker in Bigelow Township.

"Come in, Mr. Brann. I saw a dust cloud from a car coming down the road and figured it must be you. Have you ever seen it this blistering hot? It's been a tough growing season with the heat and the drought we seem to be stuck in. If it's all right with you, we can sit at the picnic table under that maple," Sam said, leading the way across the lawn.

Sam watched Brann take the paperwork out of his briefcase.

"None of my business, Mr. Brann, but I couldn't help but notice your hands shaking. My brother, Merton, has the same problem. The doctor said it was an issue with nerves in his hands. The doc told him there wasn't much he could do to help him. Said it would likely get worse over time."

"My hands are fine, Mr. Decker. They're shaking because of what one of your neighbors in Dead River told me a short time ago."

"Well, it must've been something terrible, 'cause you also look a little green around the gills. By the way, you might as well call me Sam, 'Mr. Decker' sounds a little stiff. I'd call you by your first name if I could remember it."

"It's Don. I normally don't talk about personal issues with clients. But to tell you the truth, Sam, what was said bothers me badly."

Brann told Sam how Austin Titcomb had become extremely upset about his property valuation and said he was lucky no one had taken a shot at him.

"Mind telling me who said those things?"

"Austin Titcomb."

"Why doesn't that surprise me? Don, it's no secret that Austin has always been a bit off. Some people say he has an overly active imagination. Others believe his issues run much deeper than that.

The word *loner* is often used when people speak of Austin. Austin took his wife's death hard. After Emma died, he froze up inside. He and Emma had been married for forty-five years. When Emma passed away, Austin disappeared."

"How do you mean, 'disappeared'?"

"Dropped out of sight. No one saw him around town for six months. You'd have thought someone would have spotted him at the town dump. Saturday's dump day, though it's only open on Saturday mornings. Every person in Flagstaff and Dead River goes to the dump on Saturdays. You have a better chance of seeing friends and relatives—and some you'd rather not run into—than at Leavitt's Store. It's like old home week, except it only lasts from eight to noon. It's where you catch up on the happenings in the Valley since the last dump day. Anyway, most folks didn't think much about not seeing Austin there. They assumed he must be using a burn barrel to get rid of his trash so he wouldn't have to drive all the way to the dump on the other side of Dead River."

"You said no one saw him for six months. Then what?"

"One day last July, he walked into Leavitt's Store. I remember it real clear. It was a sweltering-hot day. The Valley was right in the middle of a heat wave. We get one or maybe two heat waves a year. It's been that way for as long as I can remember. Always in July, too. Usually, it's the third week of July."

"I'm sure it was very uncomfortable. What Did Austin say?" Brann said, remembering what Leavitt had told him about keeping Sam on track.

"Uncomfortable isn't the word for it. I can't get out of my own way when it's as hot as that. Sticky, too. Clothes cling to you like a wet sheet. Usually, I wouldn't go to town when it's that hot and clammy. I'd rather sit at the kitchen table, let the fan oscillate across my face, and hope the dynamo at Bryant's Mill doesn't give out. But I needed to pick up laying mash for my chickens on this particular day. The heat had me so hot and bothered that I completely forgot that I had run out of grain the day before. Anyway, when I walked into the store, Austin was talking to Mr. and Mrs. Leavitt. Or I should say arguing with the two of them."

"What about?"

"The dam, of course. That's about all anyone talks about these days. Austin was on a tear about how the power company had no business building the dam and that they were playing everyone for suckers by taking their land. Leavitt tried to reason with him, but Austin would have none of it. No one was going to tell him anything different. Finally, Austin got so mad that Mr. Leavitt wouldn't agree with him that he stormed out of the store, telling Leavitt it would be the last time he'd get his business. After that little episode, Austin went missing again."

"Let me ask you something, Sam. Do you think Austin is so angry about the dam that he'd try something drastic?"

"You mean like take a shot at a company man?"

"That's what I mean."

"From what I saw at the store, with him yelling and making ridiculous claims about what the power company was up to, I'd say he just might do something that crazy."

Brann measured and evaluated the condition of each of Sam's buildings to determine their value. He told Sam that he would return to discuss the appraisal next week. He passed by Austin

Titcomb's farm on the drive back to Skowhegan. As Brann drove by the driveway, he glanced toward the homestead just in time to see Austin enter the barn carrying what Brann thought was an ax. Brann was finished trying to work with Austin. His supervisor had instructed him to avoid any landowner who gave him a hard time. Further communication with Austin Titcomb will be through CMP's attorney.

A small patch of woods a quarter mile beyond Titcomb's home separated two hayfields. Parked by the roadside in the middle of the strip of trees, Brann spotted a dark-green pickup he recognized as belonging to CMP's surveying division. The company had six survey crews marking the 142-mile perimeter of the 20,000-acre reservoir that Long Falls Dam would create. Once the high-water mark was established, loggers would cut all the trees and burn the tops below the blazed survey line.

Brann rolled down the window to say hello. He knew many of the men by name, as they frequently crossed paths when he drove from one property to another. Suddenly, two sedans sped past him and stopped in front of the CMP pickup. Four men jumped out of the vehicles and ran into the woods. A third vehicle approached from the opposite direction and stopped behind the company pickup. The driver then vanished into the forest, chasing after the others.

Brann assumed there had been an accident and stopped to see if he could help. He had served as a medic during World War II and was knowledgeable about emergency first aid. While searching for the others, Brann ran by a transit set on a tripod. Ahead, he heard men talking, but the thick vegetation concealed them. Finally, he came up behind six men huddled over a man lying on his back.

"I'm trained in first aid. Can I help?" Brann asked.

"See if you can stop the bleeding," said a man holding a handkerchief against the fallen man's chest.

Brann dropped to his knees. With each heartbeat, blood squirted from the man's chest. Brann stared at the injury. He had treated enough men in the military to recognize a bullet wound. The man had been shot. This was not the time to ask questions. The issue at this moment was to try to save the man's life. It would take a miracle for him to stop the bleeding. Brann noticed one of the men wore a sweatshirt.

"Give me your sweatshirt, fast!" Brann demanded. He held it against the wound to control the bleeding. "Has anyone called for an ambulance?"

"Yes," came from a man standing off to the side. "When I flagged down a car, I asked the driver to call the police and for an ambulance."

"Should we get him to the road to make it easier for the ambulance crew?" another man asked.

"I wouldn't do it. I don't think he would survive the trauma of being moved. The ambulance will have a stretcher," Brann said.

"I can hear the siren. I'll go to the road and bring them in," someone said.

Fifteen minutes later, the ambulance doors closed and left for the forty-mile trip to the Redington Memorial Hospital in Skowhegan. As soon as the ambulance was out of sight, Sheriff Sheridan Smith and Deputy Pike arrived. Once Smith understood the situation, he instructed Pike to gather statements from the others while he interviewed the CMP employee.

"Let's sit in the car. You can tell me what led up to the accident," Smith said, opening the car door. "Tell me your name and what happened."

"Wendell Stinson. I work for Central Maine Power Company as a surveyor. Jim Norris, the guy who was shot, was my rodman."

"Wait a minute. What makes you think he was shot?"

"I heard the gunfire."

"Start from the beginning," Smith said, reaching for his pen.

"Jim and I arrived around noon. We had been here earlier but needed to set grade stakes at the dam so the shovel operator would know how much material to remove. Anyway, I walked into the woods to set up the transit where we had left off yesterday. Jack grabbed the machete and the ax and followed me into the woods. Once I was ready, I lined up the instrument in the direction we needed to go and told Jack to clear the brush with his machete so I could see where to set the next benchmark. Once I determined the elevation, Jim pounded a stake into the ground and started working back toward me, scabbing the trees with his ax while I recorded the distances and bearings."

"How far apart were you?"

"About a hundred feet."

"Then what?"

"It was then I heard the gunshot. It was really close. I looked for Jim but didn't see him, so I ran toward where I last saw him. I found him on the ground, face up, staring at me. He tried to speak, but no words came out. A second later, he passed out."

"Did you see anyone?"

"I looked around, wondering if I would be next. I didn't see anyone except…"

"Except what?"

"I saw movement, or at least I think I did, moving toward the field," Wendell said, pointing in the direction of Austin Titcomb's farm.

"What kind of movement?"

"The motion of someone or something walking through the undergrowth. As I said, I'm unsure whether it was real or just my imagination. Everything seemed so surreal. Maybe it was a deer spooked by the blast. Or maybe it was the shooter making his escape. I just don't know."

As the two continued to talk, Deputy Pike knocked on the window of the police vehicle.

"Sorry to bother you, Sheriff. I just received a call on the two-way. The man died before they reached the hospital."

"I'll call the State Police. A murder investigation is above my pay grade," Sheridan said.

It wasn't long before everyone in the Valley had learned about the shooting. The people's reaction to Jim Norris's murder was markedly different from the two previous incidents at the construction site. The shooting of the bulldozer operator, while tragic, did not cause significant concern among the public. Some residents thought it was just an accidental shot from someone target shooting or hunting squirrels, rather than a deliberate act to harm the equipment operator—a thoughtless shooter at worst. The vandalism of the contractor's equipment was even less disconcerting to people living in the three communities. Most people were convinced it was joyriders from Kingfield or Madison out looking to make trouble, certainly not any of the young people from Dead River and Flagstaff who had been raised to respect other people's property.

However, the killing of the CMP employee hit too close to home to ignore. Nearly everyone in the Valley wondered if one of their own had murdered Jim Norris. No one believed that someone from outside would drive to Dead River with a rifle, intent on killing a surveyor's helper who was just doing his job.

The Maine State Police, however, needed to explore all possibilities to determine who had fired the weapon. Warner Bridges from the Homicide Unit in Augusta was assigned to the case. Bridges, a ten-year veteran, began his career as a patrol officer in the Traffic Division and worked his way through the ranks to become one of the State Police's most respected detectives after solving two longstanding homicides classified as cold cases.

After meeting with Sheriff Smith and reading the case files of the other two incidents involving the power company, he decided to investigate the possibility that the three were related and that the same person had committed all three crimes. Bridges would approach the investigation in the order in which the offenses happened. His first stop would be the Long Falls Dam construction site.

When Detective Bridges arrived, Ralph Clark was in the general contractor's office trailer talking to one of the foremen. Once he left, Bridges rapped on the door and stepped inside the trailer. After a few pleasantries, the two men sat at the drafting table.

Detective Bridges asked Clark if there had been any trouble recently.

"Since our equipment was vandalized six months ago, it's been business as usual. There have been no incidents or attempts to gain access to the construction site."

"Do you think the shooting of the dozer operator and the vandalism are related?"

"I have no idea. It could go either way. However, my gut tells me the shooting of the bulldozer operator, Bruce Olson, was an accident."

"What makes you say that?"

"It seems to me that if someone's intent on killing someone, they would use something other than a twenty-two rifle. Besides, there were at least six other workers nearer to the woods from where the shooter likely fired. If you wanted to kill someone with a twenty-two, there were plenty of other targets much closer than Bruce. Don't get me wrong, whoever did it needs to be held accountable, and the company will press charges if that person is found. However, Headquarters believes the shooting was a freak accident."

"Still, it's not out of the range of probability. People have tried crazier things with a low powered rifle," Bridges said, even though what the superintendent had said was likely to be the case.

"What about the vandalism? Any ideas on who might have done it?"

"When the sheriff asked me that question right after it happened, I said no."

"It sounds like you might have changed your mind."

"Let's just say there are two people that might have been pissed enough to have done it."

"Why didn't you call the sheriff Smith with your suspicions?"

"Two reasons: First, I have no idea if it was them or not. Second, the company has moved on. The insurance covered the damage, and fortunately, no one was seriously injured. I have enough headaches trying to keep this job on schedule. Our contract includes a penalty clause saying Central Maine Power will withhold five percent of our quarterly payment if we fail to meet the construction milestones. And guess who is held accountable if the job falls behind?"

"I hear what you're saying, but I need to determine if there's a link between the incident at the construction site and the murder in Dead River. So, why don't you tell me what makes you suspect these two individuals might have been involved in sabotaging the bulldozer?"

Clark recounted the events of the January morning when he arrived at the construction site, discovered the break in the fence, and then learned that the two security guards had intentionally skipped their assigned rounds.

"After I told those two birds to leave, I called the Hendrick Security Company and told them what happened. An hour later, the security company president called me and said both men had been fired. He fell all over himself, trying to apologize for what they did. He could have saved his breath. Later the same day, I received a call from CMP headquarters in Augusta saying that the Hendrick Security contract had been canceled, and they'd hired a different company. The new company didn't staff the site for another two days, meaning the old lock stayed on the gate.

"Now, here's where my speculation comes in. It's possible that the two characters were so mad about being fired that they wanted revenge. It's likely they still had the key to the gate padlock. They could have returned the night after they were fired, let themselves in, and sabotaged the dozer."

"That's an interesting theory. Perhaps they weren't satisfied with just vandalism and decided to escalate their revenge for being fired by killing the surveyor's assistant. What are their names?"

"Fred Stevens and Barry Dubord—both live in Skowhegan. If you want their addresses, you'll have to contact Hendrick Security."

Detective Bridges obtained Dubord's street address from the Somerset County Telephone Company directory. There was no listing for Fred Stevens.

"Good morning, my name is Warner Bridges. I'm a detective for the Maine State Police. Is Barry Dubord home?"

The woman Bridges believed to be Mrs. Dubord glanced at him and then at the State Police license plate on the car parked in the driveway. Still holding the door open, she turned toward the living room and shouted.

"Barry! Get out here! There's a State Police detective that wants to talk to you."

"What are you talking about, Louise? A detective wants to talk to me?" he said as he walked into the kitchen, not noticing Bridges in the doorway.

"*That* detective wants to talk to you," his wife said, pointing at Bridges.

"Are you Barry Dubord?"

"Yeah, I'm Barry Dubord. I suppose my lovely ex-wife sent you to serve me papers for back child support. You can tell her I've moved to Alaska and left no forwarding address. She got enough money in the divorce settlement to put them both through medical school."

"That's not why I'm here. I need to talk to you about when you worked at Long Falls for the Hendrick Security Company."

"What about it?"

"May I come in to talk? I don't want to heat all outdoors."

Barry motioned toward the kitchen table. Barry sat across from Bridges, waiting for him to start the conversation.

"I understand your employment with the Hendrick Security Company ended abruptly."

"You might say that. I'm sure you know the reason why."

"Yes. You and your friend, Fred Stevens, were let go after the job superintendent caught you not doing your job."

"First, Fred Stevens is not my *friend*. Not since he suckered me into skipping our rounds that night in January. I should have known better than listening to that lazy bastard. But it was bitterly cold and windy, so I went along with his dumbass idea. That little fiasco still haunts me. Thanks to Fred's brilliance, I can't find a decent job. Everything looks good until they check where I worked last. Once Hendrick tells them why I was let go, that ends any chance of being hired. I can't even get a job sweeping streets for the town."

"Did you hear about someone sabotaging a bulldozer and nearly costing the operator his life?"

"Yeah. It was in the paper."

"Do you know who might have done it?"

"No. I don't know who might have done it," Barry said, mocking the detective.

"I've heard stories that you and Fred did it."

"That's a damn lie! I had nothing to do with it."

"Does that mean Fred did?"

"You'll have to ask Fred."

"I will. Do you know about the CMP employee shot dead in Dead River Plantation three days ago?"

"Yes. Not having a job gives me plenty of time to read the newspapers."

"Is Fred Stevens capable of doing something like that?"

"Fred is a complete jerk and has done some nasty stuff since I've known him. But to kill someone would be a new low for him. I would never rule anything out that Fred might do, but I can't imagine even him being that stupid. Besides, what motive would he have to kill someone?"

"Payback for being fired."

Barry had nothing to say.

"That's it for now. If you want to tell me anything else, you can reach me at this number," Bridges said, scratching his phone number on the back of his business card. "Call me if you want to talk. Now I'll see if I can catch Fred at home."

Barry walked to the kitchen window. "He's home, his car is in the driveway."

"You mean he lives next to you?"

"No, he lives on the next street, but I get to look at the side of his house. Lucky me. I watch him leave for the Arnold Tavern each afternoon and hear him drive into his yard after the dive closes."

Two minutes later, Bridges pulled in behind Fred Steven's Plymouth. He stepped onto the glassed-in porch and knocked.

"Are you Fred Stevens?" Bridges asked when a man opened the door.

"Maybe. Who wants to know?"

"I'm Detective Bridges of the Maine State Police. I want to talk to you about someone vandalizing equipment at the Long Falls Dam construction site."

Stevens hesitated. "I don't know about any vandalizing at Long Falls or anywhere else. You're talking to the wrong guy," and he started to shut the door.

"I wouldn't do that. You're under suspicion for criminal mischief. If you don't talk to me now, the Somerset County District Attorney will want to speak to you. It's your choice," Bridges said, hoping his bluff would work.

"Outside. My wife doesn't need to hear this." The two men continued their discussion behind the garage, out of sight of Fred's wife and nosy neighbors.

"Like I said, I don't know anything about any vandalism."

"Were you let go from Hendrick Security in January?"

"Yeah, I got 'let go,' as you put it, but it had nothing to do with putting sand in that bulldozer's fuel tank."

"I never said what the vandalism was. How did you know there was sand in the diesel tank."

"I must've read it in the newspaper."

"That's funny; the Somerset County Sheriff never released what kind of damage was done to the machine, only that it was sabotaged," Bridges said, not knowing if what he said was true.

"Then I probably heard it from one of the workers at the bar I visit occasionally. A lot of the laborers who work on the dam live in the area and hang out at the tavern on Saturday nights. If anyone knows what happened, it would be them."

"Maybe. But I think you know more about it than you're admitting. The rumor is that you were so furious when you were fired that you wanted to take revenge on the company. Upset enough, you returned to Long Falls during the night and used your key to get through the gate. Then, you cut the brake lines and put sand in the dozer's fuel tank. Would you like to know what else people say about Fred Stevens?"

"Please, tell me," Fred said, gazing around the room, trying to act uninterested in what Bridges had to say.

"You weren't satisfied with just damaging the bulldozer. You wanted to send CMP a special message that no one fires Fred Stevens and gets away with it. So you ambushed the surveyor's helper. Shot him in the chest."

"Now, that is a goddamn lie! I didn't shoot anyone!"

"Is it? It's not uncommon for someone filled with rage to do something criminal. And sometimes, they'll take their revenge by hurting an innocent person. Only you took it to the extreme by committing murder."

"I told you it was not me that did it."

"We're done, for now. I have a few people I need to interview. If I find out you're lying, I'll be back with a warrant for your arrest for the murder of Jim Norris." Bridges started to walk back to his car.

"Hold up," Stevens said.

Bridges walked back to hear what Stevens had to say.

"I'm going to tell you exactly what happened. You can believe me or not. But I'm telling you right now, if you arrest me for what I say, I'll deny I ever said it."

"Go ahead," Bridges said, taking out his notebook.

"No notes. You put that paper and pen away, or I won't tell you anything."

Stevens watched as Bridges slipped the notebook and pen into his shirt pocket.

"You're right. I was royally pissed off that I was fired. I'd been a security guard for Hendrick for nine and a half years. Not once had I missed a day of work or not made my rounds. The one time I screw up, I get fired. Jesus, it was twenty below zero. I didn't want to freeze off my gonads. As far as I was concerned, I showed good judgment by not going on patrol in that weather. What if Barry and me had gotten frostbite and lost a finger or a foot? We could have been out of work for weeks. Instead, the CMP boss shows up, reads us the riot act for not doing our job, and gives us our walking papers."

"I understand you planned to fake the log entry to make it look like you had gone out and walked the fence."

Stevens glared at Bridges but didn't answer and continued telling his side of the story.

"Anyway, after Barry and me helped search the grounds we packed our personal belongings and left. The next day, Hendrick fired us, thanks to that asshole Clark. He called the company and blabbed that we hadn't done our four thirty and six thirty patrols. The more I thought about what Clark did, the madder I got. I walked over to Barry's house around ten o'clock after the wife had gone to bed. By the time I walked into Barry's kitchen, I knew what I was going to do. I tried to get Barry to go back to Long Falls with me. They'd treated him just as rotten as me, and I figured we had the perfect right to get even for letting us go."

"Did Barry go with you?"

"No. He whined that messing with the equipment wouldn't be right, and if we did, we'd only get into more trouble. Screw you, I said. I'll do it myself.

"The next night, I went back to the worksite and used my key to get inside the fence. I knew it would be a few days before CMP found a new security company, so there was no chance of getting caught. I spotted the bulldozer parked next to the maintenance garage and…" Stevens hesitated. "I've told you enough." He knew better than to confess what he had done to the equipment. By not admitting to the sabotage of the dozer, he believed the worst charge he would face would be illegal trespass.

"Did you shoot the surveyor's rodman?"

"No. I read about it in the paper the same way everyone else did. If you try to pin his murder on me, it'll never stick. I know exactly where I was when Japan attacked Pearl Harbor, and the same with D-Day. And I know where I was the day the CMP guy got shot."

"Where were you?"

"With a friend, perch fishing on Sibley Pond in Canaan. He'll back me up that I was there."

"What's your friend's name?

"Kevin Black. He lives on the Outback Road in Canaan, next to Hillman's Dairy."

"He better back up your story, or I'll be back with a warrant for your arrest."

"He'll back it up. Don't forget, you try to push the case against me for what happened at Long Falls, and I'll deny it. I'll tell the judge you misunderstood what I told you."

"Don't *you* forget I'm a detective with the Maine State Police, and I have a job to do," Bridges said, opening the car door.

Bridges drove to Canaan to speak with Black. Both Black and his wife confirmed that he and Fred Stevens were fishing on the day Norris was shot. Bridges was convinced that Stevens hadn't killed Jim Norris. As far as the vandalism at the construction site was concerned, it would be up to CMP to decide whether to press charges. All he could do was tell Construction Superintendent Clark what Stevens had said.

⇀

Next on the detective's list of potential suspects in the murder investigation was the backwoods clan that lived south of the

Ledge House. If the three Barton brothers were even half as crazy as Sheriff Smith made them seem, it would be wise not to go alone. Bridges took two State Troopers and the sheriff with him to serve a search warrant for the .308 caliber rifle used to kill Norris.

"Which of the three is the leader of the pack?" Bridges asked Smith as they made the ten-minute walk to Backwoods Haven.

"That would be Jake Barton. He seems to be the spokesman for the three families."

"Okay. I'll talk to him while you and the troopers check the premises for anything incriminating, like a 308-caliber rifle. Have his brothers go with you so we're not accused of stealing something."

Barton's dog began to bark, announcing the strangers' presence. Jake, Ken, and Tim Barton stood on the porch when Bridges and Smith stepped into the clearing.

"I told you not to step foot on our property again," Jake said, recognizing the sheriff as one of the two men he had told to leave two weeks earlier.

Detective Bridges took the warrant from his shirt pocket.

"I'm Detective Warner Bridges with the Maine State Police. This is a warrant to search your property," he said, holding out the warrant.

"For what?" Jake asked, clearly getting madder by the second.

"It's all in the warrant. The three of you are under suspicion of shooting Jim Norris. The warrant specifies that we seize all high-caliber rifles on the premises."

"I'm warning you. You're in for big trouble if you put one foot in my house."

The two troopers looked at Detective Bridges, waiting for instructions.

Bridges nodded, and the two men started toward the front door. Molly, Lolly, and Dolly, standing to the side, began screaming at the troopers. Ken rushed the sheriff, who had started down the porch stairs to check the outbuildings for guns, hitting him in the back and knocking him to the ground, while at the same time, Tim grabbed the arm of one of the troopers attempting to open the door. As the trooper tried to get free from Tim's grip, Jake reached behind his back and pulled out the revolver he had wedged in his pants belt. He pointed the weapon at Bridge's stomach. Seeing what was about to happen, the second trooper drew his revolver. As the trooper was about to shoot Jake to save the detective's life, the first officer freed himself and shoved Tim, sending him staggering backward between Bridges and Jake. At that instant, Jake pulled the trigger, intending to kill Detective Bridges. Instead, he shot his brother in the back as he crossed the line of fire. The scene played out in a matter of seconds.

The scene went from complete chaos to dead silence except for the thud of Jake's gun hitting the porch floor. Lolly rushed to her fallen husband and dropped to her knees, sobbing. Detective Bridges collected himself and instructed one of the troopers to return to the car and call the Skowhegan Hospital to request an ambulance.

The following day, the State Police returned to the Barton compound to continue the search for the weapon used in Norris's murder. Although two of the seized rifles were .308s, neither was the murder weapon: The rifling was different from the bullet that killed Norris. What was meant to be a routine search in a murder investigation had ended with an innocent man dead and Jim Norris's killer still on the loose.

What the residents of Dead River Valley didn't need was additional turmoil. The stress on families being forced from their homes and searching for new places to live was overwhelming enough. Knowing that two men had been killed and that the murderer of one of them was still at large only heightened the anxiety. Although the locals hardly knew the shooting victims, the two incidents tore at the fabric of the close-knit communities.

Over the years, there had been several accidental fatalities during deer hunting season, but never a homicide. Now, with only a year remaining before the towns were to be doomed by floodwaters created by Long Falls Dam, two people had died. The townspeople wanted to be remembered as three safe, content, and patriotic communities willing to sacrifice their homes for a cause greater than themselves. Not as three drowned-out towns haunted by two unnecessary deaths. However, as newspaper reporters descended upon the communities to cover the two shootings, it appeared that this was likely how they would be remembered.

Detective Bridges came close to losing his job due to the incident at Barton's backwoods retreat. A Board of Inquiry into the shooting released a report indicating that Tim Barton's death might have been prevented if the detective had adhered to State Police protocol while executing a search warrant. Knowing that six individuals were at the cabin, Bridges should have had at least eight officers with him in case of trouble. Thanks to a letter of support from the Chief of the Maine State Police, Bridges only received a letter of reprimand and was allowed to continue his investigation.

After the incident at Backwoods Haven, Bridges was more determined than ever to solve the murder of Jim Norris. He decided to stop at Leavitt's Store and ask Jim Leavitt if any new rumors had surfaced about the shooting.

"If there are any, I haven't heard about them. However, Don Brann, the agent assessing properties for CMP, wants to talk to you. He always stops at the store to pick up a coffee before going to work. He should be here most any time," Leavitt said, glancing at the wall clock. "This morning's paper is in the chair by the woodstove. You're welcome to read it while waiting for him."

Fifteen minutes later, Brann walked into the store. The two men moved to the far corner of the store to talk.

"Like I was telling Jim, it's probably nothing, but I wanted to tell you about what happened to me the same day Norris was shot."

"At this point in the investigation, any possibility is worth considering."

"I had stopped at Austin Titcomb's place to give him the appraisal for his property. When I told him what the company would pay for his farm, he became extremely agitated and accused me of trying to steal it from him. He said the land was worth twice again what I had valued it. Then, in no uncertain terms, he told me to get off his property and stay off. He even mentioned something about someone taking a shot at me. There are two reasons why I wanted to tell you this."

"Which are…?"

"The guy that got shot—"

"What about him?"

"He was on land that belonged to Austin Titcomb."

"And the second?"

"When I drove back by Austin's place after meeting at a neighboring farm, I saw Austin walking into the barn."

"And?"

"Well, at first, it looked like he was carrying an ax. But now, thinking back on it, it could have been a rifle."

Twenty minutes later, Bridges pulled into Austin's driveway. He knocked on the front door, but no one answered. Austin's Dodge pickup was parked in the yard, but he wasn't home. As he walked down the porch steps, he heard a scraping sound coming from inside the barn. Bridges went inside to investigate. The sound came from inside the tie-up. Through the open door, he saw someone he presumed to be Austin Titcomb cleaning the cow manure from the stalls.

Bridges rapped on the partition that separated the tie-up from the rest of the barn, not wanting to startle the man.

Austin never missed a scoop with his barn shovel. He glanced up to see Bridges standing in the doorway and kept shoveling. Satisfied the job was done, he stood the shovel next to the wall and walked over to Bridges.

"Who are you?" Austin asked, looking up and down at the man who didn't appear to be from around here, dressed in his khaki pants and pressed shirt.

"I'm Detective Warner Bridges of the Maine State Police. I'm here to talk to you about the shooting that took place on your land three weeks ago."

"What about it?"

"I thought you might be able to provide a few answers that could help me find out who murdered Jim Norris."

"Now, why would you think a thing like that?"

"The killing was on your land, wasn't it?"

"What of it? It doesn't mean I know what happened. All I know is if those two hadn't been trespassing, the man wouldn't have been killed."

"Sounds to me like them being on your land bothered you."

"You're damn right, it bothered me. I own that land and every other acre for a quarter mile in every direction from the home place. Not Central Maine Power Company, not the State, and not Joe Blow from Idaho. I'm the one that pays the taxes. I'm the one who works the land from sunrise to sunset and has done so for nearly forty years. The CMP crowd has no business being on my land unless I give them permission, and they don't have it."

"Did them trespassing anger you so bad that you shot the rodman?"

"Look, mister. I have every right to stop anyone from cutting trees on my property. And that's exactly what the surveyors were doing—cutting down trees and blazing the ones they didn't cut with an ax. I wrote to the power company and the governor half a dozen times, saying I'd take matters into my own hands if it didn't stop. Neither the governor nor CMP bothered to write back. They likely took my letters as just some old man trying to stand in the way of progress and figured the best way to deal with me was to ignore me. Well, I don't take too well to being ignored."

"You didn't answer my question. Did you shoot Norris? Yes or No. Before you answer, you should know someone saw you lugging a rifle into the barn about the time of the shooting."

"No."

"What about you walking into the barn with a rifle?"

"You need to tell that would-be snitch he better get his eyes checked. I remember the day of the shooting very clearly. I was finishing up splitting a pile of cedar for this winter's kindling. I recall beating on a stick full of knots when I heard a rifle shot down the road. At the time, I didn't pay much attention. I thought maybe someone had hit an animal with a vehicle, and the driver stopped to put it out of its misery. Later, I heard about the shooting and figured the shot I heard was the one that took him out."

"Did you threaten Don Brann, the CMP appraiser? He said you warned him never to show up at your door again, and you were surprised no one had taken a potshot at him."

"I ain't going to deny I said that. It was only an idle threat made in the heat of the moment. And it worked, too. Brann left the yard like a scared rabbit being chased by a hound. Laid rubber when he popped the clutch on his car, he was in such a hurry to get away from my property."

"Any others in the Valley so upset about their homes being flooded out that they might try to take the matter into their own hands?"

"Nowhere near enough, as far as I'm concerned. People around here have been all too willing to roll over and play dead instead of fighting for their right to live in the Valley. I know most folks think I'm just a troublemaker. Some want me to keep quiet. They don't want an old bastard like me to make such a stink that it causes the project to be scuttled and them not get their money.

"Sure, more than anything, I want to stay in Dead River. It's the only home I've ever known. However, if I'm forced to leave, I expect fair compensation, and I don't just mean the property's appraised value. CMP should pay double the appraised value. Call it goodwill money for tearing communities and people's lives apart. They shouldn't be allowed to steal our heritage. To answer your question: No one I know would kill someone thinking that would stop the project. I know a few that might go up to that line to get people's attention as to just how one-sided the whole effort to flood us out has been for the past twenty years, but not murder."

Bridges believed Austin's story. He appeared to be a man who stood by his principles and would have admitted to the murder if, in his mind, he thought it was justified.

His next stop would be to visit Arapaho Nell Beattie. Leavitt had told him about a previous incident where she'd threatened two CMP surveyors with a rifle and sicced her dog on them to chase the two off her land. Her involvement in the Norris murder seemed like a long shot, but Bridges had to pursue every lead, no matter how unrealistic it might seem.

Bridges followed Leavitt's directions to Nell's farm in Bigelow Township. When he stopped in front of what he thought was Nell's home, he wondered if he had misunderstood Leavitt's directions. The small cape-style farmhouse was long overdue to be painted. Only a random smattering of faded white paint covered the weathered gray clapboards, some missing or dangling from the dwelling held by a single nail. The front yard was overgrown with burdock and weeds so thick that the rickety porch was barely visible from the road. Bridges couldn't believe someone lived in the derelict structure. To be sure it was Nell's home, he drove back to the main highway and rechecked his directions.

Satisfied it was the right house, he followed a narrow beaten path to the side door, stepped gingerly across the rotted porch floor, and rapped. The knock touched off a dog inside the house that came on a dead run to investigate. The dog didn't bark but let out deep, throaty growls as it bounced off the entry door, trying to get a look at the intruder through the door's window.

"Pretty Boy! Move away from that door!" came a muffled voice inside the house. "There's no one there. It's only the wind."

Pretty Boy didn't give up. He kept growling and standing on his hind legs, peering at Bridges through the glass and showing his exceptionally long, pointed canines.

"Land's sake, Pretty Boy, what has you so excited?"

She saw Bridges standing on the porch, waiting for someone to come to the door.

"Why didn't you tell me someone was at the door, Pretty Boy?" She rushed to the door and studied the man's face through the dirty window.

"Pretty Boy, it's Bill! Bill has come home!" As she started to open the door, Pretty Boy wedged his nose in the opening, trying to force the door open to get to Bridges. Detective Bridges grabbed the doorknob and yanked the door shut, knowing if Pretty Boy made it outside, he would be easy pickings for the German shepherd. The dog yelped and backed off briefly, then again charged the door. This time, the woman took control and led an unwilling and noisy Pretty Boy into the pantry and shut the door. Now, she could turn her full attention to welcoming home the man she thought to be her long-lost husband.

"Bill, your home! Thank the Lord you've come back to me!"

Bridges took a step back, unsure of what the woman, whom he presumed to be Nell Beattie, was talking about.

Suddenly, Nell's excitement turned into disappointment.

"You're not Bill," she declared, looking at Detective Bridges. "I don't know you. What are you doing here?"

"My name is Warner Bridges. I'm with the Maine State Police. May I come in?"

"State Police? Has something happened to my husband?" Nell said, almost in hysterics.

"No. It's nothing about your husband. I want to talk to you about a shooting that happened three weeks ago in Dead River," Bridges said, regretting he had bothered to stop to talk to Nell about the murder.

"I don't know anything about any shooting. Did someone get hurt in a hunting accident? You see, I haven't been out much since Bill left. I must stay close to home, so I'll be here when he returns. He should be here any moment now," she said, glancing at the wall clock above the sink, its hands frozen at two thirty-five.

Bridges knew there was no way Nell, given her mental state, could have been involved in the shooting. However, his training to become a detective had also taught him that people can be very clever when faced with a crime, often attempting to mislead the authorities. It's an opportunity for some to showcase their acting skills by adopting new and believable personas. He decided to study her reaction when he asked her about any firearms in the house.

"What an odd question, Mr. Bridges, asking me if I have any guns in the house. Would you like to see the rifle Bill gave me on our first wedding anniversary? You wait right here, and I'll go to the bedroom and get it for you."

Bridges didn't know what to expect when Nell returned. He unbuttoned his jacket, ready to grab his revolver from his shoulder holster in case she had thoughts of using the weapon on him.

"Why, here it is, Mr. Bridges. I'm afraid it's very dusty. I don't believe I've shot it for some time. Although I did threaten to use it once to scare off two mouthy trespassers. I used to shoot red squirrels trying to get at my bird feeders. Nothing drives me crazier than a brazen squirrel who thinks it has a right to take a sunflower seed from a junco. I don't feed the birds anymore. I guess I just lost interest after Bill left home."

"May I see the rifle?"

Bridges took the weapon. It was a J.C. Higgins .22 caliber, single-shot, bolt-action. "Is this the only rifle you own?"

"Why, yes. My husband told me this was the best weapon to stop squirrels from stealing birdseed. Do you think I need a more powerful rifle, Mr. Bridges?"

"No, Nell. This is the perfect weapon to use on squirrels." Bridges passed the weapon back to her. There was no reason to stay longer. Nell was not a suspect. She had her problems, but they were more related to schizophrenia than to physical violence.

"I have to go now. It was nice meeting you, Nell."

"Do you have to leave so soon? You can stay for supper. I made a fresh pot of baked beans just last week. Why don't you join me?"

"Thank you, but I can't stay. I told my wife I'd be home early. Today is our anniversary and we're going out for the evening to celebrate," Bridges said. It was his favorite line when he needed to get out of an awkward situation or away from someone who wouldn't stop talking.

June 27, 1949
Leavitt's Store
Flagstaff

While Detective Bridges struggled to determine his next move in the murder investigation, a new threat to Flagstaff and Dead River residents was about to emerge. More customers than usual stopped at Leavitt's Store, not to buy goods but to inquire about the sudden influx of men into the Valley.

"What's going on with all the trucks tearing through town? I nearly got hit backing out of my driveway," Charlie Dennison asked.

"There's a front-page story about it in today's Waterville paper. Great Northern Paper has hired seven hundred men to cut down all the trees in the Valley where the lake will be once the dam is built. What they can't sell for logs or pulp they're going to burn," Leavitt told him. "Not only that, but CMP is allowing the cutting crews to live in the houses they've bought up.[7] There'll be four times more of them than us living in the Valley."

"That company has done one piss-poor job of keeping us informed about what's going on. They kept us in the dark for twenty years whether they'll build the dam, they've gone around the Valley buying up land as if it was some big dark secret, and now, without telling us, they're going to cut all the trees and burn them while we're still living in our homes."

---

7. The Great Northern Paper Company owned the cutting rights to the 15,000 acres to be cleared for the Dead River Reservoir. Garret Schenck, founder of the Great Northern Paper Company and owner of the Madison Paper Mill, was also one of the corporators of the Kennebec River Reservoir Company.

"You can't fight city hall, so you might as well go with the flow; besides, you need to remember that half the state will benefit from the electricity the dam produces. People living in rural areas will have electricity for the first time, and those who already have it will now have a reliable source. All thanks to Long Falls Dam."

"That dam ain't going to produce a watt of electricity. It's only going to store water so the power company can use it to make it somewhere else," one of the other customers said.

"Even if that's true, it doesn't make no difference. The dam is still making electricity in a roundabout way," Cline said.

"Well, I don't like it," someone else said. "I thought I was giving up my land to make power at Long Falls. If I'd known I had to pull up roots just so they could have a lake to store water, I would have never supported the idea. And I doubt if half the Valley would have either."

"It's all about turbines spinning at Wyman. Whenever Wyman Lake gets low because of a dry spell, water will be released from Long Falls Dam. Every other hydro dam on the Kennebec will use the same water. The longer and faster the turbines run, the more electricity is made, which means greater profits for Central Maine Power Company."

"I don't care about whether it will make power or not. Right now, I'm more concerned about what might happen cutting all the trees and burning the brush. That sounds scary to me—the burning part, I'm talking about. The Valley has hardly seen a drop of rain the entire month of May, and April wasn't much better. You take the dry spring and below-average spring runoff like we've had, and you've got a disaster waiting to happen. Those men better be careful when they burn the slash. If those fires get away from them, the whole Valley will go up in flames."

12.

"By the time we got to Walter's farm, which was nothing but blackened earth and tree stumps from the previous weeks' devastation, we could see the awful monster across the river. Flames were jumping from tree to tree in such rapid progression that we couldn't keep track of them. We could see the Stone House and Dad's shack, and through the smoke, we could see they both stood. But it was like a swift flood, it spread quickly and seemed alive."

—Olena Taylor
Last Summer in Flagstaff,
There Was a Land

May 2, 1949
Flagstaff, Maine

"Look at these clothes! They're covered in soot from those damn fires," Ruth said, holding what was meant to be a white T-shirt. "They've been on the clothesline for hardly two hours and are almost black!"

"Why are you so surprised? That's how it's been almost every day since they started burning brush," her husband, Walter, said. "Look at it this way: Some people have it a lot worse. The Rands had a fire come within fifty feet of their home. They would have lost everything if Martha and Fred hadn't beaten the fire out with brooms as it was coming across the lawn. As it was, old man Clark lost his barn and mower while at a doctor's appointment. I don't believe the company is the least bit interested in controlling those slash fires. Every acre of trees that burns is an acre they don't have to cut, which saves time in clearing the Valley."

"I'm just sick of keeping one eye on the horizon looking for flames bearing down on our place. When are we leaving, Walter? This is starting to be too much, constantly worrying if we will get trapped by a fire and be unable to escape."

"As soon as we find a place to rent. There's nothing available unless we move to Farmington or Skowhegan. We both agreed we wanted to stay close to home, but so do a lot of other families. Everything is spoken for."

"Then let's move to Farmington. There are more jobs there. We can both work and perhaps return to the area in a few years."

Ruth stepped into the kitchen to answer the phone.

"That was Maude Havener. She said Erwin and Judy are missing. When she went outside to check on them, they were gone. She was wondering if we had seen them."

"Those two kids are always off somewhere. I think they have great futures in exploration. Perhaps they could join Admiral Byrd on one of his Antarctic expeditions."

"Well, Maude is concerned. She wants us to call if we see them."

"My prediction is they'll show up at just about suppertime. Food is a great magnet for five- and seven-year-olds."

Walter and Ruth were finishing supper when Maude called again.

"They're still not home, Ruth. I've called everyone on our road, and no one has seen them. Enoch has searched every area from here to Jim Eaton Hill. He's organizing a search party to find them and wants to know if Walter will help."

"Of course he will. I'll send him right over. I'll come along as well to keep you company while the men look for Erwin and Judy."

Twenty men joined the search party. They spent the night looking for the children between Stratton Road and Dead River but found no trace of them. At daybreak, others from Flagstaff village and Dead River Plantation arrived to replace the exhausted search party. Only Enoch and Walter stayed.

Isaac Blanchard was one of the men who came to help with the search. Nine years had passed since the death of his friend at Hayden Landing. Now, at twenty-six, Isaac works with his father, cutting wood in the winter and taking on odd jobs in the Valley during the rest of the year.

Isaac took charge and directed the men to spread out in a single line. At his signal, the search party advanced, calling out to the two lost children. The morning was hot and humid. One thing worked in their favor—there were no runaway fires. The men prayed it would stay that way. At ten o'clock, a breeze began to blow from the south.

"Look!" a man yelled, pointing toward the search area. "There's smoke over the next ridge!"

The men gazed at the billowing clouds of pinkish-gray smoke less than two miles ahead. A sense of urgency shot through each man, knowing there would be little chance the children would survive if they became trapped between the search party and the raging wildfire. The men's pace quickened, but Isaac kept them in a line as they advanced toward the fire, checking behind every boulder and tree.

Soon, only a quarter of a mile separated the rescuers and the raging fire. Tree limbs crackled as the flames jumped from treetop to treetop. As they advanced closer to the raging inferno, the men held one hand over their faces to shield themselves from flying embers.

Suddenly, the wind shifted, driving the blaze toward the Dead River. The search crew pressed into the charred woods. No one spoke; there was no need to. Everyone understood the gravity of the situation. They continued through the scorched vegetation for half an hour, searching for what they feared they would find.

"Everyone, stop!" Isaac shouted and motioned the men to join him.

"From the distance covered by the men last night and us this morning, it doesn't seem as if kids as young as Erwin and Judy would be ahead of us. Would you agree, Enoch?"

Enoch nodded.

"Any ideas about the direction they might have gone, Enoch?" Isaac asked.

"Flagstaff Pond is the only place I can think of. Maude and me had taken them swimming there a few times this summer. Perhaps they tried to go there."

"Okay. We'll swing north toward the beach. If we don't find them before we get there, we'll search back to Enoch's house," Isaac instructed.

The men resumed their formation and headed north toward Flagstaff Pond. After a while, they left the burned area and entered a maple and beech forest. Twenty minutes later, the man at the end of the line shouted.

"There's a shack off to my right! Someone just went inside."

"It's over there, to the right of the big pine."

"Oh, that's Sid Morton's place. Sid's a bit daft but harmless enough," Isaac told the men. "I'll go talk to him. Maybe he's seen Erwin and Judy. The rest of you regroup and stay left of his house. It's only another half mile to the beach. I'll meet you there."

Isaac navigated through the obstacle course of scrap metal and other assorted junk clogging Sid's yard. After several loud knocks, Sid opened the door, appearing as shabby as ever.

"What is it? I'm busy."

"Hello, Sid, I'm Isaac Blanchard; I live in Dead River. I need to ask you a question.?

"What?"

Isaac told Sid of the two missing children and asked if he had seen them.

"I haven't seen anyone in two weeks. So, if that's all you want, I'll get back to what I was doing," and he shut the door.

Jim again rapped on the door. "Just one more thing, Sid."

Sid partially opened the door. "Now what?"

"If you see them, please let Jim Leavitt know at the store, okay?"

"Yeah, I'll be sure to do that," he said, closing the door.

Isaac hurried off to intercept the search party, finding them gathered at the small sandy beach at Flagstaff Pond. Walter, Enoch, and Isaac stepped away from the others to discuss their next steps. The three men decided to search back toward Enoch's house, and if they didn't locate Erwin and Judy, Isaac would call the sheriff's office for extra help with the search.

Twenty minutes after leaving Flagstaff Pond, the men entered another area where an earlier fire had burned. It was narrow, maybe two hundred yards wide. They had just reentered the stand of beech and maple when one of the searchers hollered that he had found something.

When the others arrived, the man was gazing at the ground. Isaac instructed Enoch to wait until they could figure out what the man had discovered.

The men in the search party circled the body of a man lying face down. One of them dropped to his knees to get a closer look at the corpse.

"Don't touch anything, George. The State Police will want to investigate the scene before he's moved."

George either didn't hear Isaac or decided to ignore him and rolled the body onto his back.

"Why, that's Sid Morton. He must have got caught in that burn we just come through and made it out of the fire this far before his lungs exploded from the heat," George said.

Isaac stared at the lifeless man. He looked just like Sid. But it couldn't be. Isaac had talked to Sid less than an hour ago at his shanty. This man appeared to have been dead for several days, judging by his pasty skin and rigid body. Isaac was perplexed about who this doppelgänger was. Still mesmerized by the corpse, he instructed the others what to do.

"We'll let the police investigate the cause of death. We need to find Erwin and Judy. Joe, head back to Flagstaff and contact the State Police. While you're at it, let the sheriff know about the two missing children and that we need help to find them. Hank, you stay here with the body until the police arrive. The rest of you line up and space yourselves apart so you can still see the man beside you and continue searching back to the main road. Lauriston, it's up to you to keep everyone together."

"What are you going to do, Isaac?" Enoch asked. "We need everyone looking for Erwin and Judy."

"I'll be right back, Enoch. First, I'm going back to Morton's place to see if I can figure a few things out."

Fifteen minutes later, Isaac was back at Sid's cabin, pounding on the door.

Sid cracked the door open to see who was at his door. All Isaac could see was Sid's head cocked at an odd angle so he could focus on Isaac using his good eye.

"It's you! I told you I'd tell Leavitt if I saw the two kids. So, go away."

"It's not that, Sid. I need to talk to you about a dead body we found not far from here. I thought maybe you could help explain a few things. Please come out so we can talk."

After a long pause, Sid came out of his cabin. "Who is it that's dead?"

"You. At least the body looks exactly like you. Maybe you can explain what's going on."

"It could be Milford. "

"Who's Milford?"

"My twin."

"Your twin?"

"Yeah, we're identical twins. People say we even have the same annoying laugh. The one thing we don't have in common is a prison record."

"Was your brother staying with you?" Isacc asked, ignoring the prison reference.

"Hell, no, he wasn't staying with me. Milford showed up at my cabin three weeks ago. I had no idea he was out of prison. He was dead set on living here, but I wanted nothing to do with him after what he did to that old man."

Isaac wanted to learn more about his brother but decided that the State Police should ask those questions. However, Sid had told him enough to understand who the dead man was and why they bore such a striking resemblance.

"All right, the State Police have been notified about your brother's death. I'm sure they will want to talk to you."

"Hey! You leave me out of this. I've told you all I know."

"That's not how it works, Sid. You're next of kin, and you know your brother's background. They'll need to talk with you to help sort things out. Now I have to go. We still have two lost kids to find."

The search party was nearly back at Enoch's Farm when Isacc caught up with them. Ten minutes later, the homestead was in sight. After two days of searching for the missing children, the volunteers had not found them. Enoch was at a loss as to what he should do next, but as a discouraged group of men walked past the barn, Walter noticed three people in the yard.

"Enoch! Look! They're home!"

Enoch ran, recognizing Erwin and Judy beside their mother. After a long embrace, Enoch stood up and hugged his wife.

"Where did you find them?"

"I didn't. They walked into the kitchen about an hour ago. Erwin said they were going to Flagstaff Pond to swim but got lost trying to find the beach. Just before dark, Judy spotted an old horse hovel that must have been left over from a logging operation. Anyway, they curled up in the leftover hay and this morning followed a brook to the river and made their way home. They're both fine except for a few scratches on their arms and legs."

Everyone was so focused on listening to Maude recount what had happened to the children that no one noticed the State Police car pull into the driveway. Detective Bridges and a uniformed officer got out of the cruiser. Isaac stepped away from the group to speak with them.

"What's this about a body someone found in the woods?" Bridges asked.

"That's right. Follow me, I'll take you to it."

―

"No sign of trauma," Detective Bridges said, inspecting the corpse. "Looks to me like a heart attack got him. Any idea who he is?"

"Yes," Isacc said. "His name is Milford Morton. His twin brother lives a short distance from here. I can take you there if you want."

"Let's go. Trooper Billings, stay with the body while I talk to this guy's brother."

"Jesus. You mean someone lives in this dump?" Bridges said, glancing at Sid's hovel and the piles of junk around it.

"This is the place. His name is Sid Morton. He enjoys his solitude, so be patient when speaking with him. Now, I need to get back to the farm. Good luck."

Bridges watched Isacc disappear into the woods and knocked on Sid's door. After much coaxing, Sid came outside to talk.

"You've heard that a body has been found not too far from here."

"Yeah, I've heard."

"I understand that the deceased was your brother," Bridges said.

"It kind of sounds that way."

"Well, there's only one way to be certain. Why don't you come with us to see if you can identify the body."

Reluctantly, Sid followed the detective back to the corpse.

"Is that your brother?" Bridges asked.

"Yeah, that's him. Milford Morton. I thought he was long gone."

"Why don't you tell us the whole story about Milford."

"My brother and I hadn't spoken in nearly twenty years. Not since he bludgeoned that old man over a five-dollar bet."

"Tell me the rest," Bridges said, taking a notebook from his shirt pocket.

"Milford and some old guy went to the St. Lawrence County Fair in upstate New York to watch the horse races. They watched a couple of races and then agreed to bet which horse would win the third race."

"You mean they went to the window and placed a bet?"

"No. It was a side bet between the two of them. Anyway, Milford's horse won, but the old man wouldn't pay up, claiming the winning horse's jockey used an illegal whip. A big row erupted on the drive home, and according to Milford's confession, he pulled onto a dirt road, got the tire iron out of the trunk, and beat the man's head to a bloody pulp. And for that act of stupidity, my brother got thirty years in the New York State Penitentiary."

"How did he end up in Flagstaff?" the detective asked.

"He got out early for good behavior. Good behavior—can you believe it? Milford commits second-degree murder and gets cut loose after twelve years because he was such a model prisoner and didn't give the guards a hard time. Anyway, he tracked me down, thanks to my lovely sister.

"He wanted to move in with me, but I'd have no part of it. I let him stay for the better part of a week before I decided I'd had enough of the lazy slob. I knew it would take most of my savings, but I decided to ship him to Savannah, Georgia. That's where our cousin lives. I figured my sister dumped him on me, so I thought I'd do my cousin the same favor.

"Monty Young drives a taxi from Flagstaff to Farmington several times a week. I told Monty I needed a ride to Farmington to catch the bus. I paid him three dollars in advance for the ride and said I'd see him the next day. When I got back home, I told Milford to pack his belongings. He was leaving on a morning bus trip to the sunny south. He didn't like it, but he knew I meant business. Before he left, I gave him what I figured was enough money for the bus trip to Georgia and reminded him to keep his mouth shut and let Monty think it was me he was driving to the Farmington bus station. After that, I had no idea what had happened to my brother. Now, it seems he never left Flagstaff and hid in the woods. That would explain why supplies were missing from the storage shed. Looking back on it, I think he was coming around while I was asleep and stealing things. I'd seen stuff missing and figured I had just run out or had forgotten that I'd used it."

"Do you think your brother was the person that killed the surveyor?"

"I'll put it this way: I think my brother was capable of just about anything. He'd already proven that by killing his friend. But killing that surveyor, he didn't do. He couldn't have. He was in prison up until three weeks ago. If you have any other questions, ask them now. I have things I need to do at home."

"No questions; however, as next of kin, you need to claim the body for burial."

"No, I don't. I'm not paying for any burial for that lowlife, even if he was my brother. Let the town bury him. There's a pauper's section in the village cemetery. They can plant him there," Sid said, turning toward home.

As Detective Bridges walked back to Enoch and Maude's farm, he vented his frustration to the trooper about his inability to solve the murder of the CMP surveyor.

"Look at it this way, Detective. In about a year, the whole Valley will be flooded. People will have moved to God knows where, and CMP will have their dam. Any physical evidence of the murder will be resting at the bottom of a lake. The murder of Jim Norris will be added to the dozen other unsolved murder cases in the state," Trooper Billings reasoned.

"That may happen. But for the sake of Norris's family, I hope it doesn't. They deserve to know who killed their son and to see that the person pays for what he or she did. I don't want to be forever known as Warner Bridges, the Maine State Police Detective who couldn't solve the murder case."

Bridges wasn't the only one concerned about his ability to solve the murder investigation. Two weeks after his conversation with Sid Morton, Detective Bridges was asked to meet with the State Police leadership in Augusta, along with an aide to Governor Horace Hildreth.

13.

"Old Home Days and Fourth of July Celebration Serve as Wake for Flagstaff Before Obliteration"

—News article headline
Lewiston Daily Sun, July 2, 1949

"Let me get right to the point, Detective Bridges. There is a lot of pressure in the system to solve the Jim Norris murder," Colonel Benner said, glancing at the governor's representative. "I've read your weekly investigation reports, and I believe you still have no clear suspect after eight months on the case. Is that a fair assessment?"

"I'd say it was a fair assessment. I've had a few leads, but none of them panned out. The case is pretty much at a standstill."

"That's my feeling as well. We need to move this investigation forward. I want you and Sergeant Henderson to review the case documentation," Benner said, gesturing toward Sergeant Bruce Henderson, who sat off to the side. "There might be something you overlooked. If there is, then the two of you are to dig deeper. I want a report on my desk in one week with your findings. One other thing you and Sergeant Henderson should know: Jim Norris, the man who was shot and killed, was to be the future son-in-law of the governor. However, that doesn't change how we handle this case. The Maine State Police vigorously pursues every murder of a

Maine citizen, regardless of a person's status in life," Chief Benner said, with another glance at the governor's representative.

The next day, Warner Bridges and Timothy Henderson met in a conference room at State Police Headquarters to review the evidence in the Norris murder.

"I read your reports about the murder at home last night, Warner. From what you wrote, it seems to me that there are three individuals we should take another look at."

"And who would they be?"

"Tim Barton and his brother Ken have both shown a tendency toward violence during each of your attempts to interact with them. Their backwoods survivalist lifestyle demonstrates they are society misfits and would likely do about anything to preserve their solitary way of life. Perhaps they, along with Jake, saw the building of the dam and the resulting lake as a threat to how they wanted to live and would try anything to stop it."

"Who else?"

"Austin Titcomb. His feelings against the dam were well known. He threatened CMP's appraiser and kicked him off his property. Most importantly, the survey crew was on Titcomb's property when Norris was killed and was seen by the CMP appraiser going into his barn carrying a rifle at about the time of the shooting."

"Correction. With what *looked* like a rifle. When I questioned Titcomb about it, he told me it was an ax. Even the appraiser who saw Titcomb entering the barn wasn't positive it was a rifle."

"What else was Titcomb going to say?"

"Why didn't you search Titcomb's property for the murder weapon?" Henderson asked.

"Because to get a search warrant, you need probable cause," Bridges said, irritated by the question.

"I understand that. However, in the case of Austin Titcomb, I believe there is probable cause. He was seen walking into his barn with what is presumed to be a rifle at about the time of the murder. Look, let's ask the judge for a search warrant based on what appeared to be a rifle. We'll get it. Governor Hildreth appointed District Judge Mallet, if you catch my drift."

"I get it. Okay, I'll ask the State Police Council to write the request this afternoon. Chief Benner will need to approve it."

"Benner will sign. He wants to add a feather to his cap by being able to tell the governor that the State Police arrested the person responsible for the murder of his daughter's future husband."

"That assumes we can find the murder weapon and prove that Titcomb was the one who used it."

Detective Bridges and Sergeant Henderson pulled into Austin Titcomb's driveway three days later with the search warrant neatly folded in Henderson's shirt pocket. Titcomb was sitting in a rocker on the front porch.

"Mr. Titcomb, you may remember me from my last visit," said Bridges.

"I remember," Titcomb said, slowly rocking and staring at Henderson.

"This is Sergeant Henderson. We want to ask you a few questions about the Jim Norris shooting. May we come onto the porch?"

"I'd rather you didn't. You can ask your questions from there."

"That's fine. Do you own any firearms, Mr. Titcomb?" Bridges asked.

"Yeah, is that a problem for you?"

"May we see them?"

"I see no reason to show 'em to you."

"I'm afraid you have to. Sergeant Henderson, please serve Mr. Titcomb the search warrant."

Henderson held the paper out to Titcomb, but he refused to take it.

"Mr. Titcomb, regardless of whether you accept the warrant, we can search the premises for weapons. Sergeant, you check the house while I inspect the barn."

Titcomb's face turned beet red, yet he stayed silent, only staring at the yard while rocking back and forth.

Thirty minutes later, Henderson stepped out of the house carrying a .32-caliber rifle. He walked past Titcomb, still sitting on the porch, on his way to the barn to see if Bridges had found other weapons.

Bridges was coming down the ladder from the hayloft when Henderson walked into the barn.

"Anything?" Henderson asked.

"Nothing. I probed every square inch of the place, even the hayloft, and all I have to show for it was a shirt full of chaff. How about you?"

"Only this antique Remington thirty-two."

"Well, that doesn't do us any good. We're looking for a 308 caliber, according to the ballistics lab. You might as well return it to Titcomb. It looks like either Titcomb isn't our man, or he got rid of the murder weapon. Let's check the two outbuildings. If we draw a blank, then we'll leave."

Walking past Titcomb's two jersey cows, Bridges stopped.

"What's up?" Henderson asked, watching Bridges study the two animals.

"I was thinking cows typically receive a few pounds of grain in the morning and again at night, along with their hay. The only place I haven't checked for the murder weapon is the grain bin," Bridges said, lifting the cover to the wooden box next to the door into the tie-up. "Henderson, roll that barrel over here. It's a long shot, but let's see if anything of interest is buried under these oats."

Bridges scooped out enough grain so he could reach the bottom of the bin.

"There's something there, I can feel it. Now to get a grip on it," Bridges said, working the object up through the oats. "Henderson, I think we have what we've been looking for."

Bridges held up a rifle wrapped in burlap. He passed the weapon to Henderson. "Check the caliber," he said, brushing the chaff from his shirtsleeve.

"308."

"I believe we've found the murder weapon and our man. We'll drop it off at the Crime Lab. They'll tell us if the bullet's rifling matches this gun. I'm banking that it will. We'll take Titcomb in and book him for the murder of Jim Norris."

Bridges and Henderson walked back to the house to arrest Austin Titcomb.

"Damn it! He's gone. You check downstairs, and I'll head upstairs. Just be careful. If he suspects we're onto him, he might try anything," Bridges said, sprinting onto the porch.

Five minutes later, Bridges ran down the stairs and found Henderson in the kitchen.

"I don't believe this! We find the murder weapon, and the suspect disappears. Where in hell could he have gone?"

"Wherever he went, it was on foot. His pickup is still in the yard," Henderson said.

"Let me think." Bridges paced around the kitchen, frantically rubbing his forehead, trying to come up with a plan to find Titcomb. "Okay, this is what we'll do. You call division headquarters in Skowhegan. Talk to Captain Snyder and tell him what happened. Ask him to send every available Trooper to Flagstaff. Then, call the County Sheriff and ask him to send help to find Titcomb. I'm going to Leavitt's Store to see if anyone knows where Titcomb might head. Perhaps he has a hunting camp and is hiding out. I'll meet you back here."

A half hour later, vehicles from the State Police and County Sheriff's Department began to arrive at Titcomb's farm. Soon, twenty-three law enforcement officers gathered in the farmyard, waiting for instructions. Soon, Bridges returned. Leavitt had told him that Titcomb only owned the home place and said he had no idea where the man would go to hide from the police.

Bridges divided the men into two groups. Henderson and his men searched the woods and fields on both sides of the farmhouse, while Bridges focused on the area between the main road and the Dead River.

At sunset, both groups returned to Titcomb's home without finding evidence of Austin.

The following day, the canine unit arrived, but Titcomb's scent had long gone cold. At noon, the game wardens loaded the dogs back into their kennels and returned to Augusta. Two hours later, the State Police and the sheriff's men also left. Henderson and Bridges watched the last police cruiser disappear down the road.

"Now what?" Henderson asked.

"All we can do is put flyers in local stores and post offices and hope someone calls with a lead. I have a nagging feeling that my time on this case is running out. Benner will need to hold someone accountable for losing the likely killer, and that someone will be me."

In the distance, a car raced toward them, honking its horn. The driver swerved into the driveway, clipping the corner fence post, and came to a sudden stop beside Henderson and Bridges.

"They found Austin's canoe!" the young driver hollered, jumping from the car.

"Slow down and tell me what you're talking about," Bridges said.

"Mr. Rand and his friend had paddled up the river to fish Hurricane Brook. When they returned to their canoe, they spotted a green canvas-covered canoe floating upside down, no more than twenty feet away. Mr. Rand and his friend dragged the canoe to shore. After they righted it, they noticed *A. Titcomb* carved into the gunnel."

"Where's the canoe now?" Henderson asked.

"It's just down the road, sitting in Mr. Rand's yard."

Five minutes later, Bridges and Henderson were inspecting the canoe.

"Bruce, take a look at Titcomb's name. Notice how bright the letters are compared to the rest of the cedar? Those letters were carved into the gunnel not long ago."

"It makes you wonder if Titcomb did that to throw us off track trying to find him. Perhaps he wanted the capsized canoe found, hoping we'd think he had an accident and drowned while making his getaway."

"You're right. But we can't risk the chance he didn't drown. Maybe he had a heart attack while trying to escape and tipped the canoe when he fell out. I'll ask Sheriff Smith if he could send a couple of his men to help us search for a body," Bridges said.

Bigelow, Dead River, and Flagstaff residents faced pressure from all directions: low appraisals, the challenge of finding new homes, wildfires, and flooding when the gates at Long Falls were closed.

After days of uncontrolled fires, the remaining Flagstaff and Dead River residents reconsidered staying until the Central Maine Power Company ordered them out of the Valley. Families grew weary of evacuating when fire threatened their homes, only to return once the immediate danger had passed and be forced to leave again days later. Many of these families had still not found a place to live, and several held out, hoping for a better offer from the power company. Now, they realized that if their property burned, it would have no value and they could end up with nothing.

Nearly two dozen buildings sold to CMP were bought back by the owners for ten cents on the dollar. There was a frantic rush to lift them from their foundations onto flatbeds and transport them to a nearby town before rising waters or a destructive wildfire destroyed them.

May 19, 1949
Leavitt's Store
Flagstaff, Maine

"There goes Charlie Olson's house," Eric said, watching the two-story home slowly going down Main Street precariously balanced on a flatbed trailer. "Charlie bought a lot in Eustis, right on the shore of the new lake, once it's filled up. He'll have a view of Mount Bigelow just like before, only from a different angle. He told me yesterday that they'd already moved his grandfather

Olaf's body to the new cemetery. Charlie said it's only a mile from his new lot. He told me he and Gladys could walk there in less than ten minutes. That will make it handy when they need to water the flowers around Olaf's headstone."

"Sure will. Anyway, Charlie's house is the third house that's been moved out of the village this week. At this rate, the only place left standing in town will be the store," Leavitt said.

"By the way, did you hear about the big celebration the town fathers are planning for the Fourth? It will be a combination of an Independence Day celebration, a homecoming, and a farewell to the Dead River Valley, all wrapped in one. The towns even raised a thousand dollars for the event. Everyone who has already moved out is invited back for the big day. It will be our first homecoming. Everyone wants to end living in the Valley with a big bang and not a whimper."

14.

The Dam is surely coming. Now we're all sorry and wished they'd never come up here. Every time we go anywhere now, we cherish the view and the good times because after this summer, things will never be the same again. It's just like dying, isn't it? In a way, it is the dying of the town. Sad.

—Notes from the Diary
of Olena Viles Taylor, June 22, 1948.
There Was a Land,
Flagstaff Memorial Chapel Association, page 23

Detective Bridges remained the lead investigator in the murder of Jim Norris, although the case was technically recategorized as inactive until new information surfaced. The murder of the surveyor's helper was never far from Bridges's mind, as was Austin Titcomb. He still blamed himself for allowing Titcomb's escape. Most authorities believed Titcomb had suffered a heart attack and drowned the day he fled his farm, while others speculated that he managed to leave the area unnoticed. However, his disappearance remained purely speculation.

Bridges learned of the Flagstaff Old Home Days celebration in the daily newspaper. At first, he read it with only a passing interest. Then, the more he thought about it, he wondered if Austin Titcomb might take the opportunity to return to the Valley one last time, assuming he was still alive. Bridges reasoned it would be foolish for Titcomb to walk into town and mingle with the crowd, but he could hide in the shadows and observe the celebration. He'd probably killed the rodman out of frustration for having his home and land taken from him, and seeing the Valley one last time before it was lost forever seemed to be a reasonable act for a desperate and despondent man. Bridges requested his supervisor's permission to be in Flagstaff on July 4th. Permission was denied. State resources would not be spent on the case based solely on a wild idea that a killer might appear for a homecoming celebration.

Bridges couldn't let go of the idea. He would attend on his own if he couldn't go on official time. Bridges called Sheriff Smith and told him about his plan and asked for help. The sheriff was dubious that Titcomb would dare to appear; however, he agreed to be at Flagstaff for the homecoming celebration.

Finally, July 4th arrived. It was a magnificent summer day, marred only by a pall of woodsmoke obscuring Mount Bigelow—a reminder of the reason for the homecoming celebration. A large crowd gathered in front of Leavitt's Store and Hazen Ames's Pool Hall. Almost every family that had left the Valley returned one last time. Although everyone gathered to acknowledge the impending demise of the three settlements, it was anything but a somber occasion. Stories were exchanged, and memories were shared among family and friends. A parade of decorated tractors, pickups filled with children, and a band from Waterville marched down Main Street. At two p.m., a band from Pittsfield performed in the small memorial park. After the concert, people headed to the ballfield to watch a Flagstaff and Dead River baseball game.

Sheriff Smith patrolled the village perimeter as Bridges mingled with the crowd, watching for Titcomb. The day had gone smoothly and without incident. It was starting to seem like Bridges's theory about Titcomb making a secretive appearance wouldn't materialize.

After the ballgame, the crowd began to move back to Main Street to continue the festivities and wait for the start of the street dance featuring music from another band out of Farmington.

PART ONE: Washed Out   207

Sheriff Smith also made his way back to the village when he noticed someone walking just inside the tree line at the far end of the ballfield. Initially, he believed it was one of the locals taking a shortcut to his car. The sheriff stepped behind one of the pickups and watched. Whoever it was didn't leave but appeared to be working along the wood line, stopping periodically to observe the remaining people on the ballfield. The distance was too great to know who the stranger was or what he might be up to. However, the sheriff couldn't take the chance it wasn't Titcomb. He scanned the ballfield, looking for Bridges, and spotted him talking to Isaac Blanchard by a parked car behind home plate. Smith realized that if he shouted to Bridges, he could alert Titcomb that something was wrong, causing him to vanish into the forest. Similarly, he couldn't rush to inform Bridges that the man in the woods might be Titcomb. Off to his side, he noticed a lone Dodge pickup. He would drive to Bridges. When he opened the door, he came face to face with a couple making out in the front seat.

"Push over; we're going for a drive," he told the two teenagers, forcing them to the passenger side as he slid behind the wheel. Slowly, he drove around the infield to Bridges and Isaac, where his passengers jumped out of the pickup the moment it stopped.

"Warner, there's someone beyond the ballfield acting suspicious. Look over third base, just inside the woods."

Bridges scanned the area until he locked onto what appeared to be someone hiding behind a tree. The distance was too great to identify who it was. Bridges watched as the stranger began to creep along the edge of the outfield, hunched over as if attempting to avoid detection.

"That could be our man. This is what we'll do. Sheriff, you drive the pickup toward the highway as if you're leaving town. Once you reach the main road, park and walk into the woods toward whoever it is. Isaac, you can walk around the parking lot, head into the woods, and make your way toward him. I'll give both of you five minutes to get in position, and then I'll cross the ballfield directly toward him so he can see me. He's bound to make a break; when he does, it might be toward one of you. If you have the chance, grab him. I'll be right on his heels.

"Isaac. You don't have to do this if you don't want to. If it's Titcomb, he's already killed once, so he has nothing to lose if he decides to take out someone else."

"I'll do it. I don't think he's going to shoot anyone else. His beef was with the power company. I think he's a scared old man that doesn't know what to do. If it is Austin, maybe he'll listen to me and give it up."

Bridges waited while Isaac and the sheriff moved off, then checked his watch. Assuming they were in position, he started slowly across the ballfield, heading straight toward the man standing among the trees. Halfway across the outfield, he saw the man disappear behind a large maple tree. Fifty yards separated them. Suddenly, the man broke from his cover and ran deeper into the woods. Bridges gave chase, hoping he would veer left or right toward Sheridan or Isaac. He didn't. He kept running straight ahead. Bridges gained ground. He closed the gap to within fifty feet. Unaware that Bridges was closing in on him, the man stopped to look back. In that instant, Bridges recognized it was Austin Titcomb and ran harder to catch up with him. He closed the gap to twenty-five feet. He was so close, he could hear Titcomb gasping for air as he ran as fast as a sixty-seven-year-old man could. Bridges knew he had him. A few more feet and Bridges could grab Titcomb's arm and drag him to the ground. Only feet stood between them. As he reached out to grab Titcomb, the chase abruptly ended. Bridges was so intent on catching Titcomb that he didn't see the dead sapling. He hooked his foot under the tree and fell headfirst to the ground, spraining his ankle. Bridges lay in agony while Titcomb ran deeper into the woods.

Bridges grabbed hold of a sapling and pulled himself up to his feet. Unable to put much pressure on his right foot, he realized it would be tough to make it out of the woods without help. He had struggled forward for a hundred feet when he heard someone calling his name. It was Isaac. A few minutes later, Sheriff Smith arrived, and together they helped Bridges back to the village. It was nearly dark when the three men reached Bridges's car. As they discussed what to do next, a hundred yards away the orchestra played, and people laughed as they danced the night away, unaware of the mad chase through the woods after a killer.

Bridges wanted to call his supervisor at the Maine State Police Headquarters to request permission to form a search party for Titcomb. However, he was already on thin ice with Augusta for allowing Titcomb to escape the day he and Henderson had discovered the rifle, and everything he had done today was without authorization. Instead, Bridges convinced Smith to assemble a search party to catch Titcomb before he was long gone.

At daybreak the following morning, fifteen deputies and game wardens started the search for Titcomb while Bridges nursed his swollen ankle in his car. This time, he was confident Titcomb would be captured. Sheriff Smith and his men returned six hours later without Austin Titcomb.

"No sign of him?" Bridges asked, not attempting to hide his disappointment.

"There was sign, all right. We stumbled across where he's been staying for the last two months—an abandoned farmstead about a mile and a half back in the woods. I don't know what he survived on. What food we found wasn't enough to keep a woodpecker alive. We searched for a mile in every direction from the place and didn't see hide or hair of him. He's gone. I'm afraid all we can do now is get the word out to law enforcement in Maine and the rest of New England to be on the lookout for him."

The unsuccessful search ended any further attempts to find Norris's killer and also ended Warner Bridges's career as a detective with the Maine State Police. Chief Benner caught wind that Bridges had been working on the case after being warned not to do so. Bridges and the Chief had a closed-door meeting to discuss Bridges's future with the Maine State Police. The reprimand was more than Bridges could tolerate. He signed his resignation letter a week after the meeting and took early retirement.

15.

No, we old-timers in Flagstaff don't give up that easily. Our homes may be going, our fields and orchards so to lie under the flood waters, but you can't kill the spirit of a people in a community as closely knit as we have been. Takes more than flood waters to drown memory and put an end to loving things you have always loved.

—An anonymous resident of Flagstaff

Flagstaff Township
Flagstaff Lake
August 27, 1972

"I think you and Mr. Hasting will like this lot. I listed it two days ago, and you folks were the first people I thought of that may be interested in the property," said Chuck Fenderson, owner of Standard Gauge Realty Company.

"It's a long boat ride to get here from Eustis," Mrs. Hasting said.

"As it turns out, the paper company that owns all the backland will be cutting wood in the area and needs a haul road to get it out. The company is willing to grant a road easement to whoever purchases the property. Now turn around and take a gander at the view."

"It's beautiful! You can see the entire Mount Bigelow Range," Mrs. Hasting said.

"For my money, one of the best views in the state. It's hard to imagine that three small towns were flooded to make Flagstaff Lake. It would never happen today. People would scream bloody murder and spend a lot on lawyers to stop it," Fenderson said.

While the three walked the property, the Hastings' nine-year-old son went exploring on his own. A short time later, he came running back to his parents.

"Come see the hole I found!"

The three followed the boy through a pine stand to see his discovery.

"Right there! It's deep! I can't see the bottom."

"You get back from there, now!" Mr. Hasting yelled. "You could fall in and get hurt."

Mr. Fenderson walked to the four-foot-wide opening and peered in. "It's an old stone-lined well. It was probably the water supply for the house and barn. The cellar holes are right over there," Fenderson said, pointing up the knoll. "Whoever buys the property better plan on filling it in; if someone ever fell in, no one would know what happened to them."

Fenderson returned to the boat while Mr. and Mrs. Hasting walked over the property again. Soon, they joined him.

"We'll take it. It's exactly what we've been looking for. A log cabin overlooking the lake at Mount Bigelow will be the perfect place for us to escape from Portland," Mr. Hasting said.

On the boat ride back to Fenderson's office to sign the purchase-and-sale agreement, Mrs. Hasting told her husband that before filling in the well, they should use the stones for landscaping and making rock gardens. Mr. Fenderson added that telling visitors where the rocks came from would make a great story.

The following summer, the Hastings had their log cabin. The last job before the excavator left the site was to remove the rocks from the well, as Mrs. Hasting wanted. Their son, Jimmy, watched the large machine pluck buckets of rocks from the old well and place them in small piles for his mother and father to use to make walls and gardens.

PART ONE: Washed Out

The machine was nearly at the bottom of the well and had only a few more rocks to remove when Jimmy noticed that one rock dumped from the bucket looked different. When the operator swung the boom back to the hole for another scoop, he hurried over to take a closer look. This rock was chalky white, while the others were slate-colored. Jimmy picked it up and rolled it in his hands. He took off running when he saw two large holes and the remnants of teeth.

"Mom! Look what I found!"

October 17, 1972
Maine State Police Headquarters
Augusta, Maine

Former Detective Bridges was invited to the State Police Headquarters to meet with the Chief of the State Police. Still bitter about how his former employer had treated him, Bridges almost declined the invitation.

"Please, sit down, Warner. You're probably wondering why I asked you to come in."

"Yes. After being retired for twenty-three years, it did make me wonder."

"Well, Warner, I think you'll be pleasantly surprised by what I'm going to tell you. Do you remember the James Norris case?"

"I remember it very well. The Norris homicide was the reason I quit my job. What about it?"

"As you're aware, the evidence at the time pointed to Austin Titcomb as the person who murdered Norris. You were the last person to see Titcomb the day you chased him through the woods north of Flagstaff village. We now know what happened to him."

Bridges sat upright, anticipating the Chief's next words. Not knowing what had happened to Titcomb had haunted him for twenty-three years.

"Several months ago, a nine-year-old boy found his skull among an excavator's bucket full of rocks that was removed from an old stone-lined well. We have determined that it and the other bone fragments at the bottom of the well are the remains of one Austin Titcomb."

"Are you certain it was Titcomb?"

"More than certain. Forensics are positive that it's him. There was a wedding band still on the bone of his third finger. The inscription on the inside of the ring remained readable after it was cleaned: *AGT and EVT 1897*. Austin Gregory Titcomb and Emma Violet Titcomb."

"But how did he end up in a well?"

"On that, we can't be certain. However, the Case Review Team has a theory. They believe Austin likely fell into the well on the day of the chase, which was twenty-three years ago on July Fourth. They believe, and I agree, that Mr. Titcomb was so intent on avoiding you that he didn't see the well cover. Given the decayed boards and rusty nails surrounding the skeletal remains, the team suspects he stepped on the well cover, fell through, and landed at the bottom of the twenty-two-foot shaft with no chance of escape. I like to think he died from the fall; if not, it would have been a long, agonizing death."

Bridges was speechless, struggling to process what the Chief had told him. He had agonized over how that one case had ruined his otherwise stellar career as a detective with the Maine State Police. Now, he'd learned that Titcomb hadn't drowned in the Dead River as many had assumed, nor had he moved to parts unknown to start a new life; instead, he had died from a fall into a four-foot-wide hole in the woods.

"So that is why I asked you to come in today. Any questions?"

"No questions. But I'll admit, this is the first time I've been glad to be asked to meet with the Chief."

"Before you leave, Warner, there are two more things. First, your personnel file has been updated, and all references to insubordination have been removed. I'll make sure you get a copy. The second item is: How would you like to be reinstated in the Maine State Police?" said the Chief with a smile. "We could use a detective who knows how to get the job done."

"Thanks, anyway, but at my age, catching three-pound brook trout is more to my liking than catching the bad guys."

November 15, 1949
Dead River, Maine
The home of Bill and Olena Skilling

"Let's take one last ride through Flagstaff before we leave. I want to permanently etch in my mind what the town looked like before it gets drowned out," Bill Skilling told his wife.

"I don't think so. Almost everyone has left. Why would I want to torture myself by seeing demolished houses and all the trees that used to line Main Street cut down? Flagstaff is nothing more than a ghost town. I want to remember when I'd go to Leavitt's Store to check to see if we had mail or to buy a yard of material to make pajamas for the kids. I don't want to look at a bunch of hollowed-out buildings."

"Just imagine, Olena, how few people in Maine can say the place they called home ended up at the bottom of a lake."

"How many people can say they had no say if they wanted to be flooded out and forced to find a new place to live? How many can say they lived on the edge for months, wondering if fires would destroy their property before the rising water did? How many can say their lives were being controlled by the likes of a power company?"

"Okay. I get it. I feel the same way. But things change. All we can do is promise ourselves life will be even better living in Anson."

"Bill. This is home! You and I were born here. We raised our children here. What right does anyone have to tell us that all we have done means nothing and that we must find a new place to live? Who do they think they are?"

"Let's just take a ride to Flagstaff. I want to see if the Honor Roll Monument has been dug up. The selectmen are going to relocate it in front of the new Flagstaff Chapel. We'll ride down Main Street, then up to Flagstaff Pond. We'll be home in an hour."

Reluctantly, Olena went with her husband. Agreeing to drive to Flagstaff didn't mean she had to look at the carnage. She sat silently, staring through the windshield while Bill gave an annoying progress report on the dismantling of the town.

"They've taken the roof off the Walter Grines place. It looks like the crew will salvage what they can and burn the rest. Too bad. It was a nice home, probably too large to move on a flatbed." A few minutes later, "They moved the Pearsons' house. Nothing left but the foundation. I remember my father telling me that Ed was the first person in Flagstaff to have a poured concrete cellar."

Olena didn't want to hear anymore. She only wanted to go home.

Bill had just turned onto the Pond Road when he met a pickup truck coming toward them.

"Hello, Justin," Bill said, stopping to speak to the driver of the new Ford pickup. "That's one fancy truck."

"Thanks. I bought it in Farmington last week. I wanted to put a few miles on it, so I drove up to see what was left of the Valley. I'll tell you, Bill, that selling out to CMP and moving to Farmington was the best thing that's ever happened to me. I've got a job at the Bass Shoe Company in Wilton, hand-stitching Weejuns. Pays well, too. Although it is one monotonous job."

Olena remained focused on the windshield, unwilling to engage in conversation with anyone who didn't view the loss of living in the Valley the way she did.

"Do you think you'll miss living in Dead River, Justin?" Bill asked.

"Going to? Heck, I miss it already. I mean, a man's got to do what he has to do to make a decent living. I made the right decision to leave the area, but home will always be here, in the Valley. I intend to drive up every chance I get to hunt and fish. If there had been a decent job in the area, I'd have stayed closer to home, but a guy can't always get what he wants. Farmington is a decent place to live, but many of those folks don't look at life like you and I do.

"I'm on my way to Eustis to have supper with my mother. She's having beans, seeing it's Saturday night, and I'm supplying meat for the pot—two partridge breasts. Ma likes her new home. She can see Bigelow from the living room just like when she lived in Flagstaff, but now she has electricity."

Bill watched Justin disappear over Big Bridge. There was little conversation on the drive back to Dead River. Bill knew his wife was still stewing about being forced to leave the Valley.

"Everyone has a different slant on CMP flooding the Valley," he said, finally breaking the silence. "People left for a host of reasons. Some, like Justin, wanted a decent job. Some saw the CMP payment as a way out of debt. Some felt that leaving was in the best interest of those families in the state who needed power for their homes. Not everyone in the Valley is as fortunate as we are. As schoolteachers, we moved just twenty miles down the road to find work. You know what I think, Olena?"

"What?" She dreaded hearing her husband pontificate about why people accepted their fate without putting up a fight.

"I bet that as time goes on, everyone will look back at living in the Valley as some of the best times of their lives."

"I suppose. But I still don't like it."

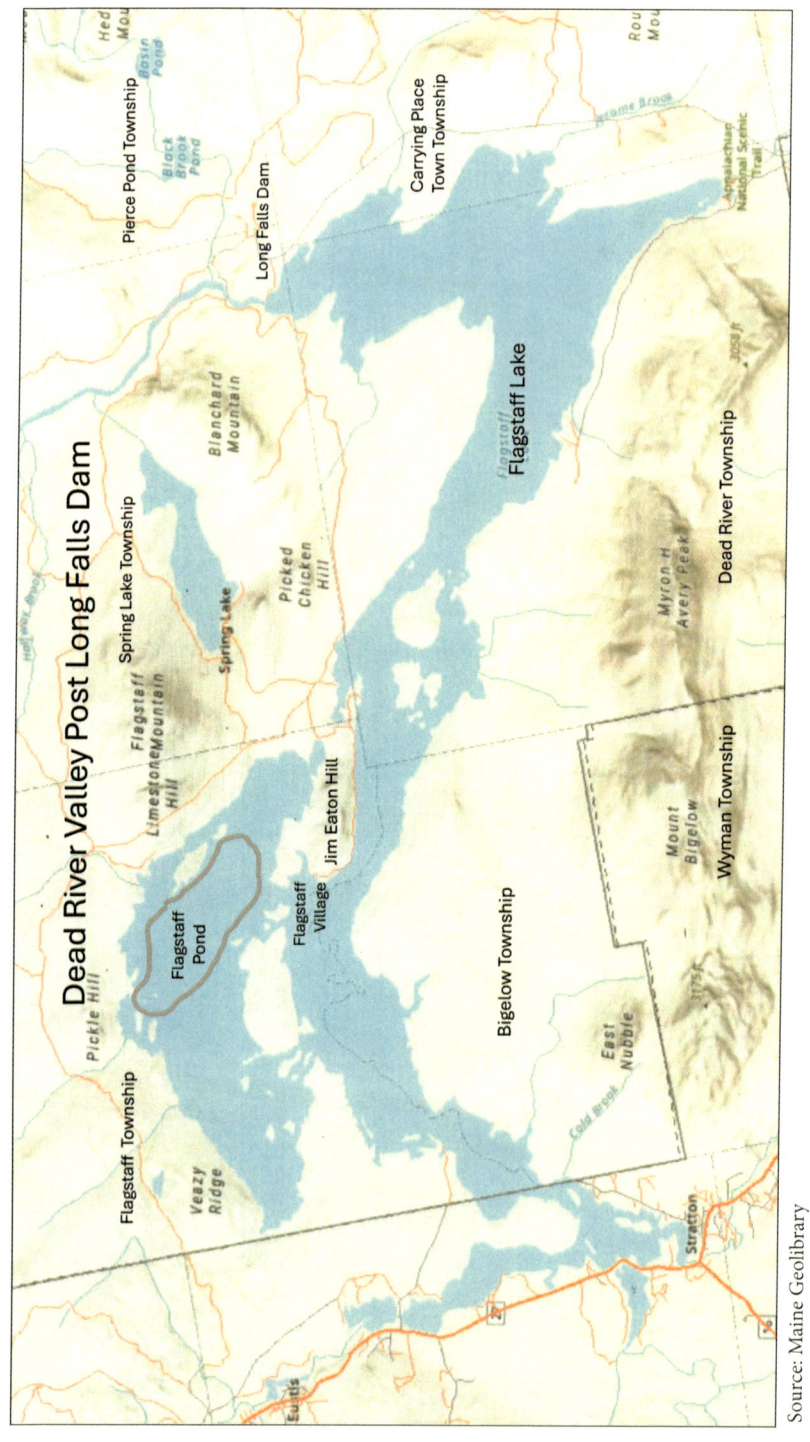

Dead River Valley Post Long Falls Dam

Source: Maine Geolibrary

EPILOGUE

On November 19, 1949, the gates at Long Falls Dam were closed, and CMP ordered everyone to leave immediately. The raging fires of summer and fall had already forced most people out of their homes, with only the most steadfast residents remaining. Some returned to collect forgotten items and visit their homes one last time. However, by mid-December, the Dead River Valley was deserted.

Buildings that were not moved or demolished slowly fell victim to the rising water. Leavitt's Store was one. Not until the winter of 1951 did crews go onto the ice and burn the former cornerstone of Flagstaff village. In the spring, the rising water lifted what had lain beneath the ice from its foundation, breaking the former store into a floating mass of boards and timbers. The other remaining buildings in the Valley suffered the same fate as Leavitt's Store. By the summer of 1952, Flagstaff Lake was full, and all evidence of the communities of Dead River and Flagstaff had vanished beneath its surface. The scattered remnants of Route 144 rise from the lake as the land undulates, an eerie reminder of the Valley's only paved road that once linked the Dead River and Flagstaff to the outside world.

The Flagstaff school, situated slightly higher than Flagstaff village, escaped the flood. Salvage rights were sold, the building was torn down, and the lumber was transported to Stratton and

Eustis to be repurposed. The crumbling foundation still stands where families and friends gathered on cold winter evenings to watch the girls' and boys' basketball games.

One step remained to complete the dissolution of the Dead River Plantation and Flagstaff Plantation. On March 5, 1951, the Maine State Legislature passed An Act to Provide for the Surrender by Flagstaff Plantation of Its Organization. A similar resolution was passed for the Dead River Plantation. By enacting this emergency legislation, Flagstaff and Dead River became unorganized townships and, in effect, wards of the State for administrative matters. From this point forward, Dead River and Flagstaff would be designated Dead River Township and Flagstaff Township.

> But whatever the fruits of the struggle
> Be it bitter or sweet, still contend,
> Stand straight and staunch through the turmoil,
> And play this life fair to the end.
>
> —The final lines of *L'Envoi*,
> a poem by John F. Moody, Jr.

AFTERWORD
by Kenneth Wing

As a fifth-generation Wing residing in the Dead River Valley, I feel fortunate to have grown up along the shores of Flagstaff Lake, deeply immersed in its local history. I grew up in Eustis and considered many of the people displaced by the 1950 flood to be close friends. Many relocated to Eustis—some moved their entire houses—while others went on to live in cities. Many secured higher-paying jobs and sent their children to college.

I often walk the old streets of Flagstaff village when the lake is drained every year to accommodate the spring snowmelt. My father was my guide, sharing countless stories as he pointed out each foundation and point of interest. My favorite place was the granite foundation of the house where he grew up. He always pointed out the remnants of his dog pen, the frame of his old Willis Knight car, and the granite steps at the front of the house. My grandparents' house was adjacent to Hazen Ames's Pool Hall, and across the street was Leavitt's Store. I've walked through those foundations many times as well. And, of course, I've wondered "What if?" and "Whatever happened to…?"

The reader might wonder what happened after the dam was closed and the lake was formed. *The Lost Villages of Flagstaff Lake*, written by Alan Burnell and me, explores this question. We interviewed former residents of Flagstaff, Dead River, and Bigelow

Plantations. Alan and I inventoried thirty-three buildings that were moved to Eustis, Stratton, Embden, and Highland. Many were complete houses, while others were sheds and small garages. Many buildings were relocated along Route 27 in the Town of Eustis, a section called "New Flagstaff."

Evan "Dutchie" Leavitt and his wife Evelyn, former operators of Leavitt's Store in Flagstaff village, constructed a new store in New Flagstaff. It remains in business today, seventy-five years since the Valley flooded, only larger than when the Leavitt's owned it. Evelyn asked me to call her Gram since I didn't have a grandmother nearby, and since she was a Wing, it just made sense. Many families relocated to New Flagstaff to remain local, and CMP sold them land at a fair price. My parents moved their small house to New Flagstaff, where we lived for several years. I still own it.

The burials in the old cemeteries needed to be relocated. The largest cemetery was located near Flagstaff village with two smaller ones at Dead River. In 1949, the Town of Eustis graciously donated two acres of town land for the new cemetery to the newly formed Flagstaff Memorial Chapel Association, located at the intersection of Perry Road and Route 27. One hundred eighty remains were relocated here over twenty-eight days in July and August 1949. Ken Taylor, a notable resident in Flagstaff, supervised the undertaking. The old church in Flagstaff village could not be moved, so CMP constructed a chapel next to the new cemetery. It still contains the three original stained-glass windows, the pews, and the bell. The Flagstaff Memorial Chapel Association owns this cemetery and chapel, which are well-maintained and revered by all.

As I grew up, I don't remember anyone discussing the flooding of their towns and homes with anger or disdain. Some, particularly those who moved away from this area completely, expressed emotion about having to relocate. However, there was no firestorm against the dam that would likely happen today. Most families move on, adjust, and have electricity full-time in their new homes.

Electricity was a big deal for those who'd never had it. Most residents living in the Valley never had electricity. Some homes in Flagstaff village were fortunate to have an electric line going to Harry Bryant's mill at the Flagstaff Pond outlet. This provided them with a few lights in the evenings. A small water-driven turbine provided electricity to the mill. After operating hours, Harry would leave the turbine running, switching it over to provide DC power for the neighboring houses. During basketball games, the lights in the school's gym were powered by Bryant's generator and shut off once the game ended.

I'm often asked what would have become of the Dead River Valley if Long Falls Dam had not been built and the Dead River Valley had never flooded. I can only speculate. The obvious difference is that there wouldn't be a 27-mile-long lake, and the area would inevitably have become more populated. Before the construction of Long Falls Dam, the main industry was logging, along with a few sporting camps that relied on local help and seasonal guides to operate. Also, there was some farming. Telephones and telephone poles were already present, so electricity would inevitably follow over time. With the advent of electricity, other businesses would likely emerge. Today, the Dead River Valley would attract recreational enthusiasts, such as mountain bikers and hikers. Hunting and fishing would continue to thrive, as in the nearby villages of Stratton and Eustis. Everything would have become bigger, and its people would have been more prosperous.

Long Falls Dam brought many positives—most importantly, an increase in electricity generation on the Kennebec River. Flooding would surely have been worse than it is now. Not only does Flagstaff Lake provide water held in reserve for many downriver hydropower projects, but it also provides significant flood control along the Kennebec River. Every winter, the lake level is intentionally lowered to make room for melting snow, which helps minimize spring floods on the Kennebec. April 1923 marked a significant flood event in Maine, especially along the Kennebec River and the communities of Flagstaff and Dead River. Walter Wyman used this catastrophic flood as one of his talking points for creating his dams at Long Falls and Moscow. Because of electricity and flood control, most Dead River Valley residents thought their sacrifice was justified for the greater good.

My father was born in 1928. He always knew that a dam and a lake would be built directly over where he was born and lived in Flagstaff village. He accepted it from day one. I'm sure his grandfather lamented over this, but he passed away before it became a reality. My grandfather built a new home on the shore of Flagstaff Lake, directly across from the new Flagstaff Chapel, and planned a life of guiding sports on the new lake. I believe the older residents felt sad about being forced to move but realized they had to do so. Meanwhile, the younger generation understood it was inevitable and planned to relocate. There were no court proceedings besides the year-and-a-half legal battle with CMP by two residents over a reneged, previously agreed-upon selling price.

The development of wind turbines on our local mountaintops was previously a topic of debate. One Flagstaff village resident commented that if electricity and its generation were so important, why not just put a turbine in Long Falls Dam as originally discussed? He argued that this would resolve the debate over the environmental issues related to wind towers in high alpine areas. He noted that the environmental damage from creating Flagstaff Lake had already occurred sixty years earlier. Doesn't it make more sense to generate electricity twenty-four hours a day using water instead of depending on daytime winds and building miles of transmission corridors through the wilderness? Further discussion on the subject was immediately terminated, with the moderator citing state law prohibiting that kind of discussion at that public hearing.

In July 1949, Flagstaff village hosted a grand celebration to mark the end of life in the Valley and the first Old Home Days. Speeches were made, bands played, and a large parade marched through town. And a promise was made. Everyone agreed that on the first full weekend in August, there would be an annual Old Home Days gathering to remember the people, places, and stories about the flooded Dead River Valley. Each get-together includes a Sunday service at the Flagstaff Chapel and various family reunions and picnics at the nearby Cathedral Pines. I remember these fondly and grew up looking forward to each annual Old Home Day. However, as with everything, time was not on our side, leading to fewer attendees and more burials in the Flagstaff Memorial Cemetery as the former residents of the Dead River Valley are laid to rest beside their ancestors. During each service, stories are shared about the old days along the Dead River. Just as it should be.

PART TWO

An Abbreviated History of Politics and Water Power in the 1920s as It Relates to the Construction of the Long Falls Dam

In the 1920s, Maine remained largely rural, and its residents were conservative and fiercely independent. Small independent power companies had electrified many towns and cities, and where there was electricity, families were eager for new products like radios, washing machines, and vacuum cleaners. However, electrification spread slowly into the countryside; it would take years before some areas could flip on a light switch. At the same time, new power sources had to be developed to meet the increasing demand for electricity. Two men emerged as leaders in this expansion. Both desired for Maine to benefit from electrification, but they disagreed on the method of achieving it. One was a visionary, confident that Maine's economy would rapidly expand with abundant, inexpensive energy. At 26, Walter Wyman and his partner purchased the first of many small electrical companies, broadening their service area to small towns and cities. Wyman envisioned a network of hydroelectric dams along with extensive distribution systems that would supply power to the far reaches of Maine's countryside and lure industries to the state to take advantage of the abundant, affordable energy. He was a businessman who understood that Maine couldn't immediately absorb all the power his facilities would generate and aimed to transmit the surplus power beyond Maine's borders.

The other viewed hydropower development as exploiting the people's water resources for private gain, monopolizing free-flowing rivers without compensating Maine citizens. Percival Baxter argued that hydroelectric power should stay in Maine to meet current and future needs, asserting that Maine should not harness its rivers to benefit other states' economies. The two clashed in the state legislature and the press, each striving to convince Maine citizens that their respective beliefs were just.

Walter S. Wyman
Born May 6, 1874, in Oakland, Maine (known as West Waterville until 1883). Wyman attended Tufts University. His first job after college was as an inspector and assistant superintendent of the Maine Water Company. By 1893, Wyman became the manager of the Waterville and Fairfield Railway and Electric Company, which started in 1892 as a four-mile electric railway connecting Waterville and Fairfield. Walter Wyman swiftly emerged as the leader of power development in Maine during the 1920s. His vision was to transform the state's electrical grid from small independent electric stations into larger interconnected power stations that would provide reliable, affordable electricity to families in Maine. Towns had little interest or the capacity to integrate their power systems with other nearby municipalities, so Wyman decided to pursue his ideas independently.

He partnered with Harvey D. Eaton, a local lawyer who shared Wyman's vision of expanding electricity into new regions. In 1899, they acquired the Oakland Electric Company, the first of the many small power producers they would obtain over the next twenty years. They built their first hydroelectric dam on Messalonskee Stream in 1901 and renamed it the Messalonskee Electric Company. After receiving a charter from the state legislature, they expanded into Waterville, Oakland Fairfield, and Winslow and eventually to the greater Augusta area.

On January 10, 1910, the company became the Central Maine Power Company and continued to buy more small independent electrical companies. By 1919, the fledgling company had 21,000 customers.

Wyman needed an infusion of capital to finance growth and expansion. He turned to the Insull Corporation, which owned the Middle West Utilities Company, a vast conglomerate with a less than stellar reputation. In June 1925, through a stock purchase, Central Maine Power became a subsidiary of the Insull Group, and with the merger came the money Wyman needed to continue the company's expansion.[8] Now, Wyman was able to go big and develop more generating capacity, including on the upper Kennebec River, one of the few uncontrolled rivers remaining in the state. His prize project would be a massive hydroelectric dam a mile above the town of Bingham that would produce a hefty seventy-two megawatts of power, more than could be consumed in the state.

Wyman needed two concessions from the State to justify the project's cost: the repeal of the law preventing power from being exported out of Maine, and a charter from the legislature to construct a reservoir on the Dead River at Long Falls. Wyman required the out-of-state market for that surplus power. The Dead River Reservoir would supply water during low-flow periods to keep the turbines spinning efficiently. A casualty of the 1929 stock market crash and the Great Depression, the Insull Corporation collapsed. Wyman and a group of investors purchased Insull's subsidiary, New England Public Services Company, of which CMP was a part, and saved the company from liquidation.

Wyman spent most of the 1920s trying to persuade Maine's legislature and citizens that his plan would benefit the state. Percival Baxter believed that the state's water resources were part of Maine's heritage and should not be developed by private interests without compensation. Baxter also believed that power generated in Maine should remain in Maine to ensure that electricity would be readily available for its economic growth. For twenty years, Baxter remained a thorn in Wyman's side, consistently blocking his attempts to control Maine's power supply.

Percival Baxter

Percival Proctor Baxter was born in Portland, Maine, on November 22, 1876, the son of James Phinney Baxter and Mehitabel Cummings

---

8. Before the pending sale to Insull, Harvey Eaton stepped down as president of Central Maine Power Company. He returned to private law practice, supposedly unhappy with the merger. At Eaton's departure, CMP had acquired thirty-seven power companies.

Proctor. He attended Portland public schools and graduated from Bowdoin College. Baxter received a law degree from Harvard Law School in 1901, although he never practiced law.

Baxter became a state representative in 1903 but was defeated for reelection. For the next twenty years, he was in and out of politics. During that period, he was a state senator and a state representative for a second time. He was reelected to the senate, becoming President of the Maine State Senate in 1921. Baxter became Maine's 53rd governor following the death of newly elected Governor Parkhurst, who passed away twenty-six days into his tenure. Baxter was elected to a full term in 1923 but chose not to run for a second term.

Percival Baxter's most recognizable achievement was Baxter State Park, 200,000 acres cobbled together from thirty-two parcels he bought and gifted to the people of Maine. His other notable bequests to the Maine people include Mackworth Island, Baxter School for the Deaf, and numerous donations to animal rights causes and libraries.

Baxter was less known as a champion of keeping Maine's natural resources out of private corporations' hands, arguing that they belonged to all Maine citizens. His political career was a constant fight with power companies wanting free access to Maine's water resources for hydroelectric development and water storage reservoirs and to be able to ship the power out of state. Percival Baxter introduced the export bill, which became law in 1909 and was named the Fernald Law after Governor Bert M. Fernald signed the act into law.

Many in the state saw Baxter's demand that Central Maine Power Company rent the dam site at Long Falls as standing up to corporate interests. Others, particularly those in the opposing party, saw Baxter as inhibiting industrial progress in the state. William Pettengill, a prominent politician from Augusta, minced no words in asserting that the state's Chief Executive was "the most dangerous demagogue who ever occupied the office of Governor of Maine." He further stated that Baxter's approach to waterpower development "attempts to create class consciousness and introduce class hatred..." by consistently claiming that whenever he discussed waterpower, the state's natural resources belonged to the ordinary Maine citizen and should not be monopolized by wealthy corporations. Pettengill stated that no obstacles should hinder the development of waterpower in Maine, and financing should be pursued through all legitimate avenues to transform the waste waters from Maine's lakes and rivers into assets that would benefit its residents.

Throughout most of the 1920s, Baxter remained steadfast in his convictions that Maine's natural resources were a part of all Mainers' heritage and should not be given away or sold to private interests. An overriding theme in Baxter's years in Maine politics was Maine energy for Maine people. One of his opponents said that if the people of Maine had either adopted or rejected his waterpower stance, Baxter would have had no excuse to continue in public life.

In one sense, the push-and-pull between hydropower advocates and Maine Governor Baxter was a struggle between the old Maine that wanted to keep life the way it had always been, and those who saw economic growth hinged on integrating Maine's economy with the rest of New England, mainly when it came to the state's natural resources.

Fernald Law
In 1905, out-of-state power interests viewed Maine as possessing limitless untapped hydropower. One enterprising company approached the legislature to obtain permission to develop Maine's rivers and to secure the right of eminent domain to construct transmission lines to "shoot" electricity into Massachusetts. In 1906, the State of Connecticut granted a charter to a company to operate in Maine to develop and transmit hydropower. The company then approached the Maine legislature, seeking a similar charter to do business in the state. In both instances, the requests failed; however, Baxter and other conservatives saw the direction in which waterpower development was headed. Baxter stated that

hydropower should be developed to benefit Maine's economy and its citizens, serving as an incentive to attract industry to the state. Baxter insisted that Maine waters were for public use and not for private and exclusive control by corporations. As a senator, he introduced and championed legislation preventing private interests from exploiting Maine's water resources. A law was passed that prohibited the export of hydroelectric power generated in the state. It would become known as the Fernald Law, named for Governor Fernald, who signed the bill in 1909. Wyman saw the law as an unnecessary barrier to the development of hydroelectric projects and said it would have the opposite effect on growth by discouraging industries from settling in Maine.

Due to concerns that the Ferland Law might be unconstitutional, the so-called Baxter Amendment was proposed to ensure the law's intent would be upheld by amending every waterpower charter passed by the legislature. This amendment stipulates that the company in question shall not transmit current beyond the stated border or join with any other company in doing so. This proposal ignited a political firestorm in the state legislature. A senator from Penobscot said that if the Fernald Law was found to be unconstitutional, the Baxter Amendment "won't amount to a pinch of snuff." Although the house passed the legislation, the senate eventually tabled the measure, thus killing it.

****

> "When we get ready to take electric current out of the State of Maine, we are going to take it out. The legislature can't prevent it; the 1909 law can't prevent it, and the Baxter Amendment can't prevent it."
>
> Harvey P. Eaton, President
Central Maine Power Company

****

By 1924, the country was working to expand the electrical grid by developing "superpower projects," a sophisticated electrical grid connected by power projects on an unprecedented scale to channel electricity from where it was generated to where it was needed. Maine was excluded from discussions regarding implementing this plan because the Fernald Act prohibited power exports beyond the state line. Politicians had convinced most residents that, at some point in the future, industries would be compelled to come to Maine for the electricity necessary to operate their machinery. However, with the proposed superpower projects, there was no reason for it to happen. Opponents of the law pointed out that since the enactment of the Fernald Act, no industry had relocated to Maine in search of a reliable power source and that electricity needed to be accessible before any company would consider moving to Maine, not the other way around. Superficial cracks began to emerge in support of the Fernald Law. However, none were deep enough to repeal the 1909 law.

After leaving politics, Baxter held firm to his view that hydropower produced in Maine should stay in the state. However, he modified his stand in 1925 when a developer proposed harnessing the tides in Passamaquoddy Bay in Eastport, Maine. The promoters of the massive project said that if it were built, major industries would flock to Washington County to take advantage of the cheap, reliable power generated by the "Niagara of the East."

Baxter supported the tidal project and its energy export beyond Maine's borders. He justified his shift in position saying that tidal power was distinct from river-generated electricity in the source and under different conditions, and technically, tidal water was not water belonging to Maine. However, Baxter maintained that river-generated electricity should be kept in the state. His selective change of position upset those supporting the development of river waterpower and transmitting it to out-of-state buyers, suggesting that Baxter was attempting to rationalize that an electron created from a turbine on a dammed river was somehow different from one generated from tidal power.

On September 16, 1925, voters in Maine went to the polls to cast their ballots on the Cooper-Passamaquoddy Development

Project. Although the act was approved by a wide margin to permit the construction of the hundred-million-dollar tidal development, it hardly began before being shelved. In 1927, Baxter had been out of office for three years but still advocated for keeping the Fernald Law. Augusta once again debated its repeal. Baxter was concerned that CMP's alliance with Insull would give the company added leverage to ram through the repeal. He was determined to keep the citizens informed of the consequences if that happened.

On February 8, 1927, at his own expense, Baxter broadcast the first of three radio addresses from station WCSH in Portland. He warned listeners that Insull wanted more than just export power. They also wanted to seek to dominate other business interests in the state, including newspapers, banks, and railroads. In short, Insull was a potential threat to Maine's industry, economic well-being, and free speech on public matters. He told the radio audience that if CMP/Insull won, "our power will be gone, gradually our industries will vanish, our communities will shrink, all that will be left us will be to become a summer resort, to which curiosity-seekers will journey to view the primitive natives in their old-fashion[ed] villages of a former generation." Much of what Baxter said appeared somewhat exaggerated regarding the potential outcomes if Insull succeeded. Nevertheless, his remarks aimed to inspire the electorate to urge their legislators against repealing the Ferland Law and to vote no if such a proposal reached a referendum.

In 1928, the legislature reached a compromise known as the Smith-Carlton Act. Central Maine Power and leading politicians backed the Smith-Carlton bill. Baxter, who had stated the previous year that he would never support the export of hydropower from the state, changed his stance and endorsed the bill. The law permitted the export of surplus power, with the understanding that as Maine's energy needs increased, the surplus would be sold within the state. Additionally, a four percent excise tax would be imposed on exported power to make the repeal legislation more appealing to voters. Proponents of the law stated that Maine would benefit by attracting hundreds of millions of dollars in capital investment and reducing power rates. Those against the Smith-Carlton legislation spoke of false promises of new industries coming to Maine and the loss of local control. Furthermore, if passed, the law was an unabashed attempt by outside interests to get their corporate noses under the tent and take control of Maine's hydroelectric power by shipping it out of state. The opponents also argued that if the Fernald Law was such an obstacle preventing new industries from entering Maine, why was Insull, the owner of Central Maine Power Company, spending millions of dollars buying up and refurbishing mills in Maine?

****

"I stand solidly for keeping all our Water Power in Maine forever and shall use my influence to maintain that position."

Percival Baxter
Radio address on WCSH Radio, 1927

****

Baxter told his critics he had switched his position on the Fernald Law because no law enacted by humans was perfect but an expression of the moment, and that changed conditions must be met by changing rules. He went on to say that the Fernald Law hadn't accomplished what was intended. Manufacturing did not come to Maine because hydropower was available. Baxter declared that it was only fair for hydropower producers to sell the excess wherever a market was found, and the Smith-Carlton Act would protect Maine people and industries by requiring the surplus to be returned to the state if domestic demand exceeded current production. Also, the four percent excise tax on the power exported would go to expanding electrification to underserved parts of the state.

The Smith-Carlton measure, approved by the state legislature and signed into law by Governor Gardiner, was put to referendum in September 1929. It was defeated even with Baxter's endorsement.

The strength of the no vote came from Maine's most rural counties. The State Grange rank and file overwhelmingly rejected the referendum, while the Grange leadership favored repeal. Portland, arguably the most liberal city in the state, could only record a slim majority who voted for exporting power. Maintaining local control of the state's resources was a deciding factor for many electorates.

Central Maine Power needed to find in-state customers to use the extra electricity without the ability to export excess power from Wyman Dam. The Company funded Bath Iron Works, Keyes Fiber in Waterville, and a shoe company in Auburn, built the Maine Seaboard Paper Company in Bucksport, and sold these companies the excess power.

The Fernald Law was twice considered for repeal after the defeat of the Smith-Carlton Act—once in 1947 and again in 1953, and both times, it failed. Finally, in 1955, with little argument, the legislature repealed the Fernald Law. Most reasons for its repeal were the same as those of twenty-two years earlier: The law hadn't done what it was intended to do and had stifled growth by not allowing hydropower to be sent out of or brought into the state. There were new reasons for repeal as well. Repeal eliminated a stumbling block for hydro development of the St. John River in Aroostook County, allowing power into Canada (a project that didn't come to fruition). Repeal also allowed hydropower producers to sell excess power in times of high flow, and input power in times of drought. Nuclear power in Maine was still a few years away; however, if Maine adopted the technology, a market was needed for the extra power such a plant would produce.

Dead River Reservoir and Why It Was Necessary

To run the turbines at peak production in the drier periods of the year at Wyman Dam and other hydro stations and mills along the Kennebec River, the water on the upper Dead River had to be stored and released as needed. Without controlling the discharge, the downriver paper, cotton, and wool processing mills would have to curtail production in drought because of the lack of water. They also had to shut down during periods of high runoff to prevent damage to the turbines. Two storage reservoirs, one at Brassua Lake and the other at Long Falls on the Dead River, would go a long way in solving this problem. Evening the flow of the Kennebec would increase the efficiency of the turbines, and that ensured more production by all the mills and hydro stations along the waterway. Another benefit of the storage reservoirs was flood control. Holding back storm runoff would decrease damage to flood-prone areas downriver.

The Dead River Valley was the only practical site for storing water on the Dead River, with Long Falls being the only feasible location for the dam. However, two public lots occupied the site.[9] Long Falls Dam could only be built with Central Maine Power Company controlling this land by buying or leasing it from the State. The legal rights to construct a dam at Long Falls consumed Percival Baxter, the legislature, and the power interests for four years.[10]

In 1923, the legislature passed the Kennebec Reservoir Charter, granting CMP and other downriver investors the authority to construct a dam on the Dead River at Long Falls, creating a reservoir that would later be named Flagstaff Lake. The proposed site for the dam was State land, which would be transferred to the power interests without compensation. Governor Baxter opposed offering State land to private companies without payment and vetoed the bill. The veto was overridden and became law. Baxter

---

9. The origin of Maine's Public Lots dates back to the separation of Maine from Massachusetts in 1820. At that time, the State set aside lots in each unincorporated township for public use, such as schools in the towns, which someday might be created.

10. A clause stating that up to five thousand horsepower of electricity could be generated at Long Falls was included in the failed Kennebec River Reservoir Charter and, again, in the new Charter without specifying horsepower. Perhaps this is where some of the residents of the Dead River Valley got the notion that Long Falls Dam would include hydropower generation. Turbines were not a part of the final design.

threatened to take the bill to referendum and let the people decide if this was acceptable.

Baxter's message accompanying his veto did little to endear him to the legislature members who had voted for the bill. His claims of "unfaithfulness to their oaths, attempts to defraud the State, and a fraudulent purpose" were particularly inflammatory. Such accusations from the governor suggested that the legislature's integrity was questioned due to their passage of the Kennebec Reservoir Charter.

A swift rebuke followed the governor's terse message. Senator H.E. Wardsworth authored a response to Baxter's claims. The senator reminded the governor that the bill had received overwhelming support from both chambers, and they voted again to override Baxter's veto. The senator stated that Baxter was mistaken in suggesting the legislature had employed dirty tricks in passing the Kennebec River Reservoir Charter.

As the referendum was being sought, the opposing parties attempted to reach a compromise. After a series of meetings among representatives of Percival Baxter, Walter Wyman, and other Kennebec River users, all agreed to the Dead River Reservoir Company proposal to replace the Kennebec Reservoir Company Act. Under the newly proposed charter, the corporators agreed to pay $25,000 each year for forty years and that the lease would be renewed if the State opted not to assume reservoir operation.

The next day, a Friday called by the *Morning Sentinel* "one of the most exciting days in the legislature since the count-out of 1879,"[11] Baxter spoke to the legislature about the agreement's details. Baxter had concluded that the agreed-upon rental

---

11. Count-out of 1879: Riot conditions existed at the state capital. Republicans thought they had won the legislature and the governorship. However, the Democrats controlled how the votes were counted and gave the Democrats both victories. Eventually, the Maine Supreme Court sided with the Republicans, and a more significant crisis was averted. The riotous event would become known as the Great Count-Out.

arrangement for the Long Falls site also applied to future reservoir development in the state. Immediately, Walter Wyman wrote to the governor, stating that the agreement was specific to the Dead River Project and not a general agreement to compensate the State for future water rights for potential reservoir construction. Therefore, he and the other sponsors would withdraw from the Dead River Reservoir proposal. What was to have been the long-sought legislation to clear the way for the construction of Long Falls Dam fell apart because of a misinterpretation of the compromise, or perhaps merely wishful thinking on the governor's part.

Rural residents supported Baxter's philosophy of self-sufficiency regarding waterpower, supporting the governor's stand on the Fernald Law and his insistence that the Central Maine Power Company pay for the privilege of building a dam at Long Falls.

In the summer of 1925, former governor Baxter hiked Mount Bigelow to view the Dead River Valley, which Central Maine Power Company sought to transform into a storage reservoir. This marked the first and only occasion on which the ex-governor visited the area, even though the struggle to flood the Valley had consumed much of his time in Augusta. Standing on East Peak,[12] he would have seen Katahdin looming nearly 83 miles away. (One day, its 5,269-foot peak would bear his name.) Dozens of other mountains framed the landscape.

With his eye, Baxter could trace the meandering Dead River from west to east and then sharply north to the constriction at the end of the Valley where the dam was supposed to be built, backing up water to Stratton, twenty miles to the west. At the base of Maine's fifth tallest mountain, the Valley stretched long and wide, surpassing the length of the Mount Bigelow Range that bordered its southern edge. Baxter could see Flagstaff village on the north side of Dead River, looking no larger than a postage stamp from this distance. Numerous farmsteads dotted the expansive floodplain,

---

12. East Peak was renamed Avery Peak after the death of Myron Avery in 1952.

each surrounded with hay land and pasture. The view was spectacular and rivaled those from Katahdin's rocky summit.

His thoughts weren't occupied by the people of Flagstaff, Dead River, and Bigelow being forced from their homes. His concern was that the Central Maine Power Company wanted to flood this valley to store water for power generation on the Kennebec River and didn't want to compensate the State for that right. At the time, he believed the power company had been blocked from constructing the Long Falls Dam when the legislature revoked the Kennebec Reservoir Charter bill in 1923. Baxter stated after visiting Mount Bigelow's summit: "To allow any private firm to flood that great territory, create a 28-mile-long lake, and obtain deeds of the State-owned land at the outlet would have been a crime against the people [of Maine]."

Although Baxter appeared to suggest that he would never support the construction of Long Falls Dam, he did leave open the possibility that if the legislature granted a charter to build the reservoir, the State should lease the dam site to CMP "for a fair and honest rental." He informed reporters that he would pursue another referendum as a private citizen if the legislators passed a bill again without providing just compensation for utilizing State land to build the dam at Long Falls.

Central Maine Power Company and the owners of the manufacturing mills along the Kennebec River remained determined to regulate the flow of the Upper Kennebec River. The company could not wait for a charter to flood the Dead River Valley. Instead, CMP opted for their second choice: a storage reservoir at the outlet of Brassua Lake on the Moose River, which flows into Moosehead Lake. By regulating the flow at Brassua Dam and Moosehead Lake, the mills enhanced hydropower production efficiency along the main stem of the Kennebec River. The Brassua Dam was finished in the fall of 1925. However, CMP and the manufacturers downstream wanted even lower rates and greater capacity and persisted in their efforts to construct Long Falls Dam.

On February 27, 1927, the state legislature revisited the contentious issue of constructing the Dead River Reservoir to regulate the flow of the Dead River. The newly proposed charter closely resembled the repealed Kennebec Reservoir Company bill that had been approved by the legislature in 1923, vetoed by Governor Baxter, overridden by the legislature, and was on the verge of going to referendum when a disastrous, last-minute compromise was reached between the governor, Walter Wyman, and the manufacturers on the Kennebec River. One crucial difference between the 1923 and 1927 charters was that the Kennebec Reservoir Company agreed to pay the State $25,000 a year for forty years to lease the dam site, the same amount as the failed proposed Dead River Charter.[13] On April 11, 1927, and with minimal dissent, the new version of the Kennebec River Charter passed almost unanimously. After years of haggling, public sentiment and political pressure shifted enough to allow for the construction of Long Falls Dam.

The Kennebec River Reservoir Charter was a comprehensive document that detailed the powers of the Corporation. In addition to the lease agreement between the Corporation and the State of Maine, it authorized the construction of the dam at Long Falls, the acquisition of property from the Kennebec River Logging Company, and the assumption of responsibility for the annual pulpwood drive between Alder Stream and the Kennebec River. The charter also mandated the removal of all growth from the flooded area (hence the massive brush fires in

---

13. In 1994, as the expiration of the original lease approached, Central Maine Power and the State of Maine attempted to negotiate a new annual rental fee. The State sought a yearly rental fee of $527,858, calculated based on the hydropower value of the water released and the annual inflation rate since CMP had made the first yearly lease payment. Central Maine Power balked at a twenty-fold increase and asked a Maine Supreme Court Justice to set aside the ruling. The ruling was upheld. Brookfield Renewables, the current owner of Long Falls Dam, continues to pay the yearly lease.

1949), and included authorization to acquire land by purchase or eminent domain within the flowage area and other lands as needed. The charter also authorized the corporation to construct new roads to replace those flooded and a provision for removing dead bodies and locating them in new cemeteries. A provision in the lease of the dam site allowed power development at the dam and the construction of all necessary infrastructure to produce that power. (Power development was not incorporated into the dam's design.)

For years, the residents of Flagstaff and Dead River Plantations and Bigelow Township had been whipsawed by the political drama in Augusta, uncertain whether they would be forced to abandon their homes or remain in the Dead River Valley to continue living as they had before the dam proposal. Even after the passage of the 1927 Kennebec River Reservoir Charter, the construction of Long Falls Dam would wait another twenty years, causing two decades of uncertainty. During this time, the Kennebec River Reservoir Company acquired property in the Valley as it became available. In 1928, CMP announced plans to build a seven-million-dollar dam across the Kennebec River between Moscow and Pleasant Ridge. The 155-foot-high hydroelectric dam would be the largest in the eastern United States at the time. The dam was completed in 1930 and named after the founder of Central Maine Power Company, Walter J. Wyman.

After the unsuccessful attempt to repeal the Fernald export law in 1929, Wyman required an in-state buyer for the surplus power generated by the new dam to justify the construction costs. He used an infusion of capital from CMP's parent company, Middle West Utilities Company, to build the ten-million-dollar Seaboard Paper Company in Bucksport, Maine. Upon completing Wyman Dam and a transmission line to Bucksport, Seaboard Paper became a buyer of the excess electricity from Wyman Dam.

In 1946, the Central Maine Power Company announced that construction of the Long Falls Dam would begin in 1948. The gates were closed in late 1949.

Wyman got everything he wanted: Wyman Dam, the Brassua Reservoir, the Dead River Reservoir, and the final piece of the puzzle, Harris Dam, built in 1954 on the Kennebec River at the southern end of Indian Pond. The only thing he didn't get was to live long enough to see the Upper Kennebec River under CMP control. Walter Wyman died on November 15, 1942.

ACKNOWLEDGMENTS

Washed Out is a work of fiction that relies heavily on the actual timeline and events leading up to the flooding of Flagstaff and Dead River Plantations and Bigelow Township in 1949. Archived daily Maine newspapers were the primary source of this history. The feelings about leaving their lifelong homes and the memories of living in the Dead River Valley came from the marvelous collection of personal accounts in *There Was a Land*, published by the Flagstaff Memorial Chapel Association in 1999. Surely, this collection of personal recollections will stand the test of time. *There Was a Land* preserves a slice of Maine history when two hundred Dead River Valley residents sacrificed their heritage in the name of progress.

The story of Frank Moody's camp and the shooting accident was an adaptation of the article "John F. Moody, Jr." by Lenwood Pete Andrews in *There Was a Land*.

A special thank you to Kenneth Wing, Historian of the flooding of the Dead River Valley, for writing the Afterword.

GLOSSARY

chance: a working area in the woods. A hard chance is one that is difficult to access and to make a profit from. A good chance is one easy to get to and more profitable.

cookee: cook's assistant

fell/felling: to cut or cutting a tree down

landing: an area to temporarily store logs or pulpwood, generally along a riverbank

longwood: saw logs, not pulpwood

notch: the initial cut to fell a tree. It has two parts: a horizontal face and a sloping face.

peavey: a wooden lever about five feet long with an iron spike at the end and an adjustable steel hook. Used for turning logs. Named for its inventor.

picaroon: a wooden handle about thirty inches long with a steel hook at the end; used to pull wood toward the person using it

pike-pole: a long pole with an iron point, used to guide logs floating in the water

pulpwood: four-foot bolts of wood used to make paper

ram pasture: sleeping quarters for woods crews; bunkroom

road monkeys: men who are responsible for maintaining haul roads, including icing and haying

rollway: on a bank where piles of logs are stacked to be rolled into the water

scaler: a person who measures logs or pulpwood

sluiced: overturned, as a team of horses that has accidentally gone off the road and piled up

tongue: a wooden shaft that connects to the front runners of a sled or wagon with the other end secured to the harness of two horses, enabling the team to steer

tote road: a woods road that is used to transport supplies from the outside to a logging camp

twitch: logs hauled by horses along the ground rather than loaded onto a sled

twitch trail: a trail used to twitch logs from the stump to the yard or landing

walking boss: a company's head man in the woods, "walking" to each logging camp to check on operations

yard: an assembling point for logs or pulpwood before being transported to the river

BIBLIOGRAPHY

Baxter, P. Percival. *Maine Politics and Water Powers*, three radio addresses given from station WCSH, Portland. February 1, 8, 15, 1927.

Burnell, Alan. L., and Kenny R. Wing. *Lost Villages of Flagstaff Lake*. Acadia Publishing, 2010.

CentralMaine.com. Archives: *Lewiston Evening Journal, Lewiston Sun, Portland Press Herald, Waterville Sentinel, Kennebec Journal*, 1907–1952.

Flagstaff and Dead River annual town reports,1930–1948. Maine State Library, Augusta, Maine.

Guide to the Central Maine Power Company Archival Collection, 1853–2001, Title: *Central Maine Power Company Archival Collection*, Historical Committee of the Old Timers Club, Dates: 1853–2001 (inclusive), Maine Historical Society, John Marshall and Alida Carroll Brown Research Library Collection, no. 2115. Accession no. 2004.090.

Hilton, C. Max. *Rough Pulpwood Operating in Northwestern Maine 1935–1940*. The Maine Bulletin, Vol. XLV, No.1, University of Maine Studies, Second Series, No. 57. August 1942.

Kennebec River Reservoir Charter, 1926; *An Act to Provide for the Surrender by Flagstaff Plantation of its Organization; An Act to Provide for the Surrender by Dead River Plantation of its Organization,1951*. Maine State Archives. Law and Legislative Digital Library, www.legislature.gov/law lib, Augusta, Maine.

Maine, an Encyclopedia, maineencyclopedia.com.

Maine's Water Policy as defined by Governor Percival P. Baxter and endorsed by Hon. John A. Peters. Letters of Governor Baxter, Congressman Peters, and Benjamin F. Cleaves. Augusta, Maine, November 8, 1921.

Pike, E. Robert. *Tall Trees, Tough Men.* W. W. Norton Company, New York, 1984; reissued 1999.

There Was a Land, 1845-1949, by former residents and friends of the Dead River Valley. Published by Flagstaff Memorial Chapel Association and printed by Knowlton and McCleary, Farmington, Maine, 1999.

Soars, Liz. *All for Maine, A Story of Governor Percival P. Baxter.* Ellsworth American Printing Services, 1995.